Myths of a Merciful God

LITTLE FEATHER BOOKS, INC.

Library of Congress Cataloging-in-Publication data on file.
ISBN 978-0-9913329-1-5

Cover Photography © Konstantin Yuganov and © Xearb via Fotolia
Cover Design by LFB Studios

The characters and events depicted in this work are fictitious.
Any resemblance to actual persons, living or dead, is purely coincidental.

This book is dedicated to
THE COMMITTEE
my own personal council of elders,
mistresses of the absurd,
and secret society of avenging angels.

Also by Cynthia Ceilán

Thinning the Herd: Tales of the Weirdly Departed

*Weirdly Beloved: Tales of Strange Bedfellows,
Odd Couplings, and Love Gone Wrong*

Unlucky Stiffs: More Tales of the Weirdly Departed

Myths of a Merciful God

A Novel

Cynthia Ceilán

LITTLE FEATHER BOOKS, INC.
NEW YORK

Everything is supposed to be very
quiet after a massacre, and it always
is, except for the birds.

—Kurt Vonnegut

One

EVEN BEFORE SHE OPENED her eyes that morning, Sarah knew she was in the wrong bed.

The coverlet smelled old and felt rough against her cheek. Her feet, still in their shoes, felt like they were on fire. She tried to think of the last normal thing that had happened to her.

The frenzied end-of-day cry of birds calling out to each other filled her memory. Wind rustling. Children squealing. A park bench. She remembered how she had been much too keenly aware of the crackle of twigs as people walked past her, the sound of bicycle tires wheeling across the pavement, the irregular hum of nearby traffic.

She remembered sitting on that park bench, hunched over and gripping the edges of the slat beneath her knees, while spring went about the necessary business of rearranging the man-made forest around her. Spring, with its joyous fury of savage greens, purposefully beating back the muddy browns and dead grays of winter into the willful earth, oblivious and uncaring of the fathomless chasm growing inside her, or her screaming need to have lived a different life. She remembered sitting there, barely able to breathe through a sorrow so unholy, so unnamable that it made every thought in her head a soup of absurdities.

She remembered looking up at the windows of her building across the street, the ones visible above the tree line. Things were happening behind those windows, things that had no connection to each other, and certainly not to her. Behind those windows, an old man napped, a faucet dripped, lovers whispered, pets waited, someone sighed. Beyond her building, beyond this city, elsewhere in the world, other people's lives went on in disjointed motion, even as random heartbeats pulsed in unison to a larger communal rhythm, perfectly oblivious of each other and certainly of her, all of them, all of it, the meaningless and the overwrought, all of it happening while she sat gripping the edges of that park bench, while a vain man plucked an eyebrow, while a Pope in hiding smiled darkly, while a goldfish pooped, while peepers peeped, while lepers wept, while a child grew ever colder in a freezer drawer in a hospital morgue just one half mile behind her. A child. A *child*.

Her child.

"Tessie," she said, and felt the word fall to the ground like the ghost of a dead leaf, evaporating like a single droplet of rain absorbed into the earth as quickly and as quietly as that.

How does one go on with life on a day such as this? How does one go home?

Sarah sat up slowly in this strange bed, swinging her still-shod feet to the floor and looking down at them, gripping the edge of the bed as she had that park bench, who knew how many hours or days ago. The flesh below her ankles was red and raw around the edges of her shoes. Her feet were swollen. She must have walked to wherever this place was. It was a hotel room, that much was evident, and not one of the nicer ones. It must have been just a place to stop walking. By the looks of it, she had simply fallen face-first onto this ugly old bed and surrendered to unconsciousness. Her large, slouchy bag lay in a puddle on the floor near the nightstand, probably where it landed after slipping from her shoulder and down a limp arm.

She winced as she made her way to the bathroom. She knew that if she took her shoes off now, she'd never get them back on, and she needed to leave this place.

After a cursory stab at morning ablutions, she limped back to the bed and rifled wearily through the contents of her purse. There were lots of papers. Things that looked like receipts. Hospital instructions. A flyer or notice printed on bright red paper. An envelope with the logo of a funeral home. She stuffed everything back and zipped the bag. She'd figure it out later.

Slowly, as if wading through congealed soup, she walked down a poorly-lit hallway that reeked of dampness, summoned an elevator, and emerged into a lobby that was determined to make visitors believe that the rooms upstairs were as nice as this small but elegantly appointed space.

A man behind the front desk smiled at her with his lips, but not with his eyes. A spray of dusty flowers at the end of the desk absurdly brought to mind Tessie's black patent leather shoes.

"Good afternoon, ma'am," the smiling automaton said to her.

Afternoon. That was not good. "What day is this?" she rasped.

"Thursday, ma'am."

Thursday, she thought with a touch of horror. She was standing in the same clothes she had first put on three days ago. The last time she had been in her apartment, police officers had been there with her. She hadn't been back since.

Had she been walking for three days? Is it possible she sat on that park bench all day and all night—except for maybe last night—without getting killed, mugged, or arrested?

The face of a bald, sallow-faced man came to mind. She pushed the image away.

"Will you be staying with us one more night?"

Sarah looked at the man as if he had asked her to disrobe. "No. No. I need to check out."

The clerk pursed his lips. "Well, it's a little past our normal check-out time, but let me see what I can do." He said this as if he were about to do Sarah a favor he would never have done for anyone else. "Room number?"

She searched his face, as if the answer to that question were printed somewhere there. "Uhh... sorry... I'm not sure..."

"Not a problem," he said, now adding a nose-crinkle to go with the pursed lips. He began clicking away at a keyboard just out of sight of Sarah's line of vision. "Your name?"

"Sarah Miranda."

More clicking. "Ah, here we are. Room 312. Was that it?"

"Umm... okay?"

"Your key card?"

She thought he said something in Greek. When he repeated it, she heard it in English. "Oh." She looked at her empty hands and felt outside the pockets of her slacks. "I must have left it in the room. Sorry."

"Not a problem," the hotel guy said again, but Sarah could tell that maybe she had presented one too many problems already, none of which he was happy to deal with right now. She wanted to leap over the desk and claw his face off.

After a bit more clicking and clacking, he announced, "We're all set. I just need to see your credit card one more time."

The transaction seemed to take hours. When finally it was done, she limped out of the hotel and into the bright sunshine. She walked to the end of the block and looked up at the sign. West 32nd Street. She had walked sixty or seventy blocks in shoes that were only barely tolerable on a well-carpeted floor. It was a wonder her feet were just swollen and not bleeding.

You call that pain? whispered a sadistic voice in her head. *How must it have been for Tessie?*

Sarah's knees buckled. She flailed and just caught the rim of a filthy, overflowing trash can, almost bringing it down with her. A middle-aged woman passing by caught her arm. "Are you okay, honey?" she asked.

Sarah nodded. "I just... dizzy, I think." She gave her head a good shake and took a deep breath.

"Should I call an ambulance?" The woman already had a thumb poised over the "9" on her cell phone.

But Sarah was already back up on her feet and walking toward a cab that was stopped at the corner, waiting for a green light. She stumbled into it, gave the driver her address, leaned back in the seat, and promptly fell asleep.

The horn of another car blared suddenly, startling her awake. It felt as though that sound had blasted inside her own head. She looked around and saw that she was still several blocks from her apartment building, but there were some stores up ahead, and she needed to get some things before going home. "Let me off at the next corner," she said a little too loudly to the cabbie. He gave her a quick look in the rearview mirror and pulled over. She handed him a twenty dollar bill without looking at the meter and got out as quickly as she could. She had no mind at the moment for calculating how excessive or stingy a tip she was leaving, and didn't care.

First she stopped at a shoe store and bought a pair of strappy, red, high-heeled sandals without trying them on. She had been meaning to do this for months, and for reasons she didn't question or dwell upon, it seemed urgent to have them right now. Next she ducked into a candy store and picked up a copy of the *New York Times*. Again, this was important, but that's all she knew. She stared at the front page for several moments before realizing that she couldn't make out any of the words printed there. Even the picture above the fold was a hazy blob. She bought it anyway.

She walked the rest of the way home, each step an agony. The pain resonated in her chest, in her temples, but she kept going, the words of an old nun echoing stupidly in her head: "Offer it up for the poor souls in Purgatory." What the hell did that mean, anyway? And, last she heard, Purgatory didn't even exist anymore.

Like Limbo, where the unbaptized babies go.

At this, she cried out.

A few people on the sidewalk glanced her way, but none of them stopped. Sarah resumed walking.

———

Sarah at last arrived at her apartment, clutching her newspaper and the bag with the new shoes against her chest, her old shoes in the other hand. She had finally taken them off in the elevator—*peeled* them off, was more like it—and saw that her feet were, in fact, bloody, especially the right one. She opened the door to find her home full of people.

"Oh, my God! Where have you been?!" cried her mother, Ana. She ran to Sarah and crushed her against her chest.

Sarah looked to the spot on the floor in front of the TV. It was clean. Maybe none of this had happened. Maybe it had all been a bad dream, the worst of all possible nightmares.

"What day is this?" Sarah mumbled into her mother's shoulder.

Ana held Sarah out at arm's length and made some sound of

panicked exasperation. "She doesn't know what day it is!" Other people turned to look at them.

"Mom?" Sarah said from some faraway place. "What's going on here?"

"We're all here, honey. Daddy, Titi Ro, your cousins... Look— even Caroline and Shirley are here."

"Yeah. Okay. We'll take a cab."

"What?" Ana looked like she didn't know whether to start wailing again or try to make sense of what she was hearing.

"I need a shower." Sarah pushed past her mother and ignored everyone else. She dropped her packages on the bed and began shedding clothes on the way to the bathroom. She closed the door behind her with only the vaguest notion that she was awake.

———

More out of deeply ingrained habit than as a conscious act, Sarah turned the hot water faucet all the way, as far as it would go. She added cold water little bits at a time, testing the temperature with her hand under the spigot before raising the lever for the shower. Next she tested the temperature of the spray, again with her hand; sometimes it was colder when it came from the shower head. Before getting into the tub, she tested the water again, first with her toes, then her foot, then all the way up to her calf. Then she checked it one last time with her hand. She entered the shower slowly, not closing the curtain completely until more of her was wet, in case she needed to leap out of the tub and make further adjustments.

She stood with her eyes closed and her hands against the tiled wall, directly under the shower spray, letting the steaming water hit the back of her neck and that place between her shoulder blades.

It was only through water that Sarah could make her peace with the world, forget everything, remember everything, begin again. She could find a meditation in any of its manifestations: a windless summer rain, a puddle in a garden, condensation on a glass.

For the big hurts, she went to the ocean.

She couldn't hear anything except the steady whooshing sound of water, couldn't see anything but darkness behind her eyelids. She hadn't turned the light on when she came into the bathroom; the only light in the room was filtered through the frosted panes of the tall, narrow bathroom window. By the quality of the light, she figured it must be one or two o'clock in the afternoon, the time of day when the sun shone most brightly into her apartment.

It appeared she hadn't abdicated her responsibilities after all. All the big things had been taken care of, if not by her, then by someone in greater possession of his or her wits. Phone calls had been made. Documents had been signed. Why else would her apartment be full of people, and why else would there have been so much paperwork in her purse? She wasn't sure whom she had called, in what order, or when, but, apparently, all the right people had been contacted, and some of them were now waiting in the various rooms of her tidy home.

The image of the sallow, bald-headed man floated to the front of her consciousness again. Again, she pushed him away.

She couldn't remember, though, if she had called Vince. Probably not. She didn't know anymore where he lived or where he worked, and hadn't seen or spoken to him in years. If she had called him, well, fine; that meant she had finally done her job as a semi-decent human being. If she hadn't, then that was going to have to be fine, too. The son of a bitch had never been any kind of father to Tessie, anyway. Their lives had been better without him.

Their lives.

There'll be no more of that now.

Sarah stood up straight and let the water hit her fully on the face.

There. That was better.

A pair of black patent leather shoes came into view in her mind's eye, Mary Janes, girls' size twelve. That style of little girl's shoes had probably come to this hemisphere with the Pilgrims. Sarah remembered owning many pairs of Mary Janes throughout her own childhood. White patent leather, black ones, other colors and textures. Her favorite had been the brownish-red ones, made of regular leather, not the ultra-shiny kind, with tiny little holes poked into the part that covered her toes in a design she could no longer remember exactly. Wing tips? Probably not. Maybe little flowers. Technically, they probably weren't even Mary Janes. These had two buckled straps across the front, not one. Were they still Mary Janes if they weren't black? Or patent leather? Or if they had more than one strap? She wasn't sure. She tried to conjure a clearer image of that favorite pair of shoes, to place them next to Tessie's shiny black ones. What came to mind instead was an obscene pair of strappy red high-heeled evening shoes.

Sarah's eyes flew open and she gasped under the spray of the shower, inhaling water in the process. She coughed violently, finding it simultaneously horrifying and comical that she should be drowning in her own shower.

"Sarah?" Ana called from the other side of the bathroom door. "Are you all right?"

Sarah coughed a few more times. "Yes, Mom."

"Can I come in?"

"No, Mom."

"I need to talk to you, dear."

"I'll be out in a minute."

"I need to go to the bathroom."

"I'll be out in a *minute*."

"I don't think I can hold it. You've been in there a long time.

Other people are waiting, too."

"I'll be out. In a *minute*."

Ana opened the door and came in anyway, as Sarah knew she would. Maybe she could stay in the shower a few more hours, until she was able to breathe water without drowning.

"I'm in the bathroom, honey." Ana turned on the light.

Sarah sighed as her shoulders slumped. "I can hear you. Please don't flush."

"I won't." Ana sat on the closed lid of the toilet. "Are you okay, sweetie?"

"I'm almost finished."

"That's not what I asked."

"I'm okay, Mom."

"What do you need for me to do?"

"I need you to let me finish taking my shower."

"No. I mean about the—"

"Mama?" Sarah managed to sound calm but her teeth were clenched. "What I need most from you right now is a little privacy. Could you please wait outside? I'm almost done."

"You've been in here much too long." Silence. Nothing but the rush of water. "Sarah?"

Suddenly the shower curtain flew open. Water bounced off Sarah's head, spraying in all directions. "What is it, Mom."

Ana almost fell off the toilet seat, as shocked by the violent way in which Sarah had torn the curtain open as by the sight of this stranger, this crazy, naked, wet woman. "All right, all right. People are waiting. We need to get going." She said this as if she were offended, and walked away on slightly wobbly legs. "I don't want us to be late."

Sarah pulled the curtain closed and put her head back under the water, thanking the gods of hundred-year-old buildings with giant boilers in the basement for massive supplies of hot water on demand,

and conservation-be-damned water pressure.

"She's out of her mind with grief," Ana announced to the guests in the living room, and promptly collapsed into the arms of the first available bystander. Ana wept copiously, quickly bringing already hushed tones of conversation to an uneasy silence.

———————

It truly was a beautiful room. Despite Sarah's innate aversion to the overwrought embellishments of antique furnishings and the oppressive darkness of Victorian decor, she had to admit this was, indeed, a beautiful room. Still, she wondered why it seemed that no one had yet thought to decorate a funeral home in any other style. Art-deco, for instance. Or Swedish contemporary. An old-fashioned room like this was fine for folks who wanted to take one last gander at ancient Uncle Harold's scowling mug, but who could feel a moment's comfort in this ornate salon when the person resting on the bier was—

just a baby.

Sarah whispered the words to herself, exhaling the words. "Just a baby."

She looked up from where she sat in the front row, a few feet from a small white casket. Why in the world would someone put a mobile over a coffin?

It wasn't like the mobile that had been attached to Tessie's crib when she was a baby. That one was beautiful, a gift from her oldest and dearest friend, Shirley. They had known each other since they were not much more than babies themselves. That mobile was a white, tented ring from which were suspended little birds in flight, accompanied by a smattering of tiny, brightly-colored butterflies. When the music box played its lullaby, the ring was set in motion. The birds circled round and round, like a miniature carousel.

But a mobile on a coffin?

Sarah blinked hard, and looked again. It wasn't a mobile. It was an arrangement of funeral flowers entwined around a tall stand with six white candles attached to a ring.

Sarah slumped backward into her chair and closed her eyes. She thought she would be sick.

"Sarah?" she heard her father say from very far away. Slowly, slowly she turned toward the sound, moving as if her head were not entirely connected to the rest of her, as if she were deep under water, many fathoms under, and the pressure made it nearly impossible to move. "Sarah?" she heard him say again.

There were other people there, too, she noticed, droves of them. They were walking as if they were all at the bottom of the ocean. Maybe this was a dream after all. Sarah nodded, in agreement with herself.

"Sarah?"

"Hmm?" There were tears in his eyes. She very gently touched one with the tip of her finger. The feel of it surprised her. It was a beautiful thing, this perfect droplet of human expression. "Oh, my God, Dad," she said suddenly, forgetting the tear and everything else. "Bitsy!"

Dan looked deeply into his daughter's eyes. "What, honey?"

"Bitsy!" Sarah shouted. "I forgot all about her! Poor little thing!" Sarah got up to leave, looking around for a handbag she had not brought with her. "She's probably starving to death! I haven't fed her in… I don't know! I didn't even see her this morning!"

Ana broke away from the small crowd that had gathered around to comfort her. "What is she talking about, Dan? The *dog*?"

"It's all right, honey," he said to his daughter. He intercepted Ana before she could begin pawing at Sarah again. He made a warning face at Ana.

Ana's incredulous eyes were wild in her head. She spoke to Sarah over Dan's shoulder. "Sarah, honey, that dog's been dead—"

"Dog's fine," Dan said over Ana. "Bitsy's fine, dear," Dan said deliberately, nudging Ana out of the way and glaring at her over his shoulder. "The puppy's fine." He took Sarah's face in his hand. "We took care of everything. Remember?"

Sarah looked at him. Something wasn't quite right, but somehow that was okay. Her Dad was here, and he was kind and good and calm, and when he was around, everything always seemed to be okay, even when it clearly wasn't. Sarah sighed. "Mm-*hmm*."

"Yes," her father agreed. He sat down with her again, keeping a protective arm around her and the opposite shoulder ready to block Ana if she decided to swoop in again. He neglected to observe that the seat to Sarah's left was available. Ana dropped gracefully into the deeply cushioned chair, a gesture perfected over many years of pouring herself exquisitely into furniture, over people, or onto whatever prop was handy.

"Mm-*hmm*," Sarah said again through her tightly pursed lips, liking the sound it made behind the bridge of her nose. It was a tiny little sound, musical even. She wondered if she could replicate it on the piano, something quick and pretty, the final syllable almost a grace note. Mm-*hmm!*

Sarah heard her parents talking over her, in a language she couldn't quite make out. Other people continued to float by, more underwater dancers. They swam down to her, and whispered things into her ear or talked through her hair as they hugged her. She had no idea what they were saying. Just the same, to each person she repeated, "Mm-*hmm*," and every time she said it, she drifted farther away. She smiled, too, like someone who knew a secret. It appeared she had stumbled upon the world's only truly magical word. The trick had been to say it with her lips pressed together and so low it was barely audible. "Mm-*hmm!*"

Some little wire had come loose in her head; of that much she was certain. Far from troubling her, as it might have in another life, the realization was rather comforting.

As the next person drifted into her periphery, she remembered trying to read a newspaper recently, just the headlines on the front page, and it had been as if that day's edition of the *Times* had been written in some poor imitation of Russian. Most of the letters looked familiar, but some of them were backwards, and, strung together as they were, they formed no words she could recognize. Now something similar was happening with people's voices. "Blublug jurblug barbloosim," the person crouching beside her was saying.

"Mm-*hmm*," Sarah replied, studying the ugly carpet with the faded pattern of trampled roses, and thinking how much nicer a clean, vanilla-ice-cream colored rug would have been in its place. Flooring like that could make the somber décor of this room almost forgivable. Too much traffic for such a light color, though. "Mm-*hmm*."

Then, all at once, it seemed like the world had been taken over by people who needed to touch her, to whisper their garbled messages into her ear, to hold her hands and pat her face and stroke her hair. Now that she was fully aware of it, it was unbearable. The world had become a barrage of faces, a tornado of hands. And those maddening puffs of breath against her face whenever they leaned in close to mumble at her… it was too much, too much. "Mm-*hmm*," she said in a slightly higher key and with the initial tremor of panic tingeing the sound. She stood up too quickly, teetered a bit, and the overly perfumed and brightly lipsticked matron who was blurb-blurbling at her at the moment almost took a tumble. Sarah looked at the startled woman, whose eyes were now very round and bulging, and said, "Mm-*hmm*!" again as she began to stumble away.

Outside this room, at the other end of the hallway, there was another viewing room. A dozen or so people were milling around the anteroom just this side of the double doors where, presumably, another body was laid out in an oblong box. *Such a strange custom,* she thought, *getting all dressed up to cavort with the dead.* No one ever looked like they wanted to be at a funeral, least of all the corpse. Yet, there they were, the living and the dead, dutifully and deliberately not glad to be there.

Three young people in the seats closest to the doors were whispering and giggling into their fists. An old woman sitting at the edge of a chair on the opposite side, cane locked between her legs, looked like she was composing a grocery list in her head; she seemed neither sad nor happy; just pensive. The old woman looked up at Sarah as she walked past and scowled suspiciously at her. Sarah felt a momentary unease, but kept on walking.

She went into the room and stood just to the left of the double doors, surveying the crowd. There were several generations of people here who shared more than a passing resemblance. There were a few uniformed men talking to each other; one was a cop; the others looked like firemen. A couple of grade-school aged children were chasing each other, trying not to make noise and not succeeding as they traced the random patterns of the ugly rug, weaving through pairs of long legs belonging to the adults standing near the back of the room. Sarah couldn't see who was in the box, but the coffin looked rather feminine, in an old-fashioned way. People were murmuring and burburbling here in much the same manner as the ones in the room Sarah had recently vacated.

Then a noise like an old, rusty siren began to rise slowly from somewhere near the front of the room. The siren became a keening wail. The wail became a howl. The howl disintegrated into a choked tangle of wet words, cried out loud, that could just as likely have been a tirade as a prayer, maybe both. No one reacted to this noise, as deeply distressed and distressing as it was. Not a single head turned. It was incomprehensible to Sarah that people would pretend not to notice such a thing.

Was it possible that she was the only one who was hearing it?

"Mm-*hmm*," she said very quietly.

A terrible sensation began to overtake her. She felt as if she had been injected with something icy, and it was freezing her from the inside out as it coursed through her veins. She began to tremble. She took a few slow steps backward, until her back pressed against the wall.

Without warning, the scowling old woman with the cane was before her. She hissed something ugly at Sarah, inches from her face, spittle flying from deeply wrinkled lips. Then, just as suddenly, she turned and began making her way toward the coffin.

Sarah began to wonder: do crazy people know they're crazy? Does a crazy person feel like she's the only normal person in a world full of babbling and possibly dangerous lunatics, like she was feeling now? Or had the whole world, in fact, gone mad? What was real? Had this funhouse world existed all along, behind some secret curtain she was never supposed to notice or peek through, but that now for some reason was fully revealed to her?

There was a new commotion at the front of the room. The scowling old woman with the cane had thrown herself on the corpse. She was screaming something Sarah couldn't understand.

"Don't worry, Sadie!" the old woman was screeching. "I'm gonna get 'em for ya! I'm gonna get 'em *all* for what they done to ya!"

A boy of about twelve was standing near Sarah. He said to an older man beside him, "What's wrong with Aunt Moira?"

"She's nuts," said the man in a perfectly reasonable tone. "Sadie was eighty-three and diabetic. The only thing that 'got' her was the pound-and-a-half of butter she put on her scone every morning."

Aunt Moira continued ranting and swearing vengeance as she wept on the corpse of the departed Sadie. Everyone else in the room carried on as if nothing at all was amiss. Everyone, that is, except Sarah, who was becoming increasingly certain that she was, in fact, going insane. She wanted to run from this place, but her feet were anchored to the carpet. The tremor in her body ratcheted up a few more notches.

Eventually, one of the firefighters and a large, middle-aged woman went over and pried Aunt Moira off the corpse. They convinced her to take a seat, where she promptly began her own keening wail, in competition with the rusty siren. Aunt Moira's version, however, was shrill enough to peel the wallpaper.

Sarah took a jagged breath. The plodding normalcy of life had been replaced by wailing, mumbling people, stinking bedspreads and dank hallways, illegible newspapers, bleeding feet, and the living and the dead mingling at some macabre, compulsory cocktail party no one seemed in a hurry to leave.

Her vision began to fade to shades of gray. She forced her feet to move, and succeeded in inching her way back to the door, feeling her way along the wall behind her with her fingertips.

Careful, careful. No swift motions in the vast depths of this underwater dream because, yes, this is a dream and, no, not another thing but a dream could this be. Mm-hmm!

Just then, a hand touched her shoulder. She jumped and looked up into the eyes of a sallow, bald-headed man, the keeper of this fine zoo, a creature who was born to be stared at.

"Is there something I can do for you, Ms. Miranda?" he said gently.

Sarah's heart was pounding. Everything was distorted. She tried to smile, but only one corner of her mouth curled slightly. "Mm-hmm."

He waited, watching her with concern. He often feigned this sort of gesture, but not this time. "Yes?"

Sarah opened her mouth to speak and heard her jaw crack.

"Why don't you come with me?" he whispered, leading her out of the viewing room.

Sarah cocked her head as she looked up at this odd man. She cleared her throat in an effort to find her long lost voice. "Do you…" she croaked, then tried again. "Is there a bar here?"

The smile that washed over the sallow man's face transformed him into something entirely warm and human. "Come with me." He placed a hand under her elbow and led her away.

He ushered her into a small room quite unlike the ones where people assembled to view their recently departed. This room had lovely large windows through which bushels of late-afternoon sunlight poured in. Here were her warm, welcoming colors, her clean lines and soft edges. Not a trampled dusty rose in sight. As she seated herself at the large, plush chair by the window, she heard the sound of small ice cubes tinkling in a glass. She closed her eyes. She wished the sound would go on forever.

"Here you are." The sallow man offered her the glass he was holding.

"Thank you," she said, and took a sip. Then she looked at him questioningly.

He chuckled and shook his head. "It's just a little mineral water. It's all I can offer you right now, I'm afraid."

She smiled back and nodded. "You should smile more often. It changes you."

And with that, he went from sallow to warm pink. "Small sips are best," he said as he pulled a chair closer to her. "As for smiling, it's too often a difficult thing to manage in my field. How would it look if I were suddenly to become the Great Grinning Mortician?"

"What…?" Sarah almost dropped her glass.

"Pardon?" He stood up quickly and held his hands out to catch the glass, but her grip held.

"You're a mortician," she said as if he had just removed his mask.

"Yes. Funeral Director, actually. Theodore Bremer. We met, a couple of days ago?"

"Oh. Right. Yeah. I just... I..." Sarah peered at him again. "You're the mortician."

"Yes. I am."

"Oh." She closed her eyes tightly and lowered her hands to her lap. "Oh."

Theodore Bremer took the glass from her and set it on the window sill. Sarah had gone limp where she sat. "Right," she said again. A flood of tears poured down her face when she let her eyelids flutter the tiniest bit.

"I am so deeply sorry for your loss, Ms. Miranda," he said to her.

She heard the words clearly, and yearned for incomprehensible mumbling.

———

Embalming a child was the only part of Theodore Bremer's job that made him wish that, earlier in life, he had developed a greater affinity for live human beings. He might have made a good tax advisor, or a restaurateur, any job that would have brought him a little closer to people who still moved of their own volition, but who didn't necessarily require a long-term, personal relationship with him.

He allowed Sarah to weep quietly in her own world, knowing there was nothing he could say to make things right for her. When at last it did feel like the right time, he said softly to her, "Would you like me to find someone to come sit with you for a while?"

Sarah shook her head slightly without looking at him. "At what time will the people leave?"

"The viewing is scheduled until nine this evening."

"Hmmm." Sarah knew by the light in the window that nine o'clock was still a long way off. "Can we get them out of here sooner?

Like now?"

"Well..." He wasn't quite sure how to respond to this request. "It's possible, I suppose. Are you sure that's what you want?"

"I want some time with my little girl without people falling all over me, blubbering nonsense at me. A quiet space. Just the two of us."

"Of course."

"It would be weird, though. Wouldn't it."

Sarah was asking if it would be weird to ask the visitors to leave. Theodore Bremer thought she was asking if it was weird to want to spend time alone with her dead child.

"Not at all," he said to Sarah. "We'll do whatever you'd like."

Sarah considered this a moment longer. "Let's wait a little while. Just a little while."

"As you wish." Theodore Bremer stood up and gently placed a hand on Sarah's shoulder. "I'll be right outside if you need anything. You can stay here as long as you like."

Sarah nodded and tried to say, "Mm-hmm," but she had no voice for it anymore.

She slept for a while, curled up in the chair by the window. Occasionally, Theodore Bremer opened the door a crack to allow Dan or Ana to peek in and reassure themselves that she was all right. Just past dusk, though, Ana threatened to call the police if Mr. Bremer didn't step aside and allow her to wake her daughter and bring her back to the viewing room. Theodore Bremer congratulated himself on having successfully kept Ana at bay this long, and then he let her in.

———

"I want to thank you all for coming," Sarah said to the considerable crowd still gathered in the room. There were a thousand things she knew she should say, a few dozen she thought she actually could say, but all she really wanted to say was, "Get out."

Some of the people in the room would have forgiven her for that. Some would have been grievously offended. One or two might have ventured to chide her about it, years from now. All of this occurred to her, too. She wasn't up to entertaining any of these possibilities, however. So, when she opened her mouth again to speak, all that came out was, "I want to… thank you. Thank you for coming."

Some people began to gather their things among murmurs and nods. Enough of them understood. But when some of them started to make their way to the front of the room to say their good-nights to her, to express their condolences one last time, a look of panic crossed Sarah's face. She whirled around quickly and knelt before the casket, folding her hands and closing her eyes as if she were deep in instantaneous prayer. "Make them go away. Now," she commanded no one.

When she opened her eyes again and looked behind her, only Ana and Dan remained. Theodore Bremer was still holding the doors open for them.

"I need just a moment alone," she said to her parents. Dan nodded and turned to leave. Ana was outraged.

"What is the *matter* with you?! I will never understand—"

"Take your time, dear." Dan intercepted Ana and shepherded her out of the room. Theodore Bremer closed the doors softly after them, leaving Sarah to take care of business on her own terms, in her own way, and in private.

She stared blankly at the oaken panels of the closed doors for a long time. The quiet of the room seemed enormous, endless. The cloying scent of flowers filled her nostrils. She turned around slowly to look at her daughter for the first time in many days, and for the last time in this life.

She wasn't sure anymore what she had expected to see, but she was surprised at how familiar this felt. Tessie sleeping. Her lips were a little too dark, the cheeks a little too rosy, but not a lot. Not a lot. Just enough for a mother to notice.

A sense of peace washed over Sarah, totally unexpected. There was no horror in this moment, no pain. She reached into the casket and very, very lightly touched her daughter's dark, shiny hair.

It felt dry. It felt stiff. Like a doll's hair. Sarah's brow furrowed.

She wanted to hold Tessie one last time, to cradle her, to rock her. This would be her only chance.

Sarah reached into the coffin with both hands.

She expected her baby's flesh to feel cool to the touch. She was not expecting it to feel like stone. Sarah pulled her hands away and closed her fists. This was not her child. This was someone's sick idea of a child, a mannequin, a wax figure. Sarah pressed her hands to her chest, her dream of rocking Tessie in her arms one last time completely dashed. She peered closely into the falsely sleeping face of this imitation of a little girl, and saw no trace of the being with whom she had shared a life for five and a half years. That wonderful, loving, cheerful creature was gone, along with her often maddening questions, her unending chatter, her wonderment, the simple and surprising profundity of her wisdom, her warmth, her laughter, her tears. Gone. Gone. This artificial figure in a satin-lined white box, this *obscenity*, was not that child. Not her nose. Not her lashes. Not her cheeks, not her hair. And that was not a real blush.

Sarah took a few steps back and looked around this horrible, empty room, disbelieving that she could ever have thought of it as beautiful. She began to stumble up and down its length and its breadth, with hands as heavy as lead weights flailing futilely at her sides. "Where are you, baby girl?" she wailed. "Where *are* you? *Where ARE you?!*"

Two

IF SARAH HAD BEEN PRESENT at the burial, she had no memory of it.

On that sunny Friday morning, Ana had dressed her daughter in a plain black dress she had found in Sarah's closet the night before. Ana had hastily packed a few other things in a weekend bag while Dan and Sarah waited downstairs in the car; Sarah had refused to come up to her apartment. Refused to move, in fact. She hadn't spoken since Dan and Ana had burst into the viewing room last night, where they found Sarah wailing, screaming, tearing at her clothes and hair, wandering the room, upending chairs and knocking over flower arrangements. They managed to calm her down after a while. Ana had popped a Xanax into Sarah's mouth when Mr. Bremer brought her a glass of water. Sarah hadn't uttered a word since.

Dressing Sarah now in the guest room of her home in New Jersey, Ana was awash in a flood of sweet memories. It was harder to dress Sarah now, of course; Sarah was a lot taller, and she was limp, her arms and legs rubbery and heavy, and Ana wasn't as nimble as she used to be. Still, she went about this bit of business with the same care and loving efficiency as she had when Sarah was little.

Ana was deeply disappointed and shocked that Sarah had not arranged for a funeral Mass for Tessie. She feared for the immortal soul of her beloved granddaughter, as well as for Sarah's. It was unconscionable, an act of deadly defiance, as far as Ana was concerned. Unable to make sense of it, she attributed Sarah's decision to the insanity of grief. She was sure Sarah would regret this egregious oversight once she was able to think clearly again. So Ana took matters into her own hands, as she had that weekend a few years ago when Sarah was out of town and she and Dan had Tessie baptized without Sarah's knowledge or consent. Ana invited Father Luciano, the same priest who had baptized Tessie in secret and in a not entirely official way, to the graveside service and arranged for him to officiate.

The priest arrived at the cemetery with a small contingent of West African nuns. The three gray-clad sisters stood solemnly off to the side, weeping like paid mourners for a child they had never met. One of them, Sister Mireille, came over to Sarah at the end of the service, after the coffin had been lowered into the ground. She took Sarah's limp hands in both of hers. The large crucifix of the rosary she had been holding in the palm of her hand pressed against the back of Sarah's hand. Sarah stared straight ahead at nothing, glassy-eyed and absent.

"Your child is with Jesus and the angels now," Sister Mireille said to Sarah in a strangely musical accent. "We must rejoice in God's goodness and His eternal love. Your child is in a better place."

Something twitched in the corner of Sarah's eye. She sat up a little straighter, turning her head slowly until she locked eyes with the small, wimpled woman. Sarah pulled her hands away roughly from the nun's grasp, causing her rosary to drop to the ground in a rattle of beads. Sister Mireille bent quickly to retrieve it. She kissed the cross, and blessed herself with it.

"In a better *place,*" Sarah rasped. She stood up. "A better *place?*"

she growled. Sister Mireille cowered. "My baby is DEAD!" Sarah screamed. "My baby is *DEAD!!!* That is not a better *PLACE!!! THAT IS NOT A BETTER PLACE!!!* You *stupid, fucking—*"

"Sarah!" both of her parents shouted over her in horrified unison.

"*—ignorant BITCH!*"

The word echoed through the cemetery like the crack of rifle fire. Ana was too stunned to move. Dan leapt out of his chair and restrained his daughter, who appeared to be about to hurl Sister Mireille headfirst into the open grave, right onto the top of Tessie's coffin. Sister Mireille ran away, into the arms of the two other nuns, trembling, and weeping in earnest now.

After that, all was silence in Sarah's world. This moment would remain buried forever in her subconscious, as deeply and as quietly as Tessie's body now lay beneath the indifferent earth.

For her part, Sister Mireille would never attend another funeral without remembering this encounter.

————

Days, perhaps weeks passed, all of them lost in a dark fog. Sarah slept excessively, wandered aimlessly, or simply sat in a state of near catatonia.

Ana's meddlesome and often obsessive nature actually served a useful purpose during this time. She couldn't get Sarah to eat more than a bite or two of anything at any meal, but she passed a warm washcloth over her daughter's face and body when she couldn't coax Sarah into the shower, and made sure she slept in clean pajamas every night. Dan worried about how much weight Sarah had lost, and grew fearful of her silence. Late at night, in bed with his wife, he debated with her whether it would be best to call a doctor, who might suggest putting Sarah in some kind of facility. Ana would have none of that.

"She's fine here. We'll take care of her." Dan could not dissuade her.

Finally, one early morning, just as the sun was coming up, Sarah woke to the sound of birds in the tree just outside the bedroom window. It sounded like they were having a convention, perhaps a meeting to decide what they would do today, how far they should travel, or whether it was time to teach the chicks to fly.

Sarah ran a hand through her hair and grimaced. She needed a good shampooing. Out of the corner of her eye, she caught sight of her weekend bag on the floor near the dresser. The last time she had seen it, it was on the top shelf of her own bedroom closet. She could not remember the last time she had used it. She walked over to inspect it. The bag was empty except for a few pieces of underwear. She pulled out a pair of panties, and then opened the closet door. There she found a couple of pairs of her own slacks and some blouses, and a black dress hanging neatly on a hook on the inside of the door. The rest of the closet was crammed with out-of-season clothes and boxes of things that belonged to her father.

She found a pair of her mother's sweatpants and one of her father's pullover sweaters in a basket full of clean, folded laundry in the basement. This was good enough for now. She trudged back upstairs for a shower.

Dan found Sarah an hour or so later in one of the Adirondack chairs on the back deck, her hands around a large mug of coffee. "Hey, sweetheart." He kissed the top of her head and took a seat next to her. "How are you doing this morning?"

"Good, I think."

"Are you cold? You want a jacket?"

"Nah. It feels good. I feel... awake."

"I'll bet." Dan resisted the urge to stare at her, to search for signs of progress or more trouble in his daughter's face. He stole furtive glances at her instead, whenever he could.

They sat in comfortable silence for a long while. Sarah spoke first. "I've been thinking, Dad."

Dan waited a beat, and when she seemed to fall back into her reverie, he prompted her for more. "Yeah? What about?"

"Taking a little trip. To the water. Maybe Montauk. Maybe down the Shore."

"There's a perfectly nice duck pond up the road," he offered.

Sarah shook her head minutely. "Not big enough."

"Big enough for what?" He hoped his voice didn't betray his alarm.

"I need the ocean. The bigness of it."

"You want to go on a cruise? I really wish you'd go with us sometime. I think you'd like it. It's like being on a big, floating hotel. Or a mall, but with nicer restaurants."

"Sounds too much like a big, floating prison."

Dan ran a hand across the stubble on his chin. "Well, a trip to the beach sounds kind of nice, actually. It'll be quiet this time of year. I'm sure we can arrange it. I bet Mom would like that, too. A nice family trip, like we used to do?"

"Can I borrow the minivan?"

Dan could feel himself tensing up, not too unlike when she was a teenager and asked to borrow the car, making him wish he had never taught her how to drive, which he had done only as a way of getting her to come out of her room during those awful days when they had lived in Florida. "You want to go down the Shore by yourself?"

Sarah remained quiet for a while, lingering a bit in her thoughts. She knew her parents rarely used the minivan anymore, not since gas prices ticked up past $3.50 a gallon. They had purchased a little hybrid car not that long ago, and now probably spent thousands of dollars a year on electricity instead of gas. Still, they used the hybrid now almost exclusively. They used the minivan mostly to haul large purchases home, and to "round up the old girls," as Dan referred to Ana's Bingo

Night carpool. It was Ana's turn to drive only once every four or five weeks, and they hardly ever bought anything huge anymore. "What if I bought it from you?" Sarah asked.

"What, the Odyssey?"

"Yeah."

"I thought you said it was pure idiocy to own a car in the city. And that minivans should be outlawed altogether, just for being ugly."

"I don't want it for the city. I think I'm going to sell the apartment. Move away. For anywhere but Manhattan, I'll need a car." The Odyssey would make an excellent moving van, especially since there wasn't much she planned to take and she didn't know where she was going.

Dan wanted to choose his words carefully. "That's, um… that's a pretty big step." This was absolutely not the best time to make decisions like this. In fact, he couldn't think of a worse time. He went for more neutral ground. "The housing market is still kind of a wreck. Maybe you could wait a while? Wait for a better time?"

"Now's the perfect time."

They heard Ana clanking dishware in the kitchen.

"I have some money in the bank. I could pay you cash for it."

Ana poked her head out the door. "Sarah! How wonderful! You're up! Cash for what?"

"Nothing," Dan said.

"For the car," Sarah countered. "The minivan. I want to buy it."

"Don't be silly. What do you want that thing for?" Ana pulled the robe around herself tighter and stepped outside to give Sarah a hug and a kiss on the cheek. "Breakfast will be ready in a jiff." She scooted back inside.

"So what do you say, Dad?"

"It's not about the money, Sarah. Or the car, even. Hell, you could probably sweet-talk me into just giving it to you. Though you'll need a second job just to keep the tank full."

"Well… it's all relative, I guess."

"How about if we both think about this for a while. How's that sound?"

"All right," she said after a bit.

Dan stood and gave her hand a little squeeze as he walked past her.

But Sarah had already made up her mind. There was no way she was going back to that apartment.

––––––––––

Something cold and steely took over Sarah's composure in that week or so after "waking up," a little more every day. She felt as if she had emerged still trembling from some unspeakably bad dream, and the only way to move forward was to convince herself that the events of the recent past were, in fact, a terrible dream. And now that she was in this state of greater awareness and regaining possession of the kind of clear-headed rationality with which she had lived significant portions of her life—or so she liked to believe—she felt capable of taking care of business.

Almost all of life was an exercise in project management. She had made a career out of that skill, and she had been very good at it.

First, she made a list of the easy tasks: cancel newspaper subscription, cable, and utilities; calculate how many mortgage payments could be made through auto-pay before bank account is depleted; quit job (if she still had a job).

The second list was harder, the "keep/sell/donate" list. This required her to do an inventory entirely from memory, and there were a lot of things she did not want to think about or remember. It would also require her to stretch the limits of friendship with whomever she could recruit to help her do this; the alternative would be for her to do it herself, which meant that it would not be done at all. She would simply abandon all her possessions if it came to that. It was just stuff, after all, every bit of it replaceable. Perhaps she could make the task worthwhile to someone by offering a commission on whatever could be sold, and first-pick at anything worth having at no charge. Whatever was left could go to Goodwill or the trash; it didn't matter to her anymore.

Selling the apartment was a little trickier. Once again, it would require the involvement of a trusted—and willing—friend or relation, as well as a realtor, a lawyer, and the usual slew of ancillary professionals required for what, anywhere else in the world, would be a relatively straight-forward transaction. Nothing in New York was simple, least of all the transfer of real estate.

The apartment was the only possession she could not reasonably abandon. Even in a post-bubble housing market, it was now worth at least three times more than she had paid for it. It had been pure, dumb luck that she bought it when she did, still in her twenties and still single when the building went co-op. Renters were offered the opportunity to buy their own apartments for a price she considered extraordinarily high at the time, and now seemed incredibly cheap. If she sold it now, she was sure she would never be able to buy another place in Manhattan again, not without hitting the lottery. At its current value, however, she could probably live for a few years off the profits and the equity—assuming, of course, she was willing to roam the earth as a secretly rich bag lady. This option was not entirely unappealing at the moment. Fortunately, she didn't have to make this decision right this minute. She had enough money in the bank to cover her mortgage and other expenses for at least six months.

There were other accounts she could raid. A 401(k) plan she had previously not considered touching, suddenly seemed very touchable. It was full of money that had come mostly from her employers, so it was easy to think of it as "free money," even after taxes and penalties. She had borrowed a little money from her parents and used her first 401(k)—much of which she would have lost the following year if she had left it in the investment plan—for the down payment of her apartment. Even so, she promised herself and Suze Orman on TV that she'd never do that again, not until retirement, though she never regretted that first raid.

After Tessie was born, she had opted instead to put as much money as she could into a tax-deferred college fund, reducing her own contributions to her retirement fund. Sarah pushed the college fund out her mind. No need to think about that little pile of cash right now, except as the last of all possible safety nets.

Looking over her notes and lists, which would surely horrify the most open-minded of financial consultants and cast some serious doubts on her reputation as a responsible business manager, Sarah saw nothing but freedom and wide open spaces. The freedom to leave everything behind, a brand new emptiness to fill with anything she wanted, or with nothing at all. How often does an opportunity like that come along in a person's life? It felt right. It felt necessary. It was the only thing left for her to do.

———

At Ana's insistence, Sarah took a small cooler packed with soda cans and water, and a picnic basket full of snacks and sandwiches. "I'll only be gone a few hours," Sarah had protested.

"Who goes to the beach without a picnic basket?" Ana countered. "Who goes to the beach in April, for that matter?"

"It's already May," Dan pointed out.

"Let us go with you. We'll go with you. Dan?"

"Leave her alone," Dan said. "She'll be fine." He emerged from the kitchen with a set of keys in his hands. "I took 'er in for a tune-up and oil change this morning. Tires are fine. Tank's full."

"Thanks, Dad. I'll bring it back full."

"You'll get no argument from me on that." He had just dropped seventy bucks into that tank. "Be careful," he said as he put the keys into her hand.

"I will."

"Here! Take a blanket!" Ana came rushing from the laundry room. "Who goes to the beach without a blanket? In *April* yet. Who *does* that?"

"People who like to have the beach all to themselves." Sarah smiled and kissed her mother on the cheek. "It's even better in December."

————

Sarah was an hour or so out of Ridgewood now, heading south on the Garden State Parkway, about a half hour left to go. She hadn't been to the Jersey Shore in years, preferring the waters off Montauk for her city getaways, liking the idea that the next thing after the ocean, due east of The End, as Long Islanders called it, was Portugal. That was one big puddle of water.

But Long Island held memories she didn't want to recall today. She didn't want to be anywhere near it.

————

She had forgotten how short a distance there was between sand-dusted pavement and shoreline. There was hardly any beach at all, even now, at low tide. Not much at all, at least compared to her memory of it.

She walked down to the water anyway, hugging her jacket tighter against herself. It didn't smell the same, either. She had been yearning for a crisp, salty breeze, cool and clean. What she got instead was a clammy, fish-infused mist.

The day was overcast and the horizon was a blur. All that water, but there just wasn't enough of it, no sense of the enormity in which she so desperately needed to lose herself. She stood there for a long time, willing the mist and the clouds to lift and show her the edges of the world. They would not oblige.

Then a single word popped into her head:

PACIFIC

If there wasn't enough sand and water there, then she was just flat out of luck.

Do you dare?

"Do I?" she asked herself, looking back at the bleak smudge of a horizon.

She got back into the car and pointed the headlights west.

Three

S HE CHASED THE SUN ACROSS the sky, heading westward, no idea if the highway beneath her canted to the north or the south, if she would see mountains or deserts first, or both at the same time. What she did know for sure was that wherever she was going, it was still far away.

From her vast reserves of mostly useless trivia, she drew a factoid: even-numbered highways go east-west, and odd-numbered ones go north-south. The direction of the setting sun was confirmation enough that she should stay on I-70 for now, at least until she could get her hands on a map, or pass some mall with a big Best Buy or Radio Shack sign, someplace where she could buy a car charger for her cell phone and get online. For now she was staying on the road.

Something about not knowing exactly where she was or where this highway ended felt good. For the first time in a long time, she felt the first stirrings of excitement, something hopeful inside her itching to come out and see what existed outside the concrete cocoon in which she had been living for so long.

The sun set for good that evening as she was passing through the weary-looking landscape between Napier and New Baltimore, Pennsylvania. She was determined to put at least two states behind her before calling it a night, and Pennsylvania was enormous. So she decided to drive until something like a city or town appeared before her, preferably after she crossed the state line into whatever came next.

It was past nine o'clock when she started to see signs with the name of a town she had actually heard of: Wheeling. "I thought West Virginia was in the South," she said to herself. Maybe she was wrong about the odd- and even-numbered roads, too.

She wasn't especially tired, or even that hungry. She did have to pee, though. When she had stopped for gas and a bathroom break, fifty or sixty miles ago, she parked for a few minutes in front of the station's convenience store. She ate one of Ana's sandwiches and washed it down with a soda. She had emptied another can of Diet Coke on the ride since then.

Also, it was dark in this part of the world, and most people were probably already in bed. The thought of stopping to relieve herself by the side of the road or at some country gas station in the middle of nowhere (if she could find one that was open), was not at all appealing. She got out at the next exit, and hoped Wheeling wasn't too small a town for a motel.

Her Yankee prejudices conjured up images of wiry but strong cowboys and fat farmers in bib-alls, all of them looking upon her with a hint of sneering disdain and suspicion, none of them happy to exchange pleasantries with the driver of a minivan with New Jersey plates. Like most New Yorkers, Sarah's perception of America, except for a few of the larger cities she had visited on business trips, was that, west of the Hudson River, it was a land full of skinny cowboys, pot-bellied farmers, and large, doughy women who shopped at Wal-Mart. She was also aware that these were the same people who were most likely to think all New Yorkers were rude, Jewish, angry, liberal, and full of meaningless, self-righteous contempt.

Just a short distance from Exit 2A she saw a familiar sign: It said *Hampton Inn*—not *Bates* or *Motel Hell*. It would be clean and, she hoped, reasonably priced. She took it as a good sign that things would continue going her way, despite her guiltily guarded misgivings about West Virginians and other "real" Americans.

While the front desk clerk checked her in for a night's stay, Sarah dug around her purse and found her cell phone. "You wouldn't happen to have a charger for one of these, would you?" she asked the fresh-faced young woman behind the counter.

"I'm sorry, ma'am. We don't," she said, sounding sincere and full of regret. "You're welcome to use our business center if you need a computer. Or you can place a call directly from your room, if you'd like."

Sarah thanked the young woman and counted her blessings. It was the first "no" she'd gotten since the disappointment of the Jersey Shore.

She hesitated for a moment once inside room. An unwelcome flashback to another hotel threatened to overwhelm her. She quickly went about turning on every light and lamp she could find.

This was definitely a lot nicer than that other place. That's all she would allow herself to think about for now.

The phone call to her parents' house from the in-room phone would probably cost as much as the night's stay, but there was no other way around it. They would be worried.

It was Ana who answered the phone, and on the first ring.

"Sarah? Is that you?"

"Hi, Mom."

"Jesus Christ, Sarah, we've been worried sick. Are you all right? Where are you?"

"I'm fine. And I'm sorry. I—"

"It's her! She's all right!" Ana shouted to Dan. "Do you need us to come get you?"

"No, I—"

"I've been calling your cell phone all night. I must've left eight hundred messages. Why didn't you pick up? Do you have your phone? I was about to call the police." Ana looked at the Caller ID display. "You're in the *Hamptons?*"

"No. Mom, I—"

"Have you eaten? Are you hungry?"

Now she was tired. "Can I talk to Dad?"

"No. Talk to me."

"Okay, then *listen.*"

Neither one of them said anything for a few seconds. Ana was holding a hand firmly against her closed mouth, trying not to speak. Sarah didn't know what to say. "I'm listening," Ana said through her hand.

"Okay. Well… first, I'm sorry I didn't call sooner. Time just got away from me. But I'm okay. No need to worry." Sarah heard her mother suck in a breath. She could imagine Ana pursing her lips.

"I feel a 'but' coming on," Ana said tightly.

"Not a 'but.' An 'and.' I'm going to stay here for a while." She felt like she was twelve again, trying to talk her parents into letting her spend the night at Shirley's house. "Would you and Dad be terribly mad at me if I kept the car for a few days?"

"I don't care about the car. I care about you. Where's 'here' and how many is 'a few days'?"

"I just need to be by the water, you know? It helps. It helps me think. I have to… sort some stuff out, is all."

There weren't very many things that left Ana speechless, but this, apparently was one of them. She was quiet for a moment too long. "I don't know, Sarah. I think you should come home, do your thinking here. I promise we won't bother you. Stay as long as you like. I'd feel better if I could see you."

"You mean *watch* me," Sarah said, not unkindly.

"No! No! ...Okay, maybe a little. Would that be so horrible? Really?"

"No. But it wouldn't help me the way I need... the way I need for that to happen right now. I just didn't want you to think I was in trouble, or that I got carjacked or something."

"Carjacked! God forbid!"

"The car's fine."

"Enough about the car! Although now I have to walk everywhere, you understand. Or make your father drive me. I don't understand that electric car. It scares me."

"You always make him drive. Even the other car."

"Yeah, but now he *has* to."

Sarah heard her father in the background. "Tell Dad I'm all right, and that I love him."

"Just him?"

"I love you, too, Mom." She thought that if she spoke to her father she'd start to cry, and that would be a bad thing. "I have to go. I'll call you tomorrow, after I get my phone charged. I have to buy a charger."

"Okay, but—"

"Gotta go, Mom. I'll call tomorrow. Promise. G'night." She hung up before Ana could say anything more.

Bright morning sunlight roused her into wakefulness at about seven-thirty. She awoke from a deep, dreamless sleep, feeling like she had just closed her eyes to the darkness, but was grateful for the crisp, clean sheets and the state of restfulness she felt in her body and in her mind.

She rolled onto her back and stretched every part of herself that moved or bent.

Practicalities came to mind: she had no toothbrush, no change of clothes, no clean underwear. There would be tiny supplies of shampoo, lotion, and soap in the bathroom, and she was pretty sure she saw a single-serve coffee maker somewhere in the room, but she'd have to stop somewhere and buy some stuff. She had driven for many hours the day before, but she was still thousands of miles away from her imagined destination.

Is this crazy?

"No, it's not."

She got up and brushed her teeth with a washcloth and warm water. This would just have to be good enough for now. Then she spied a tiny bottle of Scope mouthwash on the counter. That made it better.

A pair of khaki slacks that felt a size or two too big all day yesterday was now puddled on the floor, next to her mother's rubber gardening clogs. The shoes were loud and ugly—they probably glowed in the dark—but they were surprisingly comfortable, and a much better choice for a walk on the beach than the dress shoes she had left in her parents' guest bedroom.

Sarah had slept in her white cotton blouse and panties. The blouse was now desperately wrinkled, but still wearable under the jacket that was now draped over a chair.

She wanted to take a shower, but was repulsed by the idea of putting dirty underwear back on.

She searched the room for the white athletic socks she had borrowed from her father's drawer the morning before, and was about to give up when she got an idea. She pulled the covers off the bed and found the socks there, near the foot of the bed. She must have kicked them off in her sleep.

She made mental notes of her small inventory and considered what to do next. Surely there was a K-Mart or Target within reasonable distance. She could stock up on a small collection of cheap clothes and other items she might need for a cross-country trip.

But wasn't this journey about divesting herself of stuff? Just a few days ago, she had resolved to walk away willingly from an apartment packed to the rafters with a lifetime's worth of stuff. What would be the point of all this if she were to start that whole silly business all over again? And where would she put all this new stuff? Why even consider it?

She reached over to the nightstand for a pen and the small pad with the *Hampton Inn* logo on it. She made a list:

> toothbrush
> toothpaste
> panties
> hair brush
> tee-shirt
> jeans

She crossed off "jeans."

There was a CVS pharmacy just a short drive up the road from the hotel. There she found most of what she needed, and some other things she hadn't thought of. She took her basket of would-be purchases to the check-out counter, and then turned back with a small apology to the cashier. She put back the large bottles of shampoo and conditioner; she would grab all the little bottles of toiletries in her hotel room before checking out. She kept the pre-moistened towelettes—a small packet to keep in her purse, and a larger tub of sturdier wipes to keep in the car. She swapped the bottle of fruit juice for a large bottle of water, and then swapped it back; when the juice was gone, she could refill the bottle with water at a rest stop along the way. She tried to put the cookies back on the shelf but couldn't make herself do it. She put back the one-time-only battery-powered phone charger and decided to wait until she came across an electronics store where she could buy a real one; she was in no hurry to call anyone. If she needed to dial 911, it would probably be too late for help, and she wasn't sure she wanted to be saved from anything anyway. She swapped the ugly souvenir-style tee-shirt for a 3-pack of plain white men's undershirts in her size. She hated that she now had more clothes, but liked that the 3-pack of tee-shirts was cheaper than her first choice. She kept the small package of white cotton panties.

Divestiture was going to be a harder skill to learn than she thought.

Sarah was anxious to get back on the road, but there was still some business to take care of. This morning's purchases brought to mind the need to check on her bank account and credit card statements, all of which she could do online in the tiny room the hotel clerk had referred to as the Business Center. That, in turn, reminded her of such pedestrian obligations as e-mail and voice mail. She couldn't remember the last time she had checked either.

In the CVS parking lot, she opened the rear door of the minivan and dropped her bags in the cargo space, next to the blanket Ana had thrust at Sarah on her way out of the house. The basket of fruit and sandwiches was also there, minus one sandwich. The sandwiches were probably inedible now, but the fruit might keep for a while longer.

As she reached up to close the rear door, a thought occurred to her: Could she sleep in this space, in a pinch? There was a row of seats already folded down, which made the cargo space seem big, but not big enough for an adult to lie down comfortably. She knew that the middle row folded down flat, but she didn't know how to do it. She would figure it out later. Maybe minivans were not such horrible inventions after all.

Her stomach rumbled just then. There was free coffee and pastries just off the hotel lobby, maybe even something more substantial. She closed the rear door, got back behind the wheel, and drove the short distance back to the neat little building with the clean rooms, free breakfast, and little shampoos.

———

Most of the charges at the top of her online bank statement were familiar: the usual monthly automatic deductions for cable, electricity, Internet access, cell phone, the weekend newspaper delivery, and a couple of bi-weekly transfers into the savings and college fund accounts; these last two were timed to coincide with her payroll deposits. She scrolled down a bit further and saw a few ATM withdrawals and small debit card purchases. None of these were recent.

She also saw that her last paycheck was deposited automatically several weeks ago. Was she even employed anymore? Sarah didn't think she was all that bothered by that possibility. It would save her from having to write a resignation letter, or speaking to the hyperventilating maniac who supervised her.

What did bother her was a check that had been paid in the amount of $8,793.62, and a bank charge for automatically moving money from savings to checking to cover that draft. She clicked on the entry and was presented with an image of the check. It was made out to Bremer & Sons Funeral Home. She closed it quickly, and moved the cursor to the LOG OFF link. A split second before she clicked on it, she went back to the AUTOMATIC PAYMENTS and TRANSFERS links, and cancelled everything she could control from here, except for the mortgage payments. She would have to contact the utility companies and other vendors separately, the ones for which she had set up authorizations for them to withdraw the monthly payments themselves. "Some other time," she said under her breath, and logged out.

With a slight tremor in her hand, she logged on to her personal e-mail account. There were close to three hundred unread messages, over fourteen hundred in all. Some were the usual spammy come-ons and sale announcements from various online vendors, but many of the messages were from people she knew. She scanned the list of Subject lines from a cluster of messages that were time-stamped in early-April.

> So Sorry For Your Loss
> RE: FWD: RE: RE: Sarah's Tessie
> heard the news...
> RE: Tess
> call me!
> lunch?
> Our Deepest Condolences
> where are you???
> RE: [no subject]

A few messages were from her (former?) boss and co-workers. Most were from friends and family.

She stared at the screen for a long time. Then, before she could change her mind, she clicked on the SELECT ALL box and deleted everything. She closed the session, grabbed her purse off the floor, and took off, glad she had already checked out. If she had been forced to speak to some pathologically cheery front-desk person right now, she might have opened her mouth and screamed, and would never have been able to stop.

She pulled out of the parking lot and made for the highway like her hair was on fire. Her determination to dump everything—her sorrow, her guilt, her *rage*—into the vastness of the ocean was renewed tenfold.

If the Pacific wasn't big enough to hold it all, she'd be in big trouble, indeed.

————

Sarah drove straight through Columbus, Ohio—a place very likely to have the kind of stores she needed for the last of her "essential" purchases—although her shopping list was now only a vaguely nagging thought that was fighting a losing battle to break through the surface of her consciousness, along with a thousand other things she kept pushing back by pure force of will. She drove gripping the wheel, teeth clenched, her attitude one of someone who had been wronged in the most egregious ways imaginable, at whom the worst profanities had been hurled. She tried to keep all of her attention focused only on the steady pattern of white lines before her, and emptying her mind of everything else. She drove in silence, with not even the radio for company.

There had been a long section of the road beyond Columbus that was bounded by what appeared to be farmland on both sides, and she began to worry that stretches like that would come more frequently, and grow longer the farther west she went. What if she was too tired to keep driving, or she needed to use the restroom and the next patch of concrete-encrusted civilization was hours—or, God forbid, *days*—away?

She was only beginning to grasp the *bigness* of this country, something that is not fully appreciable by traversing it by air at 30,000 feet. She was gaining a whole new appreciation for the people who had breached that distance on horseback and in wooden-wheeled wagons, and was in absolute awe of the original inhabitants of this land, who had done it on foot, entire tribes at a time.

At about two that afternoon, a big red Target sign loomed up ahead. She took the next exit, at a place called Huber Heights. Unlike Columbus, there would be little risk of getting lost in a maze of streets and industrial parks in search of a shopping center. The entrance to the Target store was practically at the exit ramp.

She made her purchases grimly, and paid for them grudgingly. "Going camping?" said the very large and very tall blond girl at the check-out register, startling Sarah out of her reverie. The girl ran the item back and forth over the price scanner until it beeped, then turned the item over and started to read the back of the box that contained a portable, collapsible toilet Sarah secretly hoped she would never have to use, mostly because she couldn't imagine how she was supposed to get rid of the... shall we say, post-consumer product?

"Are these any good?" the girl asked.

What the hell...?

"I have no idea," she said a bit too gruffly.

The girl eyed her over the top edge of the box. She gave Sarah a small, squinty glare and stuffed the box sullenly into an oversized plastic bag. She then scanned and bagged an airbed, a foot-powered pump, a cheap pair of dark-colored drawstring chinos, and a phone charger. The girl made a point of turning her back to Sarah. "Sign," she said, flicking a meaty thumb over a lumpy shoulder, indicating the credit card reader perched on the customer side of the check-out counter.

Sarah decided to pay no mind to the homely girl or her attitude. There were greater disappointments in life awaiting this person than people who bristled at the nosiness of complete strangers, or unforgivable breaches of customer service etiquette. The way it looked to Sarah, there were loads of insults and slights in this clueless girl's future, and probably not an insignificant number of them in her recent past.

That last thought made Sarah feel small and miserly. That wasn't who she wanted to be. She put the electronic pen back in it's cradle and said to the girl, "I'm sorry if I was rude." She was about to add something like, "It's been a rough day, rough week, rough life..." when the girl responded.

"Have a nice crap."

Whatever guilt or empathy Sarah might have felt, however momentary, vanished in that instant. She leaned toward the girl and replied warmly, "Have another Twinkie, dear."

It surprised her how much better that made her feel, just a wee bit lighter. She wheeled the big red plastic cart of the store, a little smile curling one corner of her mouth. But not before she heard the girl mutter, "Bitch."

———

A giant cross loomed in the distance, filling Sarah with a sickening sense of unease. She was about an hour west of Terre Haute, Indiana.

The cross looked like something that belonged in a scene from *Children of the Corn*. Gooseflesh broke out on her arms.

What the hell could that be? A cemetery? A televangelist training compound? The Vatican of Presbyteria?

There wasn't a lot of traffic on the highway at this hour of the early evening; mostly it was those big semis, and a few smaller (by comparison) American-made pick-up trucks. One or two normal cars rolled by once in a while. Sunset was still about an hour away, but it was coming. She didn't want to get caught out here in the middle of nowhere with nothing but that giant cross looming over her. The gas tank needle hovered just below the quarter-full mark. She kept her eyes peeled for one of those *Gas-Food-Lodging* signs.

The prospect of being stranded for the night in the shadow of that icon was beginning to feel more like a distinct possibility. That cross could probably be seen for miles in all directions, even though she had just noticed it and couldn't tell yet how tall it actually was. Her hands began to perspire. The rhythm of her breathing changed.

She wanted very badly to get off I-70 and put her back to that cross, and slap the rearview mirror away, out of her line of sight, so she wouldn't accidentally see it behind her, like the creepy hitchhiker in that old *Twilight Zone* episode. Her stomach muscles began to tense.

"All right. Enough," she admonished herself, deliberately taking deep breaths. "I'm freaking myself out over nothing. It's just a hunk of concrete or metal or something, erected by some very devout farmer with a weird way of scaring off the crows. And impressionable city folk."

She pushed the POWER button on the radio and got an earful of static.

The SCAN function made the numbers on the dial scroll by quickly. For a moment she thought there would be no radio stations at all in this vast, empty place guarded by the giant, naked cross, which now looked to be the size of a decent-sized skyscraper. She wondered how much daylight was actually left, and if there was enough of it left for her to put some real distance between herself and this creepy place.

If not for that cross, the vista might have seemed like a wistful, picture-postcard view of a vanishing America, or a single, frozen moment in time from some long-gone era and way of life, suspended harmlessly in a protective bubble. A lovely sight—if not, that is, for that ominous cross looking so much like an accusing finger, a freakish monument to inevitable death, doom, and annihilation.

The scanner stopped at a place on the FM dial where gentle voices could be heard just above the static. She tried to make out what they were saying. With any luck, it would be an NPR affiliate, where a familiar voice would be sharing a witty or engaging story, something esoteric about corrugated cardboard, or lampposts.

When she finally made out what the man on the radio was saying, she realized it was a DJ talking about the next Christian Pop tune the audience was about to be "blessed" with. She hit the SCAN button again.

Almost every station was broadcasting some kind of religious program, and that cross now looked like it held dominion over the entire planet. "All the world is a grave," the thing seemed to be saying.

One or two country music stations blared and twanged at her. She let the scanner keep running.

An idiotic commercial came on next, some guy named Big Dan Callahan screaming about an automobile "Blow-Out Extrava*GAN*za!!!" so she hit the SCAN button again, but not before she took note of the number on the dial in case this was the only non-Jesus, non-cowboy thing on the air around here.

Finally, something that sounded like a college station came through. If there was a college, there would be young people in the vicinity, and if there were young people, the population would not be made up entirely of fire-breathing evangelical farmers. She let that thought comfort her a little, and tried to be grateful for the subdued chatter of the young man currently interviewing a local artist. She lowered the volume on the radio until the voices were just audible, and tried hard not to look at the cross. She focused instead on catching up with the big tractor lumbering up the road just ahead. If there was a regular-looking person inside that vehicle (and not a black-clad little horror-movie imp… or something worse), then chances were good that she could reconnect with what was left of the normal world, and find her way back into the meandering reverie with which she had traveled most of the last few hundred miles, lulled by the mind-numbing hum of the road beneath her.

But that cross wouldn't go away.

———————

As a child, the "fear of God" had been a literal thing to Sarah. Religion and terror were inextricably linked.

She was not quite eighteen the night she dared to utter the forbidden words out loud (albeit to herself and in something not much braver than a whisper): There is no God.

In the misery of that moment, when relief and disappointment collided at the point at which she discovered that she would not be struck dead after all, right where she sat, for daring to say those words out loud, Sarah won for herself the freedom to stop believing in invisible forces at work or at play in the world, for good or for evil, and relieved her of the crushing burden of desperation when her pleas for help or comfort vanished into indifferent silence.

The doubts had come slowly, but once they had taken root, they were impossible to shake.

For a long time, Sarah believed that if she prayed hard enough, if she was sorry enough, if she was obedient and meek enough, *somebody* in heaven would finally hear her. When it became apparent that God was too busy or too important to bother with the insignificant likes of her—considering all the other horrible things that were happening in the world—she turned to the Virgin Mary and begged her for help. She also prayed fervently to Saint Jude, patron saint of impossible tasks and lost causes, and even to Saint Francis, patron saint of small animals. Of the thousands of prayers she had committed to memory, and the thousands more she made up herself in the simple language of a child, not a single one had been answered.

Sarah's parents were good people, but their blind spots were enormous. This was especially true when it came to Sarah's maternal grandmother, Liliana de la Torre.

"I don't like her, Daddy," she sometimes said to her father.

The look on his face always said, "Neither do I," but what he told Sarah was, "Blood is thicker than water, sweetheart," or, "She's your grandma. We *have* to love her." Dan never looked his daughter in the eye when he said these things.

Sometimes Sarah protested. "But she's so *mean!*"

"She's an old woman, honey. She's had a hard life. Just respect her and do as she says. She loves you in her own way."

Trying to tell her mother had been no more productive. In fact, it often made things worse. Ana could not tolerate any criticism of her mother.

About a month after Sarah started kindergarten, Ana went back to work for the first time since Sarah was born. Liliana de la Torre lived nearby, in the little apartment where Ana and her sister had grown up, above the neighborhood deli their father would run for more than forty years. After a significant amount of obsequious begging on Ana's part, Liliana reluctantly agreed to watch Sarah after school.

Those afternoons with her grandmother became a long experiment in terror for little Sarah.

On the last day that Sarah would be in Liliana's care, she and her classmates were sent, as usual, to collect their coats and jackets from the closet where all the hooks were at just the right height for little kids. The children were then to assemble neatly in two lines by the classroom door and wait to be escorted out.

That day, however, neither the teacher nor the aide noticed that Sarah never emerged from the closet. She had slipped into the farthest corner, pretending that that's where her coat was, and hid behind sheets of poster board and some easel pads that had been stored at that end of the closet. She waited there until all was quiet.

Her plan had been simple: When Miss Rita and Miss Carol came back, Sarah would ask them to take care of her until her mother came to pick her up after work. Miss Rita and Miss Carol were nice; they seemed to like Sarah as much as she liked them. Sarah could not imagine any reason why they *wouldn't* take care of her. But if they started asking a lot of questions, she would just tell them that that's what her mother said to do today. And maybe tomorrow, too. So she waited, quiet as a mouse, in the dark corner of the schoolroom closet.

When she was certain the room was empty, she crept out and sat at her assigned place at the little table where she was told to sit from the very first day, and folded her hands neatly in front of her, just as her teachers had taught her to do. If they saw how well she was behaving, and how quiet she could be, they were sure to let her stay until her mother came to get her. (At the age of five, it did not occur to Sarah that teachers did not live in their classrooms, or that they ever went to the bathroom, or that they slept at night.)

Liliana de la Torre had been standing outside in the noontime sun on that beautiful October day, under a large black umbrella—a habit developed over a lifetime so that her pale skin would not tan, like a peasant's. She stood away from the other mothers and babysitters, fully ensconced in the icy wall of unprovoked contempt that was her natural state of being. As Sarah's classmates scattered happily outside the school and ran or walked to their respective guardians, Liliana was left standing there, growing increasingly indignant at the incompetence of the morons who dared to think themselves responsible overseers of children. She stopped the two younger women just as they turned to go back into the building.

"Where is my granddaughter?" she demanded, imperious as a dowager, except now she was also growing angry, a terrible collision of storms about to brew. She closed her umbrella and wielded it like a weapon.

Miss Rita and Miss Carol first looked at this impeccably dressed, black-clad vision with the deadly glare of a panther in her eyes, and then they looked at each other.

"Which one is yours?" Miss Carol asked the woman timidly.

Miss Rita put a hand quickly on Miss Carol's forearm and was about to whisper Sarah's name, but Liliana beat her to it, and not in a whisper.

Miss Rita turned her back quickly and said quietly, "Keep her down here, Carol. I'll go check the room." She ran back inside and bounded up one short flight of stairs.

Liliana was having none of this. When she tried to push her way past the teacher, Miss Carol put a hand on her arm. Liliana pulled away with a force and speed that belied her age and diminutive size. She gave the frightened teacher a hard glare and said, "You can come with me, or you can call the police. Or should I call them myself and have you both arrested?"

In all the years Carol had been a teacher—all three of them—and had had to deal with unruly, unreasonable, and angry parents, none had ever chilled her blood the way this horrible woman had just done. Liliana stormed up the stairs. Carol followed close behind.

They arrived at the classroom just in time to see Rita take a seat in a tiny chair next to Sarah. Whatever conversation had been about to begin was immediately aborted.

After roundly insulting the teachers for their blindness and stupidity, Liliana grabbed Sarah by the wrist and dragged her out of the room. The last Miss Rita and Miss Carol saw of Sarah that day were the wide, terrified eyes of a helpless child.

"We have to talk to that little girl's mother," Carol said.

"And tell her what? That grandma's a bitch? How much you wanna bet Sarah's mom already knows that?"

"You saw the look on that little girl's face!"

"Grandma was angry because she was scared. She thought we lost her kid. And Sarah was just reacting to her grandmother's anger." Rita was doing a fine job of convincing herself that that was all that had happened. They had all been momentarily frightened, all of them, that's all. Little kids pull stuff like this all the time, hiding in the clothes racks in department stores and running off in parks and beaches in the blink of an eye. Children were exceedingly good at scaring the crap out of everybody. Just then, she caught sight of one little coat still hanging on a hook inside the open closet. She should have been able to see that when she was standing by the door.

"How did we miss her anyway?" Carol asked. "Sarah wasn't sitting here when we took the rest of the kids out. We would've seen her... right?"

"She was hiding," Rita said flatly, "from that horrible woman."

They thought about this for a long moment. Finally, Rita said, "All right. We'll talk to Sarah first thing tomorrow, see if there's something going on besides her being a normal five-year-old with a not-so-sweet old grandma. Then we'll decide if we should talk to her mother."

"Or call Child Protective Services," Carol added.

At that same moment, Liliana de la Torre was dragging her granddaughter across the street. Sarah caught the eye of the crossing guard and looked beseechingly at what she thought was a policewoman. The crossing guard cocked her head and pouted her lips. "Aww... looks like somebody's in trouble," she said amiably. Liliana ignored her and kept on walking.

Liliana practically threw Sarah through the door when they reached the apartment. "You will never do that to me again," Liliana said grimly.

Sarah had to go to the bathroom, very badly.

Liliana pushed her into the kitchen. "Kneel," she said to Sarah, pointing at a spot in front of the garbage can. Sarah did as she was told. "No! *Facing* the garbage!" Liliana shouted, grabbing Sarah roughly by the shoulders and repositioning her. "You *look* at that garbage, because that is what you are. *Garbage.*"

Sarah was too scared to move, too scared to cry, too scared to say she needed to pee. She hoped this time-out wouldn't take very long.

Liliana stomped away to some other part of the apartment. She came back a moment later with the wooden crucifix that normally hung above her bed. It was about a foot long, and had a secret compartment inside. If you pushed up on the ivory-colored Jesus with the painted-on hair and blood, the top half of the crucifix slipped upward to reveal the space where little vials of holy water and oils were stored. It was a combination wall ornament, talisman, and Last Rites kit.

"Hold this," Liliana commanded, "and *look* at Jesus. Look what you have done to Jesus, and pray he will forgive you."

For years to come, Sarah would have nightmares of a maimed and bloody Jesus trying to rip himself off the cross, sneering angrily at her, coming to get her for what she had done to him. Even as an adult, those dreams had come.

The crucifix got heavier with every passing minute. Liliana was sitting in a wingback chair in the living room, crocheting yet another white doily. She had an unobstructed view of Sarah kneeling in front of the garbage can. Every time Sarah's arms fell lower than Liliana thought was appropriate, she screamed, "Up!" at the little girl, who was doing all she could to keep from getting into worse trouble with this madwoman.

Sarah didn't know how much time had gone by, but when her bladder finally released burning urine down her legs, she begged the unblinking crucified Christ not to let her grandmother notice. And for a long time, Liliana did not.

When at last Liliana tired of crocheting, it was nearly four in the afternoon. Sarah had been on her knees in a puddle of her own urine for more than three hours.

Liliana noticed the smell first. She yanked the child up by one arm and looked with disgust at the damp spot on Sarah's pants and the congealing yellow puddle on her otherwise spotless linoleum floor.

Sarah tried to stand, but her legs gave out from under her. One of her hands hit the sticky yellow spot. The other hand dropped the crucifix. She was too tired to cry, too numb to care.

Liliana picked up the crucifix, kissed it, and hit Sarah on the head with it. Not hard enough to draw blood, but hard enough to raise a small lump.

Next she threw a roll of paper towels and a bottle of Fantastik at her. "*Cochina,*" she growled at her granddaughter. "Clean that up."

Sarah's little fingers struggled with the spray nozzle, but she finally coaxed a dribbly stream from the bottle. As she wiped clumsily at the spot, she heard her grandmother filling the tub in the bathroom. She thought she'd never been happier for a bath. She yearned for a warm bubbles.

The miracle would be that she ever took a bath again.

The water was ice cold, and Grandma scrubbed too hard, especially "down there." It would burn every time she peed for the next few days.

Sarah didn't have a change of clothes at her grandmother's house. Liliana wrapped her tightly in a towel and sat her on the plastic-encased sofa. She pulled a comb through Sarah's hair, fighting the knots with a particularly vicious zeal. "Just like Lily," she said between clenched teeth. "She was a bad girl, too. Just like you."

Sarah had heard from other relatives that she looked just like her aunt Lily. Ana always disagreed, pointing out instead all the ways in which Sarah looked like Dan's side of the family.

Sarah had never met Lily. No one seemed to know where Lily was, and no one ever talked about her when Liliana was present. Sarah would never again wonder why Lily wasn't here anymore. Maybe Grandma killed her. Maybe Lily ran away. Maybe she sent Lily to the jail for bad girls, the one where she was always threatening to send Sarah.

Liliana yanked through another knot in Sarah's hair. When Sarah scrunched her shoulders and whimpered, Liliana hit her over the head with the edge of the comb. "*Quieta!*" she scolded. Sarah was pretty sure that meant "stay still" in Spanish. She tried to clench her entire body so that it wouldn't move.

An unknowable time later, Ana finally rang the doorbell. Sarah's impulse was to throw the towel off and run screaming into her mother's arms. She immediately scooted on her butt to the edge of the sofa, the backs of her thighs making squeaking noises against the plastic slipcovers. Liliana pointed a gnarled finger at Sarah. "You stay right there. And not a peep out of you." It came out sounding like, "not eh pip."

Sarah stayed where she was while Liliana walked down the hall to open the door.

When Ana came over to her little girl, she said, "Oh, how wonderful! Grandma gave you a bath!"

Unable to hold it in any longer, Sarah began to cry. Big, wet tears streamed down her face, her mouth open in a perfect O of misery. But not a sound came out. Tiny expulsions of air through that big wide O made her shoulders jerk up and down. She wanted to tell her mother everything—everything—but she could not form words or make any sounds. So Liliana spoke for her.

"Sarita was a very bad girl today."

Ana looked over her shoulder at her mother as she sat next to Sarah.

"Shall I tell her?" Liliana said to Sarah in a mocking, sing-song voice.

Sarah sucked in a deep breath that then came out in an eardrum-piercing scream.

"What happened?!" Ana asked, alarmed.

"She ran away from the teachers," Liliana said without taking her eyes off Sarah. "We thought she had been kidnapped. And then she made pee-pee on my kitchen floor. Like a little pig. *Cochina*."

Ana looked at her mother in horror, then at her daughter. "Sarah?"

Sarah sucked in another deep breath and wailed again.

"Don't worry," Liliana said calmly. "She will never do *that* again. Isn't that right, Sarita?"

Sarah was now nearly convulsing in sobs.

"You will have to watch this one," Liliana told Ana, turning her back and strolling toward the kitchen with a self-satisfied gait. "I see Lily all over again."

That last statement raised the hairs on Ana's arms and the back of her neck. But instead of confronting her mother, she simply bowed her head. She could feel her ears closing up and shutting down, the way they did when her sister Lily was being punished for the smallest transgressions. Ana used to wonder why Lily was always in trouble, but was deeply grateful—even as she felt a searing shame for that gratitude—that she never angered her mother the way Lily always managed to do.

————

Liliana had never laid a finger on Ana, the "good" child. Lily, on the other hand, could bring out the dark monster inside their mother by simply turning her head in a way that displeased Liliana. The problem was that no one ever knew from one moment to the next what exactly would displease Liliana. This went on for years, while their father cheerily sliced cold cuts and made sandwiches for his customers downstairs, while Ana busied herself in a corner of her room, rocking a baby doll and humming a song—any song—so she wouldn't have to hear Lily scream. It happened every day, sometimes more than once a day. It went on until the day Lily finally hit back.

Lily came home from school a half hour late that day. The door slammed when she came in, the way it sometimes did when the main door to the building was open downstairs and created a wind tunnel through the stairwell. Sometimes it was strong enough to rip the doorknob right out of a person's hand. Slamming a door was one of the worst things you could do in Liliana's house. Except when it wasn't. You just never knew.

Liliana—already angry that Lily was off doing God-knows-what with boys, that whore—was waiting, pacing from one end of the apartment to the other, peeking through the curtains of every window, hoping to catch Lily in the act of doing whatever she was doing.

"Sorry," Lily whispered miserably as she stepped into the living room. It was the last word she ever spoke to her mother.

Liliana reached back and swung hard, slapping Lily across the face. The sound of it was like the crack of a whip.

For a moment after regaining her balance, Lily just stood there, her hand over the burning cheek where finger-shaped welts were already rising. Ana, who had been sitting on the floor and using the coffee table as a desk, looked upon this scene holding her breath, wishing she had chosen to do her homework in her room that day.

Something dark and dangerous cast a grotesque pall over Lily's face. She bowed her head and snorted like a bull that had had enough of the toreador's taunts. She pounced on Liliana with a screaming howl, knocking the small woman down to the floor, on her back. Lily straddled her, using her knees to pin Liliana's arms to her ribs. She began pounding on Liliana's face, chest, and shoulders, wherever she could hit her. Lily's fists moved like the pistons of a machine—left, right, left, right, so fast, so hard—as Liliana struggled to break free.

Ana was frozen to her spot, disbelieving what she was seeing, not at all certain whom, if anyone, she was supposed to save. Years later, she would remember this event as having taken place in complete silence. That was not at all the case.

"Ana!" Liliana was finally able to cry out, and that set Ana in motion.

Ana jumped on her sister's back and tried to pull her off their mother. Lily, possessed now of a rage-fueled strength, reared back and elbowed Ana in the ribs, sending her sprawling. She immediately went back to pounding on her mother. She seemed determined to put an end to her once and for all.

Ana tried again, this time wrapping Lily's long, black braid around her wrist like a rope and grabbing the rest in her fist. She pulled as hard as she could. Lily's head snapped back. She fell off Liliana. Lily scrambled to her feet and stared down at the bloody, broken face of her mother, with a look of hatred so profound that it transformed the young girl into something utterly unrecognizable. Ana cowered against a wall, heart pounding out of her chest, a loud high-pitched hum screeching in her ears. Liliana raised both hands to her face and started screaming. Lily was panting like an animal, her fists still clenched and shaking. Then she turned and ran out of the apartment, still in her school uniform.

Lily was never seen or heard from again. She was seventeen.

Liliana tended to her own injuries. She didn't leave the apartment for weeks, until the last of her bruises had disappeared. Cosmetic dentistry later fixed the gap on her lower left jaw where two or three healthy teeth had once thrived. Her nose canted slightly to the right the rest of her life.

Liliana forbade her husband, Alberto, from going out to look for Lily. Alberto did so anyway, in secret, for years. He never found his daughter. Ana told her father she couldn't begin to imagine where Lily went, but deep in her heart, she hoped it was far, far away, and that wherever she was, people were kind to her. She prayed for Lily every night. She still did.

After Lily left, life in the de la Torre home became very quiet. Eventually, it became easy to pretend it had always been that way.

Ana spent her last year at home mostly on tiptoe. She went to college Upstate, where she met Daniel Miranda and married him in her senior year, mostly so she wouldn't have to go back to her mother's house after graduation.

Fortune had smiled on her yet again; it had given her a caring companion who thought she was "good." As far as Dan knew, Ana had had a happy childhood. Ana let him think so because she had managed to convince herself that it was true. Of course, compared to Lily, Ana's childhood had been a blissful dream.

Ana never talked much about the sister she once had, and Dan was not a terribly curious man when it came to such matters. They were, in many ways, perfect foils for one another.

———

Ana now gathered Sarah up in her arms, towel and all, marveling and horrified, at long last, at how much Sarah looked like Lily. "I'm sorry," she said, looking at her child, but said it loud enough for Liliana to hear. She knew her mother would think Ana was saying it to her. She rocked Sarah in her lap and hummed softly until her little girl stopped crying.

"I don't know if I can keep doing this, Ana," Liliana said from the kitchen. "I am too old for this. I don't have the nerves."

Ana felt tears burning in her own eyes, but willed them back. Barely a week into a new job—a job she had won after a lot of hard convincing of an employer who had had his pick of candidates with much more relevant experience and no gaps in their resumes—and now it looked like she would have to give it up after all.

"I'm sorry, Mama," Ana said. Then she asked, "Where are her clothes?"

"In the garbage," Liliana said, still in the kitchen. "I told you. She peed on them. Like a pig."

Ana almost argued that pigs are not the only creatures that pee and that urine comes out in the wash, but then thought better of it. She did not ask Liliana what had frightened or disturbed her daughter so badly that she had urinated on herself, or why she now sat trembling and naked, wrapped in a cold, wet towel. Those questions came nowhere near the surface of Ana's consciousness. If they had—if she allowed herself to think them—then Ana would have no other choice but to finish the job her sister had begun all those years ago. Ana just didn't have it in her to go so far. With anyone else in the world, any stranger on the street, any monster in a dark alley, absolutely yes. She could kill anyone with her bare hands who would do harm to her daughter. But not the woman she called Mama, the woman who had spared her Lily's fate, the woman who had loved her in all the ways she could not love Lily.

"Let's go home," she whispered to Sarah. Sarah nodded limply.

Liliana came out of the kitchen with a big metal cooking spoon in her hand, the one she had used to bonk Sarah on the head when no one was looking, the one she used to slap the palms of Sarah's hands and the soles of her feet, hurting her in places where no one would see bruises. She gave Sarah a venomous look. Ana just caught it, but looked away quickly.

Ana took off her suit jacket and wrapped it around her daughter. She handed the towel to Liliana. "Thanks, Mama. I'll find someone else to sit for Sarah. I'm sorry for the trouble." She felt Sarah tense in her arms when she leaned in to kiss Liliana's cheek.

Liliana said, "Hmmph," and did not kiss her daughter back.

That night, Ana got her nerve up and knocked on a neighbor's door. She knew the family's name was Williams because it was on the nameplate by the buzzer, but she could not, for the life of her, remember the woman's first name. It was Kate, or Carla, or something with a K. She had a little girl named Shirley, the same age as Sarah. The little girls went to the same school, but were in different Kindergarten classes. The mothers knew each other from the park, where their children had played with a dozen others from the time they were toddlers. So much time had passed since they first met, and all their encounters had always been friendly but so casual, that Ana found it much too awkward to come right out and ask the woman's name now, after all this time.

She had spoken to the woman a few times more recently, warm and neighborly conversations in front of the school as they waited for their children, but they were not yet the friends they would become in the years ahead.

Ana's only hope of keeping her job was to find someone who could pick Sarah up after school and keep her for a few hours. Dan could do it in a pinch, but not every day. Ana would not be able to do it at all, not so soon after starting a new job. Kate or Carla or Something-with-a-K was a stay-at-home mom.

"I'm so sorry to barge in on you like this," Ana apologized almost as soon as the woman opened the door. "I wonder if I could talk to you for a minute."

"Sure," the woman said, a little uncertainly. "Come on in."

Ana explained about her new job and how her mother would not be able to take care of Sarah after all. She lied and told the woman her mother had recently fallen ill. "So I have a business proposition for you," Ana said, and took a deep breath. "Would you be willing to bring Sarah home with you when you pick up your little girl from school? And keep her until I get home at about five-thirty or six? I'll pay you whatever you think is fair, and it would only be until I can make other arrangements. Maybe just a few days."

Kate or Carla or Something-with-a-K thought about it for a moment. "I suppose that'll be okay. I'm happy to do it as a favor. Maybe you could babysit my kids for me on the occasional Saturday night? That would be a fair swap, don't you think?"

"No, no. I want to pay you for your trouble."

They talked about it some more, going back and forth until they reached an agreement that suited them both. A few days turned into a few years, and both the mothers and the daughters became closer than some people who are related to each other by blood. Shirley and Sarah remained best friends all the way through high school, becoming as close as sisters. Sarah and Shirley saw each other less frequently as adults, but despite the distance and distractions their respective lives had imposed upon them both, every conversation always felt as if the last one had taken place only yesterday.

Even though Ana's parents lived within walking distance until the day Alberto de la Torre sold his beloved deli (which was later turned into a Starbucks, to his utter dismay and heartbreak) and relented to Liliana's insistence that they retire to Florida, their already infrequent family visits dwindled down to a bare minimum. Ana, Dan, and Sarah visited every other Christmas Eve, every Mother's Day before heading Upstate to visit Dan's parents, and at least for a few minutes on Father's Day. Ana visited by herself on her parents' birthdays and scattered Saturday afternoons in between. All other holidays and vacations were spent elsewhere.

Liliana never visited Ana; she saw it as the child's obligation to come to the parents, not the other way around.

Ana's father remained willfully oblivious to the mother-daughter dramas and tribulations to the very end—the only way to survive being married to a woman like Liliana—never truly letting on what real joys or secret sorrows he kept locked away in his otherwise tender heart.

A couple of years after Alberto died, Liliana suffered a stroke. A doctor in Florida called Ana, who was the only person listed as an emergency contact. Liliana de la Torre would need help, he explained. She would need to be put in an assisted-living facility, at least for a while, or someone would have to come and take care of her. She was not completely incapacitated, but she would need a lot of help, especially in the first few months, perhaps longer.

Sarah was about to enter her senior year of high school when this news came. Her first thought upon hearing this was, "For Christ's sake, why doesn't she die already?"

Ana was beside herself with grief and guilt. Yes, her mother had been an unapologetic terror to some of the people Ana had loved most, but to her, Liliana had been a caring and temperate mother—at least until Sarah came along and triggered some horrible reminder of poor Lily. Things were not as black-and-white or good-and-evil for Ana as they were for Liliana. She had worked all her life to balance her fear of her mother with a measure of compassion, and a generous dose of denial.

"We have to go and take care of her," Ana explained to Sarah and Dan.

Sarah was understandably outraged, and utterly horrified by the suggestion. "Just put her in a home! If anyone deserves bedsores, it's her!"

"Sarah!" both of her parents said at the same time.

"She's a horror of a human being! Why do *we* have to go take care of her?"

Dan did not disagree, but he felt the need to find some other solution. "Why don't you go to Florida for a while?" he offered Ana as a compromise. "Sarah and I can stay here. We can take care of each other until you come back."

Ana, already teetering at the edge of reason, flipped at the suggestion. "I can't leave you alone here! A daughter needs her mother. Sarah needs to be with me, and I need to be with Mama. Besides, this is not something that's likely to get fixed quickly. She's seventy years old, a widow, living alone, and she's had a stroke. No amount of rehabilitation is going to make her independent again. That doctor said as much. It could be months, or years. I don't want to be away from either of you for that long, and I can't just leave Mama to die in some room by herself, in some horrible institution. Nobody deserves that!"

"She's sixty-eight," Dan corrected. "Plenty of good years left, with the proper treatment and care."

"Or she could live like that forever, and kill us all with her evil!" Sarah interjected.

"Enough, Sarah," Dan said gently. To his wife, he asked, "What am I supposed to do with my practice? I've put my whole life into it. I can't just walk away from that."

"We could bring her here," Ana offered.

"No!" Sarah and Dan said at the same time.

"Then you can be an optometrist in Florida. They have billions of old people with bad eyes down there," Ana responded.

"Sarah's going into her senior year. It would be unconscionable to uproot her now." He nodded to Sarah, who nodded back with great enthusiasm and gratitude. She turned expectantly to Ana.

"They have high schools in Florida. We're not ruining her education. It's just high school. College is what matters."

And so it went for the next few days. By the weekend, Ana had won the first round. She and Sarah were on a plane to Florida.

"I'm going to need your help taking care of Grandma," Ana said to Sarah once they were in the air.

"Like she took care of me when I was little?" Sarah responded with the acidic sarcasm that is the exclusive domain of incensed teenaged girls, but this had an even sharper edge to it. Ana flinched, as if slapped.

Ana put the headphones in her ears and stared straight ahead at the in-flight movie. Sarah didn't speak another word to her mother for several weeks. Ana didn't notice.

When forced to be in her grandmother's presence, Sarah only glared at her with the same vitriol and contempt Liliana had heaped upon her all those years ago.

Six months later, Liliana was still making no effort to get better. She languished in her perfumed bed or on the special cushions Ana made for her wheelchair, and refused any attempts to get her into rehabilitative services. She would not allow her home to be sold. She would not move back to New York. Her beloved "good" daughter had come to take care of her, and that was all she needed.

Dan sold his practice to his younger partner. Then he sold their house in Brooklyn. He told himself that he should have moved his family out of the shithole that New York had become a long time ago. Deep in his heart, however, it nearly killed him to hand over the keys to the new owner, who would surely turn this great old brownstone into an overcrowded tenement. He arranged for most of their furniture to be sold, and had the rest of their belongings packed and shipped to Florida. It was a temporary move, Dan told himself. In the meantime, Liliana's house was plenty big enough for a family of four, such as it was.

Sarah's last year of high school was as painful and irreparable as a botched amputation. Her new classmates made fun of her accent and the way she dressed, the way she wore her hair, the angry look on her face, and the fact that she seemed constantly on the move, pacing every square inch of the campus at lunchtime instead of sitting down somewhere and eating or talking to people. She was ridiculed and harassed by girls she neither knew nor would ever care about. Their cliques had been formed in childhood; Sarah had arrived much too late to their party, and uninvited at that. Even the school's outcasts shunned her. What few boys gave her any attention wanted only to get in her pants, because, they reasoned, "all New York girls are easy."

The last time Sarah prayed was in the days between that phone call from the doctor and the night before she and her mother boarded the plane. She begged God for a solution, for a reprieve. She prayed so they wouldn't have to leave their home, so she wouldn't have to leave her school and everyone and everything she knew, so that her father wouldn't have to sell his practice and go work for a LensCrafters in a Florida mall. The only prayer she offered for her grandmother was, "Make her well, or take her. But don't leave us here in this limbo." She begged the intercession of every saint whose name she could remember.

The response was perfect and complete silence.

Then came the night a couple of months into the school year, on the day when some giggling twits in trendy clothes and too much make-up cornered her in the girls' bathroom and plastered wads of bubble gum into her long, dark hair, and the only remedy for that was to get every bit of it shorn off. Her mother took her to an old-lady salon where they cut her hair like a boy. It was on that day that she had come home from that horror and passed by her grandmother's bedroom on the way to her room, and damned if that evil old bitch didn't sneer at her with the hideous working half of her mangled face. That was the night she sat by the window of the small room where she slept in this dark and suffocating house and dared to say out loud, "There is no God." She didn't care anymore about being struck by lightning. In fact, if that happened, she would welcome it. At least then this nightmare would be over.

And still there was silence.

Having finally uttered those forbidden words was not an experience she would ever describe as triumphant. But she found, to her comfort, that her renunciation of faith had created a much lighter load to carry than terror, powerlessness, and the humiliation of unanswered supplication. Realizing how inert—how superstitious and uselessly frightening—those words had turned out to be, allowed her to finally stop feeling like a terrified ant scrambling madly to avoid the deadly sneaker of a cruel child.

On that very night, having not been struck dead where she sat, she decided to take up the reins of her own life. Instead of giving up, or running away and rebelling as the fabled Aunt Lily had done at approximately the same age, she buckled down and went to work. Difficult as it was—nearly impossible, unspeakably *unbearable* as it was at times—she kept her nose in her books, determined to leave this swamp the right way: she was going to go to college in a place where snow fell in winter and bugs didn't eat you alive in the summer, where people didn't call her "ma'am" even though she was only seventeen. If she failed in her education at this stage of the game, she would be stuck here the rest of her life. And Liliana would live to bury them all. That, apparently, had been God's idea of a plan.

"Well, to hell with you, too," were the last words Sarah ever spoke to God.

Sarah then entered the phase of her life she would come to think of as "militant atheism," a particularly fierce and vituperative rejection of all things religious for which former Catholics seem to be especially adept.

Many years later, it would begin to dawn on her that she was no less arrogant or contemptuous in her unyielding rejection of God than the people who argued with equal vehemence, venom, and certainty that God was real. With that realization, she shed yet another layer of stone from the load she had been carrying.

Over time, her religion became the quest to become a decent and respectful citizen of the world for the simple reason that it was the right thing to do, and not because she was required to fear divine retribution, or should expect a reward for her good deeds, in this life or the next.

However, in those moments when she could stand to look honestly into that place of clearest truth deep inside herself, she found that her personal philosophy was rooted in something much less noble or poetic: the simple truth was that the prospect of eternal life absolutely exhausted her, in every conceivable way. It filled her with hopelessness, with a terrible dismay. Fifty or sixty years of swinging around the sun seemed like plenty. Seventy was stretching it, but probably still tolerable. Eighty, ninety years or beyond, frail and dependent, was utterly unimaginable. Eternity, then, was a prospect that was horrifying beyond description, even if she could do it in a young and healthy body, as so many of the fairy tales promised. Even more horrible was the idea of coming back to earth and going through the whole mess over and over again, until she got it right. She found no comfort at all in the concept of reincarnation and the thought that nothing ever ended.

What *did* comfort her—and, to some extent, even amused her— was the notion that the universe and everything in it was finite. She could look out at its vastness and still imagine that it ended somewhere. She could also feel a great love for the beauty of the world all around her, all the things in the sky or closer to the ground, manmade or otherwise, and be moved to absolute awe and wonderment. Who or what created it was not a question that kept her up at night.

And so she slept.

Most nights.

———

The sun had set and the giant cross was finally behind her, a dot swallowed up by the distance. Still, Sarah was shaken, anxious, and hungry. The needle on the gas gauge had fallen dangerously low. Where did all these farmers fill up the tanks of their pick-up trucks and tractors? Sarah thought about the sandwiches she had thrown in the trash this morning, the ones Ana had packed for her nearly a thousand miles ago, and wished she hadn't been so hasty.

She had bypassed the last couple of signs indicating that gas and food were nearby, feeling like she was not sufficiently far away from the creepy cross. She knew she was acting irrationally and taking a foolish risk. But wasn't this whole adventure a fool's errand? Why had it seemed so urgent—so *imperative*—to embark on this insane quest?

She followed the signs off the highway and down an uninviting road to a place called St. Elmo, and was about to turn around and get back on I-70 when she spotted something up ahead that looked like a gas station. It was, fortunately, attached to a convenience store, and it was still open. She could fill her rumbling belly and her empty gas tank at the same time.

While the gas was pumping, she reached into the console under the dashboard and unplugged her phone from the charger. She had plugged it in before leaving the Target parking lot, and then forgotten to turn it on. As soon as it came alive, the message indicator began chiming. Probably the eight hundred messages Ana said she had left the night before. There were probably eight hundred new ones, all of them from Ana.

The reception wasn't great, but good enough to do a quick scroll down the list of missed calls and messages. She thumbed the Internet icon and watched as the device struggled to take her there. She had been hoping to check out Google Maps to figure out where she was and how much farther she had to go. Living in New York, without a car and with easy access to cabs and public transportation, and, most importantly, where the streets and avenues were consecutively numbered, she had virtually no use for the GPS feature, so she had never used it. She'd figure it out later, whenever and wherever she stopped for the night.

When she went inside to pay for the gas, she took a gander at a dubious display of pre-wrapped sandwiches, and opted instead for a bag of chips, a Hershey bar, and a soda. She also picked up a map from the rickety metal stand by the door, just in case.

St. Louis was up ahead somewhere, or so the highway signs had promised. She had once attended a conference in that city. It had been a few years ago, but maybe something would look familiar. She decided she would get back on I-70 until it reached St. Louis, find a well-lit place to bunk for the night, and figure out an alternate route to the Pacific now that she was armed with better resources.

This was fast becoming an expensive impulse-journey, but all of the alternatives seemed too bleak to consider. She needed the forward motion. She needed to keep—

(running)

—moving. She got back in the car.

Back on I-70 and once again heading west, she found a Classic Rock station on the radio. It was playing Bob Seger's "Hollywood Nights." She cranked up the volume and rolled down the window. She breathed deeply of the earth-smelling air and felt her pulse begin to race, as if trying to match the urgent, mesmerizing beat of that song. She didn't notice how her foot was turning to stone as it pressed down on the gas pedal. It wasn't until the song was over that she saw the speedometer needle was hovering above ninety.

If any of the stories were even remotely true, there could very well be some bored highway patrol officer lying in wait, cleverly hidden in the brush, some good ol' boy who would be thrilled to bag a lead-foot with Jersey plates. She laid off the gas and tapped the brakes once or twice. Spending a night in the St. Elmo county jail (or wherever the hell this was) was not what she wanted tonight.

But, damn, she wished they'd play that song again.

She checked the rearview mirror again, just to be sure the giant cross had been safely swallowed up by the distance behind her.

Four

S ARAH WAS WAITING TO PAY for gas and some snacks at a convenience store just outside of Springfield, Missouri, standing on line behind a woman with two fussy toddlers and a shy, doe-eyed little girl. Sarah tried not to look at any of them, especially not the girl, staring straight ahead and over their heads instead, jaw set almost to the point of cracking. Just a few minutes ago, as she pumped gas, she felt herself mere inches from calling off the whole stupid trip. What in hell had she been thinking, anyway. It wasn't the whole world that had gone crazy after all; it had only been Sarah.

Suddenly, the store went quiet. There were a few people milling around the back, a few others waiting in line to pay. Behind the counter was a stocky, older man with a tidy gray beard, wearing a green-and-white cap with a John Deere logo on it. There was also a pretty young woman who looked to be in her twenties at the register, her mouth gaping, wide open. Sarah swiveled a bit and looked behind her. Why had everyone frozen in place? She started to wonder if she was entering a whole new level of crazy. She turned to look where they were looking.

All eyes were trained on the windows at the front of the store. Past the gas pumps and beyond the road, the sky had split into two distinct areas: on one side, nothing but pale blue sky; on the other, fast-moving and misshapen, dark, rolling clouds that looked to be full of black, venomous smoke.

Some people near the back of the store began to speak quietly, their voices barely more than murmurs and whispers. One word echoed with chilling clarity, making all eyes turn in their direction: Joplin.

Then came the low moan of something awakening from a deep sleep, a sound rising slowly as a distant basso profundo until becoming a higher-pitched, sustained, wailing cry.

That broke the spell.

The gray-bearded man turned to the young woman and said, "Put on KWTO," pointing to a stereo tuner on the shelf behind her.

"Oh, sweet Jesus," murmured the woman in front of Sarah on the line as she dumped her items on the counter and picked up the two smallest of her children, both of them boys, one still in diapers. The little girl wrapped her arms around her mother's leg and stared helplessly up at Sarah. Sarah clutched her bottle of soda and bag of pretzels closer against her chest, eyes darting everywhere, trying to take it all in.

The older man ran out to the gas pumps and started waving his arms, shouting to people to stop what they were doing and get inside. He pointed to the darker part of the sky. People looked at the clouds, then looked back at the man. None of them appeared to be of a mind to argue. They all did as they were told and headed quickly toward the store.

The gray-bearded man took a few running steps to the edge of the road and looked both ways. He gestured wildly at someone—maybe more than one person—somewhere on his right; he, she, or they were not visible from where Sarah stood. The gray-bearded man hopped up and down, gesturing more forcefully, then trotted back into the store.

"Cut the pumps off, Letty," he said to the girl behind the counter. Then, facing everyone in the store with his arms raised like a minister about to invoke the Lord, he said, "Listen up, folks. There's a good-sized store room in the back. I'm gonna ask y'all to follow me, nice and calm and easy. We gon' take shelter there. We got lights, and water, and a radio. Whatever's coming, we'll be fine down cellar." He turned back to the girl at the counter. "What'd the radio say, Letty?"

Letty gave him her best impression of a startled baby monkey. She was too afraid to tell her boss that she didn't know where KWTO was.

"Nev'mind," he said, waving Letty over. "Come out from behind there and help me get these good people downstairs. You bring up the rear, and keep an eye out for anyone else who might roll up to the pumps." He gave the satanic-looking clouds one more look before heading to the back of the store. "C'mon folks. Let's don't dally."

People began moving, throwing the occasional fearful glance over their shoulders as they made their way to a door marked "Employees Only." The lady with the children tried to get past Sarah, who was glued to the floor tiles. Sarah was looking at her parents' minivan, still under the awning by gas pump #4. She wondered what would happen if a tornado flattened it or carried it away, if the decision to cut short her lunatic's holiday had already been made for her, or if she would be buried alive under the rubble of this Midwestern service station with a dozen or so frightened strangers.

"Come *on,* Li'l Bit," the young mother said to her daughter, shaking her leg to dislodge the child. The little girl only clung tighter. "I can't walk with you like that, sweetheart!" The woman looked at Sarah. "Ma'am? Can you help me?"

Sarah looked at the woman, whose eyes were big as saucers and about to spill over with tears. She nodded, still clutching her pretzels and soda.

"Take the nice lady's hand, Elizabeth," the mother said in a more commanding voice. The child wouldn't move. "Come *on,* Elizabeth!"

Almost all the other people had gone through the door at the back of the store. The bearded man shouted, "Let's go, ladies. Step lively."

Sarah knelt beside the little girl and said, "Can you help me, please? I've never been in this store." She offered the child her hand.

As soon as Elizabeth loosened her grip, her mother pulled her leg free and readjusted her grasp of the smaller children, one boy balanced on each hip. "Okay. Let's go. Momma's right here, darlin'. Take the nice lady's hand and follow me." Enormous tears rolled silently down the little girl's cheeks, but she did as she was told.

The child's hand felt cold in Sarah's. Sarah took a deep breath and closed her eyes, but only for a moment.

The gray-bearded man took one last look through the front windows. The dark clouds had eaten up all that was left of the blue. "Anyone else out there?" he shouted into the store. When no one responded, he closed the door securely behind him.

The space was not so much a cellar as a slightly lowered storage area. There was a short ramp that led into the windowless space, which was lined with shelves full of paper and cleaning products, cans of motor oil, and non-perishable food. A few of the people immediately began arranging boxes of canned goods into an improvised sitting area in the farthest corner of the room, far away from the little ramp and the door beyond. Some people sat, some stood, some paced. Some looked bewildered, some seemed put-out, some were blank-faced. For at least a couple of those people, terror would not have been too strong a word to describe their current state of mind.

Sarah sat with the little girl next to her mother and brothers. The mother was bouncing the smallest of the little boys a bit too frantically on one knee; the child did not appear to find this comforting. The other little boy was tucked protectively under her other arm, his face pressed against the side of her breast. He was sucking his thumb.

The gray-bearded man began fiddling with the knobs on the special NOAA radio until he found what he wanted.

A man who would never make a living as a radio personality or sports announcer was, nevertheless, delivering information and instructions in a clear, calm voice over the airwaves.

> ...intensifying line of thunderstorms racing eastward... tornado warning is in effect...damage becoming increasingly likely as the developing squall line heads across south- western Missouri...residents are urged to take cover...brief, heavy rain...hail one to two inches in diameter...tornadoes are possible...

Sarah now realized why that single word uttered upstairs had rung a bell for her and had taken everyone else's breath away. Joplin was the town that had been practically wiped off the map by a monster tornado not that long ago. Scores of people had been killed. She wondered how close or far away Joplin was from here.

She looked around at the cinderblock walls and the boxes of merchandise stacked on shelves that almost reached the ceiling of this enclosed space. *I came all this way just to die in a ready-made tomb,* she thought. A chuckle escaped her, a loud one. It was practically a guffaw, and it somehow found a way to echo in the relative silence of this room. Everyone turned to look at her.

After a terrible, awkward moment, she said, "I'm sorry. I'm just a little nervous." But she wasn't a little nervous. She was a little angry.

A few people nodded their understanding. One woman gave her a dirty look. The young mother looked more frightened than ever. The little girl was peering at Sarah with those enormous brown eyes.

Sarah realized she was still holding the child's hand, and that it was no longer cold. She leaned in close to her and said in a whisper (but loud enough for her mother to hear), "This looks like a nice, safe place, doesn't it?" The child only stared at her. Sarah tried again. "I like those walls. What do you think those blocks are made of?"

The little girl looked. "Rocks," she said in a small voice, only it sounded like "woks."

Sarah felt something tear inside her, some big, bruised, dark purple bubble whose outer membrane had been working overtime to hold everything inside. She inhaled deeply through her nose and, in doing so, picked up the soft, baby scent of the little girl's hair. She had to close her eyes. She struggled mightily to keep the sound trapped in her throat from escaping. She tried to smile at the little girl, but could not. She nodded instead.

The little girl moved a tiny bit closer to Sarah. Instinctively, Sarah raised a slightly shaky hand to stroke the child's hair. The little girl leaned in even closer, timidly resting a cheek on Sarah's breast. The mother looked on with a mixture of gratitude and apprehension. That protective maternal instinct was already on high alert, but she was sitting close enough to pounce, if needed, if this "nervous" woman did anything weird. For now, she was a little more grateful for the extra pair of hands than she was worried.

The woman who had given Sarah a dirty look spoke. "Okay now, everybody, listen up. The Lord isn't gonna let nothin' bad happen here today. Come on now. Everybody join hands."

Sarah wouldn't look at the woman. She kept her eyes on the top of the little girl's head.

"You too," the woman said pointedly to Sarah. Sarah ignored her.

People began to move a little closer to each other, reaching out and clasping hands, some shyly, some not. The mother clutched the toddler on her knee a little tighter, and reached over the other little boy at her side. She pressed him to her with her elbow and placed a hand on her daughter's knee. Sarah felt someone behind her put a hand on her shoulder. She didn't look to see who it was, nor did she offer her other hand. She was still clutching the soda and the bag of pretzels in the crook of that arm.

"Come on now," the bossy woman said again. "Ain't no such-a thing as a atheist in a foxhole."

(wanna bet?)

The bossy woman closed her eyes and raised the palms of her large, rough hands upward. She began to invoke the Lord, Baby Jesus, and Father God himself as if they were three different people. She proclaimed that, although this room was full of nothing but lowly, unworthy sinners, they should all be allowed to see the light of day again and return to untouched homes, loved ones, and automobiles. She spoke faster and faster, and louder, until her words were a mangled blur of nonsensical syllables. Sarah imagined that some of the people in this concrete chamber would later testify in their own churches that the woman had been touched by the Holy Ghost and had begun to speak in tongues, and that was why they had all been spared, hallelujah, praise the bloody countenance of Jesus, amen. Unless, of course, any of them were maimed or killed; then they would blame their misfortune on the cackling atheist in the foxhole who had queered the deal that the babbling woman had tried to make with Jesus on their behalf.

Out of the corner of her eye, Sarah thought she saw something skittering silently across the tops of the tallest stacks of boxes. Maybe more than one something.

———

Sometimes things happened for which there was no logical explanation. There were things that existed and moved in the spaces of time between the ticks of a clock, between the atoms and molecules of all tangible matter. Whether in full possession of her rationality or as she clung to the ledges of her own sanity by her fingernails, there had been things that had laughed in the face of all that could be explained.

Sarah was twelve, still very much the dutifully terrified Catholic girl, the first time she caught a glimpse of something that couldn't be there.

There was a transom window above her bedroom door in the old house in Brooklyn where she grew up. In that moment just prior to drifting off to sleep one night, in that instant before her eyelids fluttered one last time, before sleep began in earnest, that was when she saw the terrible, grinning face of the creature clinging to the outside of the glass above the doorway.

Her eyes flew open wide, all hope of sleep dashed away to nothing in an instant.

It was not a pretty face. Gargoyle-like, sneering, mocking. A hunchbacked, gnarled, crouching thing, more face than body, a being that existed nowhere in nature, not in this world. Yet there it was.

It was a trick of the light, she told herself, frightened into near paralysis. She pulled the covers closer to her face, trembling, too afraid to look and too afraid to look away. Moonlight bouncing off the shadows, she told herself, something in her room positioned differently from the night before was what was creating a new shadow in that darkened pane of glass. Surely that's all it could be.

Minutes later, the jolt of the telephone ringing—that shrill, tinny bell that gave voice to the phones of her childhood—screeching from its perch on the small table at the end of the hall where it was tethered to the wall, heedless of the late hour.

"Someone is dead," Sarah whispered to herself as her mother's slippered feet whisked past her bedroom door. That thought was immediately followed by the weight of her own guilt for having thought such a dark and ugly thing.

Her mother's grumbling about the hour of the night suddenly became a muffled whimper, and then grew into a wailing shriek. And then her father's sure, heavy steps racing down the same hallway, toward the sound of tears. And then both of them sobbing, a sound Sarah had never heard before or even imagined possible: the sound of her parents crying. A death. A favorite aunt. Her father's aunt. Dead just like that, just two days after Christmas. They had planned to go Upstate to visit her this coming weekend.

Sarah finally dared to glance above the doorway once more. The gnarled grinning face had disappeared.

Sarah had many such visitations over the years. The nights before the death of her father's mother, the death of a cousin, the death of a mentor, the death of a friend. It wasn't always exactly the same face, but these visitors were members of the same tribe, to be sure. Grotesque, knotted, sneering, gray faces that varied very little in size or in form. Always in that moment before sleep, always in some shadowy corner she could see from her bed, always within a few hours—or mere moments—of receiving the news of someone's death.

And, every time, she tried to dismiss it as silly superstition, the hallucinations of a tired mind, meaningless coincidence, something half-dreamt, the product of an overactive imagination.

At some point in her young life, she tried to make some accommodations for her relationship with the gremlin-like messengers. Fearing them had not made them go away. Ignoring them had been impossible. Defying them would not change their form or mission. They simply were, and that was that. If she saw them, she told herself, someone would die. Or someone might die anyway, even if she didn't see them.

Maybe there was a God, and that was what he looked like. No wonder he was feared. A face like that could scare anyone to death.

There had been no face in the shadows on that otherwise ordinary night last month, and someone she loved more than anyone or anything else in her life had died anyway.

Had she simply been too tired to look? Perhaps the face had appeared and she had refused to see it, had squeezed her eyes shut and surrendered to sleep before she could acknowledge it.

Or perhaps the face, though sneering and grotesque, belonged to a merciful being after all. Perhaps, this time, it had simply crouched deeper in the shadows.

———————

The praying lady had been at it for quite some time. Sarah wondered if the woman had any intention of releasing her captive audience before the guy on the NOAA radio gave the all-clear.

Almost everyone else's heads were still bowed, eyes closed, though it appeared that the attention of one or two other people had begun to wander. Sarah thought she saw something skitter again, this time on the other side of the room. If it had been there at all, it disappeared quickly into the shadows.

That's when the lights went out.

A collective gasp filled the room as two sets of emergency lights clicked on and shed small spots of light at opposite corners of the room. The praying lady got louder and more unintelligible. Someone whimpered. Someone else got up and shuffled toward the far wall, where the NOAA announcer was still droning on in his slightly nasal voice.

A small beam of light bounced off the walls in erratic patterns. Then a series of snicking sounds were accompanied by more beams of light. The gray-bearded man started passing around flashlights of all shapes and sizes. Some people set them up on end like lamps, on the floor or on top of boxes, giving the room a dimmer but much less mortuarial feel than the cold fluorescents had. Some people clung white-knuckled to their flashlights, gripping them like talismans. The bossy woman ratcheted up the volume and unintelligibility of her prayers. She was losing the attention of her captive audience at about the same pace as her coherence.

When the gray-bearded man reached her, Sarah set the soda and bag of pretzels on the floor and accepted the flashlight he held out for her. She did so without moving the hand that was cupped protectively on the little girl's head. "Maybe you should hold this for us," Sarah whispered to her. The child wrapped both pudgy little dimpled hands around the base of the flashlight and held it in a manner that made her look like the tiniest mourner at a candlelight vigil.

Without thinking, without asking, Sarah scooped her up gently and placed the little girl on her lap. She wrapped her arms lightly around the child and, with her eyes closed, buried her nose in the soft wisps of baby hair. She began to rock slowly back and forth. Their breathing became soft and rhythmic, synchronized. The scent of that sweet angel's head was an elixir to Sarah's soul. The ache in that bruised and bleeding place inside her began to abate. If the gremlin messengers had come for them all, she would be at peace with dying right here, right now.

In her mind, she dared them to come and get her.

Suddenly, all was silent. The tongue-speaker appeared to be gagging. Even in the dim light, Sarah could see that the woman's eyes were bulging, the whites shining bright. The woman gasped for air, one arm raised above her head like a swimmer in distress, her other arm crossed at a weird angle across her chest. She fell to her knees with a thud, then fell the rest of the way, face-first onto the concrete floor. She began to convulse.

The young woman who had sat frozen behind the cash register upstairs just a few minutes ago sprang forward. She knelt beside the stricken woman and, cradling her head, rolled her over onto her back. A few other people gathered around, training their flashlights on the woman on the floor. A couple of them said, "Oooh," and "Uggh!" when they saw the blood on the woman's forehead, and the foam bubbling at the corners of her mouth. One man took off his shirt and balled it up for a pillow. He put it under the woman's head. The cashier girl went to work, seeming to know what to do.

The middle child of the young mother, the one tucked under her arm, began to sob. She picked up both boys and went to find a spot where they could sit, away from the disturbing sight. Sarah picked up the little girl and followed the mother. Crouched in a corner behind a row of shelves on the opposite side of the room, the five of them huddled in a tight cluster. The young mother distracted her babies by leading them in a whispered song that sounded like a children's hymn.

Sarah scanned the darkness above them, on the look-out for skittering shadows.

———

Sitting in the near darkness of this windowless space, it was difficult to tell how much time had passed.

The gray-bearded man was the first to leave the storeroom. From where Sarah was sitting, she could just see him as he put his ear to the door, then lay a hand flat on the surface. He opened it very slowly. He peered through a crack in the door, then opened it wider. He slipped out, closing the door behind him.

The gray-bearded man came back a few minutes later. He said to Sarah and the young mother, "It looks okay to come out now, but be careful. There's a lot of debris outside."

If the squall had spawned any tornadoes, there was no evidence of severe damage in the immediate vicinity, but it was clear that what had passed over them was no harmless spring shower. Hail about the size of mushroom caps was scattered in small patches in a few grassy places and against the curbs. The wind had strewn assorted debris, manmade and natural, all over the place. The awning over the gas pumps had held up okay and had done a fair job of protecting the cars underneath it, but the bed of the pick-up truck behind Sarah's Odyssey was littered with hailstones, leaves, broken branches of various sizes, and an assortment of trash that may or may not have already been there before the storm. All of the cars and the store windows were plastered with paper refuse and wet leaves.

The worst damage was done to the little car that belonged to the woman with the three small children. She had parked in front of the store, in the last space on the right, intending only to stop in for a minute to pick up a container of milk, a loaf of bread, and a couple of cans of Spaghetti-O's. Her car had been fully exposed to the oncoming winds, as were a few others, but it was the rear window of her car that had been the unlucky target of an ancient hubcap. It must have hurtled through the air like a Frisbee. Both of the child seats in the back glistened with rain water, melting hail, and pebbled safety glass. The hubcap came to rest in the small space between the two child-seats, where the girl called Elizabeth usually sat on the booster seat between her little brothers.

"I knew I shouldda gone to the Wal-Mart," the young mother said wearily, looking ten years older than she had before the storm. "I thought this'd be quicker."

This must be what passes for random acts of violence in this part of the world, Sarah thought.

"Momma... our *car!*" the little girl wailed.

"Step away from there, honey," the mother said absently.

An ambulance turned the corner, siren blaring, and rolled into the parking lot, crunching over branches and other debris unmindfully.

Two EMTs emerged with a gurney and followed the gray-bearded man inside.

The beleaguered mother continued to look balefully at her battered little car. Sarah felt badly for her. "Do you need a ride?" she asked her.

The young mother looked at Sarah with hope and relief. "Are you sure it would be okay? We don't live very far."

"No, of course. It's no trouble."

"My goodness, you're an angel. Thank you so much."

"That man in the store, he's the angel. A few minutes more and I would have driven right into that storm like an idiot. I've never seen anything like that in my life."

"Well, I have. And it never stops being scary. At least not to me." She looked into the store, but there was no one inside that she could see. Their fellow refugees were either out in the parking lot, doing their own version of a post-mortem of the storm, or down in the storeroom dealing with the woman who had collapsed in an apparent case of extreme zealotry. "I need to let someone know I'll send my husband to come get this car. Or push it into a ditch."

She dug around in her shoulder bag and found an old receipt. She wrote a note on the back of it. While she did this, Sarah looked westward at the brand new sky, incredulous that such transformations could happen so quickly. Then she looked through the rain-and-leaf-speckled window into the empty store, and wondered about the tongue-speaker. She didn't want to believe it, but in her heart, she knew the woman was either dead or dying.

Sarah saw the gray-bearded man go behind the counter. "I forgot to pay for my stuff. I'll be right back," she said to the woman.

The gray-bearded man was accepting payment on the honor system. With the electricity gone, he had no way of knowing who had pumped gas or had picked up a few groceries. His customers paid him gratefully, and thanked him for possibly saving their lives.

Sarah couldn't remember exactly what her gas tally had been, but she pulled out the emergency hundred dollar bill she kept in a secret compartment of her wallet. It had been tucked away in that spot for several years, so long that she had forgotten it was there until just this moment. She handed it to the man and did not accept any change.

"I'm right over here," Sarah said to the young mother as she exited the store, and led the way to her car. This is what minivans were made for, she thought: three or more kids and a mom or two to look after them; not one wandering lunatic with an air mattress and a collapsible toilet.

They got the two older kids strapped in as well as they could, considering they were both too small for standard seatbelts. The woman sat in the middle with the baby on her lap, and wrapped her seatbelt around them both.

"Make a right coming out of here," she instructed Sarah, "and then just follow this road for about a mile. My name's Jilly, by the way."

"Nice to meet you, Jilly," Sarah said and smiled into the rearview mirror. "I'm Sarah."

"I can't thank you enough for all your help. With three little ones, it's amazing how fast you run out of hands and lap space sometimes." She turned to her little girl. "Elizabeth, say thank you to Miss Sarah for keeping you safe."

"Thank you, Miss Sarah," Elizabeth repeated dutifully in a tiny voice.

She wanted to tell the little girl that she had been a greater comfort to her than she would ever know, but she could think of no way to express that to the child, or explain it to her mother without having to tell a much longer story. So she said simply, "It was my pleasure, Elizabeth. You were very brave."

"You can make a left up ahead," Jilly said, "And then after that, make a right. Ooh, watch out for that." There was a red, round, portable grill lying in the middle of the street, all three legs up in the air. "Good golly... look at this mess."

And then they saw it: evidence of a tornado's deadly and fickle nature. About two houses from the curb, the smoking remains of someone's home lay in a pile of rubble. The two houses on either side of it were utterly untouched. "Christ almighty," Sarah whispered.

Jilly hid the baby's face between her breasts and tried to distract the other two children while she herself couldn't keep her eyes away from the sight. "Just keep going," Jilly said to Sarah.

Sarah drove slowly, veering carefully around fallen branches and miscellaneous detritus. There were people beginning to come out of their homes and businesses, collecting up-ended trash cans and whatever could be hauled out of the way without the use of heavy equipment.

"I noticed you have New Jersey tags on your car," Jilly said tentatively, trying desperately not to imagine her own little house in ruins. "Is that where you're from?"

"The other side of the Hudson, actually. New York is home."

(is it?)

"This is my parents' car," Sarah added. "My other car is a subway."

"Ha!" Jilly shook her head slowly. "Wow. New York. Springfield must seem pretty dull and dinky to you by comparison."

"Springfield has been anything but dull and dinky." Sarah would never forget the sight of those black clouds rolling in as if on a flat, invisible platform, the way it had gobbled up the pale blue skies around them, or that single demolished house. Then she added, "I hope that praying lady is okay."

"Yeah, me too. Poor old Edna. It takes a real special kind of heart to love that woman, but I'm sure no one would wish her... whatever that was that hit her."

"You know her?"

"*Everybody* knows Edna Davies. But we all pretend like we don't. There's hardly a congregation in town she hasn't joined, insulted, condemned to hell, or rejected as too 'heathenous.' I know that's not very Christian of me, but, between you and me, neither is she." Jilly hid a guilty smile behind her hand. "Turn right here. Our house is all the way there at the end."

Like all the roads they had travelled on this short trip, this street was littered with debris. But there was no major damage, as far as they could tell, and the hail was already melting. The hailstones were now about the size of marbles. "Oh, thank God," Sarah heard Jilly say when they approached her house.

Sarah helped Jilly get the kids out of the car, and was about to say her goodbyes when Jilly said, "You have to stay for supper."

"Oh, no, thank you," Sarah said, though the invitation to a real home-cooked meal sounded pretty wonderful. "It looks like you already have your hands full. I should get out of your way.

"Oh, it's no trouble at all. Cooking for six is no harder than cooking for five."

"Thank you. Really. But I need to get going."

"Are you staying with friends or family here? Maybe I know them."

"No. Just passing through."

"To where? If you don't mind me being so nosy...?"

Sarah looked toward the place in the sky where the sun would soon begin its slow descent. "A little further west," was all she wanted to say.

"Well, you should get some real food in you before you go. I can have some hamburgers ready in no time. And if the lights are gone, we'll fire up the grill out back." Jilly started toward the house as if it was a foregone conclusion that Sarah would be joining them for dinner. "Oh, dang," she said, stopping midway up the front yard, "I forgot the milk and bread. Oh, well. I'll get Andy to pick some up on his way home. Which reminds me: I should call him." She said this more to herself than to Sarah.

The two older children had disappeared around the back of the house, the events of the past couple of hours apparently forgotten. Sarah could hear them laughing and squealing. She envied them their resilience.

"Come on inside, kids!" Jilly yelled to her children, holding the baby like a sack of groceries over one hip while she opened the front door. "Everybody in the tub!" To Sarah she said, "It'll be hours before I actually get them washed up." She shook her head as if to say, "It's a losing battle I'm resigned to fight every single day."

And just like that, life goes on.

Sarah stood in the front yard of Jilly's house and looked again at the brilliant blue sky to the west. Hints of pink would soon be settling above the treetops, but not yet. Earlier today, the air had been oppressively damp under the weight of a leaden sky. There was now a magical sort of crispness in the air, something almost electric, and the light was so white it almost sang. The slight chill of a passing breeze felt good against her skin. She closed her eyes and allowed it to brush against her face.

Sarah put her hands in her jacket pockets. Her right hand stumbled upon the edge of her phone. Without giving it a second thought, she took it out and called her parents.

"Sarah, baby, how are you?" Ana said instead of hello.

"Good, Mom."

"Where are you? Are you coming home? Should I make something special for dinner?"

"Uhh... no," she began tentatively. "I'm going to have dinner here."

"Where's here?"

Sarah looked around. "Missouri."

A momentary but sharp silence came between them, as if someone had snipped the conversation in half with a pair of scissors. "Missouri the *state?*" Ana asked, aghast.

"No, Missouri the spaceship."

"What?"

"Yes, the state."

"What the hell are you doing in Missouri?!"

"Just... passing through." Before she could lose her nerve or her momentum, she added, "I'm going to California."

And for the first time, the trip felt real. The simple act of stating her destination out loud had made the decision seem perfectly ordinary, and—best of all—sane. It felt so good, she said it again. "I'm going to California."

Sarah heard a minor scuffle and an excited exchange of muffled voices. Ana was probably pressing the phone against the palm of her hand or her chest. After a moment, Sarah heard her father's voice.

"Sarah?"

"Hi, Dad."

"You're in California?" he asked incredulously.

"Well, no. Not yet. But that's where I'm headed."

There was a long silence in which Dan considered this new information and Sarah wondered what else she could or should say about this. She didn't want to worry her parents, and she had no interest in being talked out of this trip, especially now that her journey had taken on more concrete dimensions. But the need to let someone know where she was at any given time had been deeply ingrained in her from earliest childhood. It was a safety measure that had become second nature; she no longer questioned it or gave it much thought. Even as an adult, she made it a point to leave the calendar open on her laptop showing her planned destination if she went out alone at night. If something happened to her, the police would at least be able to trace her likely last steps. Unnecessarily paranoid or a tad ghoulish, perhaps, but it appealed to the more pragmatic aspects of her neurotic nature. Maybe not having told anyone where she was going after she left the Jersey Shore was what had made the trip so far seem surreal and a little crazy. Now it felt perfectly rational.

"So what's in California?" Dan asked gently.

"I'm not exactly sure, Dad," she began. "I think this is more about the need to keep moving. I was feeling kind of… stuck. You know?"

He did know. He got it right away. A part of him was actually glad for her. Maybe a long trip would help her find some solace. She had been through one of the most horrific experiences imaginable: the sudden and needless death of a small child. Her only child. He had no idea how he might have dealt with such a thing himself without going mad, but he could easily imagine wanting to outrun that horror. Whether it was the right or the best thing to do, he had no idea. But he understood it. "Yeah. I do know," he said at last. "Your mother's hysterical, though."

"Yeah. Well. I think there's a pill for that."

But there's not a pill for you, Dan thought with an ache. "True. Very true. Promise me you'll be careful."

"I promise."

"Your mother wants to talk to you."

"Oh, God…"

"Now, now. Play nice."

"Love you, Dad."

"I love you more, baby girl. Here's your mother."

Ana had been crying. "I looked up Missouri on the map," she sniffed. "It took me a half an hour to find it."

"I only just told you about it two minutes ago, Ma."

"I don't understand why you're doing this."

Deflection sometimes worked to derail Ana's guilt trips. "Do you know how to text?" Sarah asked her. "On your cell phone?"

"*Texting?*" Ana said with alarm. "Isn't that for *sex?!*"

"Owya–*Gaahhdd*!" Sarah cried out and slapped a hand over her eyes. "Uggh! Never mind. I'll call you the old fashioned way. Like the pilgrims."

"Sarah, be careful. I'm not going to be able to sleep until you get back."

"You said that when I went away to college."

"And I haven't had a decent night's sleep since!"

"I love you, too, Ma."

"And I love you, dear. Wait." There was a short pause. "Your father wants to know what road you're on." More murmuring in the background. "So we can follow you on the atlas."

"Tell him Route 66."

"That's *real*? I thought that was an old TV show. Or a song."

"It's real. I'll send you a picture of the sign."

Ana relayed the information to her husband. "Don't forget to call me, Sarah."

"I won't, Mom. So long."

———

Jilly came back outside holding a small tray with two glasses and a plate of oatmeal cookies. She set it down on a little table between two chairs on the porch. "We got no lights," she called out to Sarah, "so I can't even make you a cup of coffee. But I thought you'd like a nice glass of iced tea. Come on up and sit for a little while."

Sarah obliged her, gratefully.

"I'd invite you inside, but I'm too embarrassed. The place looks like Santa's workshop exploded in the middle of a banana fight with a bunch of drunk monkeys."

Sarah laughed. "The sign of a happy home."

"Or an exhausted mom," Jilly added, "but I wouldn't trade it for the world."

Sarah nodded in agreement, and looked toward the west again.

The image of Sarah rocking Elizabeth on her lap in the cellar came to Jilly's mind, as crisp and clear as a photograph. "Do you have kids, Sarah?"

Now Sarah wished she had just gotten in the car and driven away when she still had the chance.

Jilly saw the struggle on Sarah's face, how she almost nodded yes, then almost shook her head no. "I'm sorry. I don't mean to be s'dang nosy."

Just then, Elizabeth came out to the porch and leaned against the armrest of her mother's chair. Jilly whispered something to the little girl. The girl nodded and went back inside.

"I heard you call her 'Little Bit'' when we were at the store. That's a cute nickname," Sarah said.

"Oh, yeah. She's our own darlin' Li'l Bit. When she was learning how to talk, she couldn't say her name. It's not the sort of thing that occurs to you when you're picking out baby names, that your child wouldn't be able to say her own name. When she tried to say, 'Elizabeth,' it sounded like 'a li'l bit', and Li'l Bit she stayed. We've been calling her that ever since."

"It's sweet. And it suits her." Sarah set her glass back down on the tray. "I should get going. I have a long way to go."

"Hold on just a sec," Jilly said, and turned toward the screen door. "Li'l Bit!" she called. "Did you find it yet?"

The little girl came back out with a small doll in one hand. Her mother nodded and gently pushed her daughter toward Sarah. She offered the doll to Sarah.

"For me?" Sarah asked, not really thinking it was for her.

"I make those," Jilly said. "I sell them. Mostly on eBay. Sometimes at flea markets and fairs. It started as a hobby, something to do at night after the kids were in bed and I was too tired to do anything but sit in a chair, but my hands were still itching to stay busy."

"She's beautiful," Sarah said, admiring the delicate stitches of the doll's needlework face, the hand-sewn pinafore edged in lace over a blue-and-white gingham dress, and the hair made of soft, very fine yarn tied prettily with thin satin ribbons. "You're a real artist, Jilly." She handed the doll back to Elizabeth with a smile.

"Oh, no. That's for you," Jilly said. "Isn't that right, Li'l Bit?" The little girl nodded. "Just a little something to remember us by. And for us to say thanks."

Sarah accepted the gift. "Thank you, Jilly. And thank you, Elizabeth. I will take very good care of her." Something in the corner of her eye twitched, very quickly, but Jilly saw it. "I'll tell everybody I know to look for you on eBay," she said to Jilly.

"That would be nice. There's a little label with the name of my 'store' on the side of the pinafore."

They walked Sarah back to the minivan, Jilly unable to talk Sarah into staying for dinner.

"Have a safe trip," Jilly said as she gave Sarah a warm hug. "Say bye-bye, Li'l Bit."

Elizabeth surprised Sarah with a big, strong hug around her legs. Sarah felt that thing welling up again in her chest. She stroked the little girl's hair one last time.

Five

SARAH HAD YET TO DISCOVER what kicks, exactly, one was supposed to get on Route 66.

She kept getting dumped back onto I-44 at various places, and after a while, she just gave up. She had hoped to see something memorable along the way—something other than gigantic, creepy crosses. What she saw instead were a few kitschy roadside tourist traps that might be fun if this were any other kind of trip. Mostly, though, it was the long way through a whole lot of nothing. This was not a sightseeing tour anyway. Besides, it would probably take two or three times longer to travel this storied road all the way to the end than if she just stuck to the Interstate highways.

Whether on the slightly more colorful Route 66 or the gray monotony of the multi-lane roads of the Interstate highways, the deeper she traveled into the belly of this massive country, the more she marveled at the thousands upon thousands of acres of unoccupied land, utterly baffled by the insistence of this nation's citizens on crowding themselves into the most inhospitable corners and verges. New Yorkers had nowhere left to build but up, into the air, so they built ever taller buildings whose shadows obliterated the sun at ground level at nearly all times of day, except perhaps for a couple of minutes at high noon, but only on some streets and never during all four seasons. And because space was at such a premium, people got away with selling even the most dismal and dilapidated real estate for thousands of dollars per square foot. Suburban areas weren't much better; having a patch of lawn in front of your house, however modest, with your next-door neighbor practically within reach of your kitchen window, was considered a significant gain in the struggle to achieve the American Dream. One had only to drive past the parking lot of any shopping mall in her part of the world to see that there were far too many people sharing quarters that were much too close, especially considering how vast the territory was with respect to the total number of inhabitants. Sarah thought about all the poorer people, packed like the day's haul in a fisherman's net, crammed into the smelliest pockets of America's cities, and how much happier we all might be if everybody would just spread the hell out.

On the other hand, if we *were* to spread out all nice and even, with generous amounts of space between our respective homes, would we begin to suffocate under the weight of loneliness and boredom? Would we sit on our porches and stare out at nothing—except, perhaps, the random killer storm—becoming as somnolent and unchanging as all this acreage, with not an interesting thing to say or do? It might feel like heaven for a little while, to have some room, at long last, to breathe and to stretch, to have enough uninterrupted silence for simple, quiet thought. But soon we would miss each other, because it's in our nature to resist solitude, no matter how much we find ourselves craving it at certain moments of our lives.

Sarah began to consider that it might be a fair trade after all to crowd ourselves into ever more creative configurations of vertical space at the edges of America for the occasional pleasure of smelling salt air, for the excitement of not knowing what might happen next when eight million people decide to share an island five miles wide and twelve miles long, for the communal madness of shopping for gifts or sustenance with other crazed, overextended, overtaxed consumers. For all our complaining about the exhausting busyness of city life, there is something to be said about its ability to keep our minds and bodies in perpetual—albeit relentless—motion.

The sight and scents of gently rolling hills, untouched woods, and farmland had initially aroused Sarah's senses and evoked feelings in her that she didn't even know were in her repertoire. Their discovery had initially filled her with a deep sense of reverence.

But in the same way that her ears seemed never to hear the blaring of sirens and horns in the middle of the night, her nose had become accustomed to the aromas of woods, earth, and green things growing, and her eyes had wearied of the sameness of these lonely, endless miles. She wasn't quite yearning for the oppressive crush of rush-hour commuters, each fighting for their respective ten square inches of space on a smelly, rumbling subway car, but she did wish she could get out and walk briskly for a while, and see other people doing the same. She didn't want to talk to any of them; she just wanted to see them.

———

Miles and miles rolled by, through the rest of Missouri and most of Oklahoma. The only real distraction had been a harrowing few minutes through a tangle of looping roads near Oklahoma City, their exits and on-ramps so close together that it was nearly impossible to know instinctively what to do. It looked and felt like the place where every highway in America intersected. There had been a few other places like this in other cities, but something about this one had been particularly disorienting.

Sarah somehow ended up on I-40. She would have to stop somewhere to consult a larger map and figure out this new road's trajectory, or whether she could get back on I-44 without having to go back through the Vortex of Spaghetti.

In the meantime, that fullness in her soul that she felt in a physical way, that viscous weight that wanted to crush the air right out of her, seemed only to grow larger. If she didn't find some way of releasing this burden soon, it was going to kill her. Of that she was certain.

————

At a place not far from where I-44 bisects US-81, a roadside diner with a few cars parked in front looked like a good enough place to stop for a while. She might just get something to-go and eat it standing up. Her butt and the backs of her legs were almost numb from lack of circulation and movement.

She took a seat at a booth by the window, feeling as slow and as dim as the day was overcast. It was still early afternoon, but it looked like it was much later. It was a day that wanted to rain but couldn't seem to get motivated enough to go through with it. She took her phone out of her pocket and hoped for decent reception. Luck was with her; Internet access came up right away.

She rubbed her eyes a bit to try to rid them of some of their blurriness. She squinted at the little screen as she pushed icons and images around with her finger. With her other hand, she massaged her temples.

"The letters on those screens get smaller and smaller all the time, don't they," said a man sitting in the next booth. She had not noticed him when she sat down. If she had, she might have chosen the seat on the other side of her booth, which would have put her back to him. This is something she normally did out of habit, not outright rudeness.

In the environment in which she had lived most of her non-traveling life, it was natural for each person to create a distinct zone of privacy, however minuscule, especially in a crowd. She had overlooked that trick this time.

She decided it wouldn't kill her to respond. "I'm not quite ready for bifocals, but I wouldn't mind a pair right now. Or a bigger phone."

The man gave her a warm smile. Sarah wasn't sure what to make of it. She smiled back briefly and went back to squinting at the screen and rubbing her temples. She shaded her eyes from him.

A waitress brought the man a glass of water and apologized for making him wait. As she scurried past Sarah, she said, "I'll be with you in just a sec, hon." Sarah nodded absently.

The man got up and put his glass of water in front of Sarah. "Here. Drink this. It'll help your headache."

Sarah looked at him, then at the glass. Old admonitions screamed in her head. *Never take a drink from a stranger! He could have dropped a roofie in the glass on his way to your table!* "Thanks. I'm fine."

"Really? You look terrible."

Sarah raised both eyebrows at him as he showed her both of his hands in a gesture of hasty apology. "I'm sorry. I'm sorry. That came out all wrong. All I meant to say was… that I'm an idiot and I'm sorry you have a headache. Unless you rub your forehead like that all the time for reasons that are none of my business, but you're still welcome to my glass of water."

The waitress dashed past them again, this time with an armload of plates destined for another table. "I'll be with you nice folks in just a second," she said.

"See? Nice folks. Both of us." He gave her that disarming smile again.

"Well, I only know for sure about one of us," Sarah said, relaxing just a little. This guy seemed nicer than she felt right now, but lots of bad guys were nice at first.

"May I?" he said, gesturing at the empty bench at her booth. "I promise I won't be weird."

If he did turn out to be weird, she could just get back in the car and drive away. "Sure," she said, not completely certain. They were in a public place in a seemingly harmless part of the world, and her cell phone was charged, connected, and ready. If she was quick about it, she could snap a picture of the guy and e-mail it to the FBI. She wondered how to get in touch with the FBI.

"Jackson," he said, extending his hand. She looked at it for a moment before shaking it.

"Is that your first name or your last name?"

"Both, you could say."

She took her hand back. "Your name is Jackson Jackson."

"Actually, it's James Jackson. Son of John Jackson, who everyone calls Jack, which makes me—"

"Jack's son, Jackson." Sarah nodded. "I get it." He was cute, in a middle-of-nowhere kind of way. Sandy brown hair with the tiniest hints of silver beginning to peek through, green eyes that tended more toward mossy than emerald, and with an air of harmless mirth that was difficult to resist. He also looked like a guy who knew how to chop wood, but only did it when he had to, or as a favor to a friend. Then again, Ted Bundy was cute and charming, too, and handy with an axe.

He took two menus from the holder at the end of the table and handed one to her. "To my Mom, I'm Jimmy. To my Dad and my brothers, I'm Jimbo, except to my oldest brother, Billy, who has called me Jim-Bonehead since I was seven; I believe it is because he is a moron. When I was eight, I watched an old gangster movie with my Grandpa and began channeling Jimmy Cagney, a role that would take me most of the way through my scrawny adolescence without getting beaten up more than twice a week. But Grandpa called me 'Jimmy

Jakes' because it sounded like a good gangster name and, he assured me, the world would never be big enough for two Jimmy Cagneys. He called me 'Jimmy Jakes' the rest of his life. I loved my Grandpa. Still do. Even though he's dead. Then in college, everybody started calling me Jackson, and that's what I've been ever since. I hardly ever even turn around anymore when somebody calls out 'Jim.' I just assume they're calling one of the other forty million Jims in America."

Sarah was beginning to question the wisdom of engaging this guy in conversation. Next he was probably going to try to sell her a car. Or a truck.

"I was hoping to make you laugh," he said, "Or at least crack a smile?"

She relented after a moment, and obliged him with a small smile, despite her better judgment.

His eyes twinkled above his impish grin. Oh, there was a scoundrel in there, all right, she thought. But maybe he was the good kind. "Are you from around here, Jackson Jackson?"

"Kanopolis, Kansas," he replied, and managed to sound simultaneously modest and proud.

"You're making that up."

"Nope. It's a real place. The exact middle of Kansas, which is in the exact middle of the United States. Although, if you look it up, the government will tell you Lebanon is the exact middle of the country. I never believed that, though. *I've* seen the map."

"Lebanon?"

"Lebanon, Kansas."

"Is that where the big jail is?" Maybe he was an escapee.

"Leavenworth? That's farther east, and to the north."

"Oh." She was being drawn into those smiling eyes; she didn't want to be, but she couldn't help it. She became aware of a deep yearning for a little company, and was glad that she might get it from someone who might be nice just for the sake of being nice, not because he knew anything about her or wanted something from her. What else was there to do right now, anyway? Her sense of urgency had long been overtaken by isolation and road-weariness. Still, he was not completely above her suspicion; if he could chop wood, he could chop people. She resolved to keep that in mind. "So what does one do for diversion in Cankanopolus, Kansas?"

"Kanopolis," he corrected. "One drinks a great many beers. And dreams of leaving."

Sarah turned her head and looked out on the vast, dusty vista beyond the diner's windows. "So you came here?"

Jackson favored Sarah with the most wonderful, deep-throated chuckle, full of good-natured cheer and without a glimmer of self-consciousness. She couldn't help but smile back, and then laughed out loud herself. Her laughter sounded alien in her own ears, and was followed so swiftly by a wave of guilt that it almost made her dizzy. She backpedaled from this brief moment of mirth as fast as she could, and dropped her gaze back down to the menu.

The waitress stopped at their table. "Sorry for the wait, folks." She put a new glass of water in front of Jackson. "I couldda swore I did that already," she said mostly to herself. "We're a little short-handed today. I apologize. What can I get for you?" Her warm, cheery voice belied an ancient weariness that crinkled the flesh under her eyes. She looked at Sarah expectantly, pencil poised above her little order pad.

Sarah took a quick look at the menu and picked out something fast and familiar. "I'll have the grilled cheese, please, and a cup o' coffee."

Both the waitress and Jackson looked at Sarah abruptly, with an almost identical raised-eyebrow look on their faces. It was a brief moment that Sarah missed completely as she closed the giant plastic-encased menu and put it back in its holder at the end of the table. Then she switched the glasses of water so that Jackson now had the one he brought her and she had the one the waitress had just put on the table. If he drank from the first glass and remained conscious, she would trust him a little more.

Jackson noticed the switch and smiled to himself. "I'll have the burger. Medium rare. With cheese. Lettuce and tomato. Onions. No, no onions. But you can add anything else you got back there you can legally throw on a burger."

"Okie-doke. And to drink?"

"Sweet tea. Lots of it. Heck, just bring me the pitcher and a big ol' straw."

Jackson put his own menu back in the holder as the waitress walked away. He leaned forward with his arms crossed in front of him on the table, and looked closely at Sarah. That devilish smile had the potential to haunt her for a very long time.

"Where'd you steal that accent?"

The question confused her a little. "Accent?"

"The one that likes '*caww*-fee'," he teased.

"Oh. Heh-heh…" But she wouldn't say.

He had not intended to flirt; he just hated eating alone. He hated not talking even more. She looked like she could withstand a bit of his company, even with her head in her hand and her face all scrunched up in a scowl as she fiddled with her smart-phone. Never one to shy away from conversation with whomever happened to be nearby, it didn't occur to Jackson that his company was ever entirely unwelcome. And if it turned out that it was, well, that was okay, too. Life was too short for grudges. He did know when to shut up and go away, but he so rarely experienced a flat-out dismissal or rejection that, to him, it seemed like the whole world *must* love him. How could they not? And many people, in fact, did.

"I don't know your name," he said finally, a little softer than he intended.

She looked at him, checking one last time for any traces she might have missed of a homicidal maniac lurking behind a normal-looking face. She decided there was not too much harm in telling him. "Sarah," she told him, but withheld her last name, just in case.

"Sarah," he repeated. And something about the way he said it, as if he were tasting the syllables, saying the A's a little differently than she pronounced them herself, something about that made her blush from the roots of her hair to the tips of her toes. He saw the blush and smiled. "Like a breath, that name is. Like a whisper. Like a sigh."

At another time in her life, she might have leapt across the table and straddled him right there.

She looked away, then down at her hands, utterly unsure of anything.

"You're a long way from home, then. Sarah who drinks *caww*-fee," he ventured.

She took a deep breath that caught in her throat. She had to cough a little to find her voice. "Yeah, actually. I am," she said, and immediately regretted it. Not something you should admit to a stranger. She gave her head a little shake to rid herself of the idiotic paranoid voice that so often got in the way of everything. "I've been on the road a long time."

"How long?"

"Two? Three days? Not sure. Seems like forever."

"Running from, or running to?"

Sarah considered this a moment. "A little of both, I guess." She tapped the screen on her phone and the GPS map reappeared. "It looks like I'm somewhere in the middle. Sometimes it feels too far to keep going, and too far to turn back." She looked up at him. "Is that how it felt in Konkonkomus?"

"Kanopolis. Something like that, I guess. Sometimes it's easier to just stay put. I couldn't do it, though. When you're in the exact middle of the world and you look around in every direction, your need to find the edges can get overwhelming. And sometimes the fear of never finding your way back can overwhelm you into staying. Having too many choices can be just as paralyzing as not having any at all."

Sarah had been looking at Jackson—almost *through* him—and then turned toward the window again. She nodded, almost imperceptibly. "Mm-hmm," she said in a very small voice.

The waitress came back and deftly placed their respective meals before them. "Anything else I can get you folks right now?"

Jackson admired the gigantic platter before him and nodded his approval. "I think this will do nicely to start."

Sarah looked at the flat, greasy thing on her plate surrounded by a riot of pale, shoe-string fries and wished she had ordered anything else. "I'm good. Thanks."

They dug in, he more enthusiastically.

"Is this town much different from Kon... Kan—?

"—opolis," Jackson said through a lusty mouthful of burger. He chewed a few more times and took a big sip of iced tea. "I have no idea, m'dear. Fort Worth is home now."

"Oh. We're in *Texas*?"

"Oklahoma. I've been on the road a long time, too. But not as long as you."

"Is that where you're going? To Kanopolis?"

"Um-hmm." He swallowed the bite of his burger and took another sip of tea. "Thought I'd give my old momma a thrill and give her the Gift of Me for Mother's Day."

Sarah sat back suddenly, looking at him as if he had uttered an obscenity. "Oh," she said quietly, looking down at her plate. "Right." She began to push food around on her plate slowly, her brow furrowed.

"I'm sorry," he said, startled at how fast that dark cloud came over her. He assumed she had recently lost her own mother, and felt like a fool for having been so cavalier. In fairness, there was no way he could have known.

"No, no. It's all right. I just... forgot." Her bottom lip pouted out just the tiniest bit, like she was about to cry, but she was fighting it. She found it hard to look at him now.

Jackson quickly changed the subject. "Do you know what they call teaching Shakespeare to high school jocks?"

She looked up at him, momentarily thrown. "Uhh... no," she said. "What do they call it?"

"Iambic pentathlon."

Sarah's face brightened a bit, much to Jackson's relief. She laughed softly, not too reluctantly. "That's clever."

"Ah, it's an old joke. But one of my favorites."

"Are you a jock or a teacher?"

"A little of both. But they pay me to teach. Going on fifteen years now."

"Why aren't you in school today?" *Aha,* said the voice. *This is how we catch a thief.*

"We didn't have to use our snow day this year. So they gave it to us today. Nothing better than a snow day when there's no snow."

"It snows this far south?"

"Occasionally we hear rumors of a flake or two in the vicinity. Sometimes the rumors are true, and we shut the whole city down, stay home, and watch the weatherman go crazy on TV. This was a warm winter, though. Nary a flake in sight."

He took another bite of his burger, not as big this time, and swallowed before speaking. "So you're not going to tell me where you're from or where you're going, even though I can make a couple of pretty good guesses?"

She was afraid of what might happen if she started talking about anything personal. So she began slowly, measuring her words. "I'm from New York. And a few days ago, I decided to go down the Shore."

"*To* the shore," Jackson corrected. "Sorry. Can't help it."

"*Down* the Shore, is how we say it. Where *coffee* doesn't rhyme with *copy*."

"Ah. I see," he said and popped another French fry in his mouth. "*Down* the Shore."

She nodded.

"I think you might have taken a wrong turn somewhere."

"No, I actually made it," Sarah told him. "But when I got there... I don't know... It just... didn't seem big enough."

"Big enough for what?"

"Big enough for me. So I kept driving."

"I don't think you're as big as you imagine. Also—and I hate to be the one to break this to you, but—Oklahoma has an extremely limited coastline."

"I thought I read or heard somewhere that you can drive from one coast to the other in about three days."

"I suppose. If you don't have to pee. Or sleep."

"Yeah. I didn't realize how much of that I'd have to do."

"Why'd you decide to cross the country?"

Sarah used one of the skinny fries to push the other fries around in her plate. "I'm not so sure anymore."

"So let me get this straight," Jackson said as he wiped ketchup off his fingers with the last clean corner of his napkin. "You went to the shore—sorry, *down* the Shore—somewhere on the Eastern Seaboard, found it sorely lacking, so you rejected the entire Atlantic Ocean and decided to drive to California?"

Sarah gave him a sheepish shrug. "It seemed like a good idea at the time. It sounds kind of silly when you say it."

"How does it sound when you say it?"

"Ha! Friggin' insane!"

"Friggin!" he repeated happily. "I never actually met someone who said 'friggin'!"

"Jimmy Jakes wouldda said it."

"You got that right, shweet-heart."

"That sounded like Humphrey Bogart."

" *'You dirty rat...'* " he tried again.

"That's better."

" *'Thank ya. Thank ya very mush.'* "

"No, no. Leave Elvis in Rock & Roll Heaven. I always thought he was kind of ugly."

"Ach! Blasphemy! You must leave my table immediately!" he said, doing his best impression of Henry VIII.

"It was my table first."

"Then you must stay and sup with me!" Then, in his normal voice, he added, "I hate eating alone. But you gotta stop dissin' The King." He pronounced it *Kang*.

The waitress came back for their plates. "Anything else I can get for y'all? We have a real nice apple pie up at the counter. Baked it m'self this morning," she offered.

"No, thanks. Just the check," Sarah said.

"Let me buy you another cuppa *caww*-fee," Jackson offered, and winked at the waitress. And before Sarah could object, he added, "And I believe I will have a nice big slice of that pie, Miss—" he read the name on the little plaque above her left breast. "Betty. Two forks, please."

Miss Betty smiled and nodded, and disappeared with their plates.

They talked for two more hours, sitting in that booth at that diner. He told her about his life in Fort Worth, about his students, about some of the books he had recently read, about the Pee-Wee Football team he helped to coach. Always more of a listener than a talker, Sarah found it easy to let him chatter, and was glad not to have to reveal too much more about herself. She told him about the storm in Missouri, and the gray-bearded man, and about Edna the Tongue-Speaker, who prayed herself right into some kind of seizure and who might have been fine if she had just shut up and waited for the storm to pass like everybody else had. But she didn't mention Jilly or her little girl, or how she had cradled that child in the near darkness of that cinderblock storeroom and had found, in that simple, quiet act, a moment of deep comfort for herself. She didn't mention any of the prior events that put her on the long road west and led her to this Oklahoma diner, either.

The longer he sat across from her, the more something inside him changed. And every time he made her smile, something softened in her worried face, revealing an uncommon prettiness that seemed reluctant to make itself known. There was something vaguely exotic about her. Perhaps he had grown too accustomed to the sights and sounds of big-haired, big-hearted, bold and sassy Texas women; one could reason that, by comparison, every other woman in the world was either exotic or exceedingly plain.

For Sarah's part, the ever present worry about where to stop and sleep for the night, and the hundreds of miles still to go, had drifted to the back of her mind for a while.

She wanted to hear him say *Sarah* again, the way he did it that first time.

———

The dinnertime customers were starting to fill the empty booths and tables at the diner. Jackson picked up the tab and walked Sarah to her car, neither one of them in a great big hurry to say goodbye.

"Isn't it funny how life can change in an instant?" he mused, as if he were performing a monologue at an audition. "One minute, I'm driving up this ugly road, and the day's all dark and gray... Next thing I know, I've met a lovely New *Yawkah* who tries hard not to talk funny and didn't mind me yappin' her ears off for a while. And now we go our separate ways. But my day isn't as gray anymore. I'll drive north with a little bit of sunshine in my car in spite of the darkness, and the scent of your perfume in my memory. And I'll wonder the rest of my life if Miss Betty's pie was as good as it looked."

She had, indeed, eaten the whole piece of pie herself. She would admit to that, but she was not going to tell him that she had freshened up with a baby wipe before getting out of the car a couple of hours ago. "I'm not wearing any perfume."

"Boy howdy. Even better."

"Sorry I ate the whole thing of pie."

"I'm not." He wanted to touch her, but he didn't. "There's something else I'll take with me as I make my way back to the old homestead."

"What's that?"

"The worry that you'll be all right. Wondering whether you've found an ocean that's big enough for you, and what'll happen if you don't. Curiosity about why you're going there and where you'll go after that. But mostly the worry that you'll be all right."

"I'll be all right."

"Good." Jackson started to turn around, and then stopped himself. "You know, they have this thing called the Internet now..."

"Yeah. I've heard."

Jackson reached into his back pocket and pulled out a small, wire-bound note pad. He flipped through a bunch of scribbled notes until he found a clean page, and plucked a pen from his shirt pocket. He wrote something down, folded the small sheet in half, and handed it to Sarah.

"If you think of it, or if you happen to find yourself in some greasy spoon deep in the heart of Texas, accosted by some jackass who won't shut up or leave you alone, just send me an e-mail or a text. Just so I know you're okay. Or to let me know I should shut up and leave you alone."

Sarah accepted the piece of paper with a smile. She put it in her pocket without looking at it.

"And don't feel obligated to give me your number or anything. I saw *Thelma & Louise,* and I know I'm a dead ringer for a young Brad Pitt, but I'm not going to follow you around the country begging you for a ride so I can steal your getaway money. I promise. Just call me if you'd like. If you want to. Or write. Just don't text me any dirty pictures. I prefer you e-mail those."

Sarah chuckled softly. "Tell your mother I said thank you."

He gave her a puzzled look. "For what?"

"For raising such a character." She held out her hand. "Thank you for lunch, Jackson Jackson. It was nice meeting you," she said, and she meant it.

"Ohhh," he groaned. "That sounds so much like goodbye."

"It's a big, big country. Lots of long, long roads." She looked out at the highway. And he saw that little cloud darken her brow again.

"And still our paths crossed at just the right time and place. Right here in the middle of nowhere. Isn't that something?"

Sarah smiled. "Mm-hmm. It is."

"Well, I'll tell you what: I'll be right back here on Sunday night. If not, I'm going to wonder about that pie for the rest of my life."

"It's not too late to get a slice. To go."

"Nope. I'm gonna wait." He looked into her eyes. "It'll be that much sweeter if I wait."

Sarah felt her breath wanting to catch in her throat again. She inhaled deeply. "So long, Jackson Jackson," she said, but made no move to walk away. She liked the feel of her hand in his. It was still clasped warmly in his.

"So long, Sarah."

Six

THE EARLY EVENING SKY had cleared up quite a bit while Sarah sat listening to Jackson chatter on about whatever came into his head. Or maybe the day just seemed a little brighter. Either way, she was glad for it. That sense of melancholy weariness had lifted considerably in the last couple of hours. Maybe she'd try to get back on Route 66 after all. Who knew what kicks she might have missed, or what good ones were still up ahead?

Still, she was apprehensive about driving in the dark now. She had heard of Tornado Alley, but she didn't know where it started or where it ended, or how wide a swath it cut across America. She was pretty sure she had been right smack in the middle of it back in Springfield, but that was all she would be willing to bet more than a nickel on right now. It scared her now to think that those gargantuan rolling black clouds full of mindless evil could steal over her silently and invisibly under the perfect cover of a night sky.

She drove just a few more miles and found a decent enough looking motel with a sign out front that boasted an indoor swimming pool, Wi-Fi, a fitness center, and free HBO. A swim would be heavenly. It would get her body moving and, best of all, in the water.

She checked in carrying her few bits of extra clothing in the picnic basket. With any luck, there would also be a coin-operated washer and dryer on the premises and she could freshen up her things.

There was no place for her to buy a swimsuit here, but that was the least of her worries. She would go to the pool anyway. If there were any people there, she'd just roll up her pants legs and soak her feet and calves by the edge of the pool until they left. If she had the place to herself, she'd swim in her underwear. If someone came in later, she'd wrap herself quickly in a towel; she'd just have to remember to leave one near the edge of the pool.

She dropped her things off in the room, grabbed a large bath towel, and went down to the lowest level of the building. She was delighted to find that she did have the pool area to herself. She slipped out of her pants and her mother's ugly gardening clogs, but left her tee-shirt on over her bra and panties. The water was cooler than she expected or would have liked, but if she entered slowly down the steps at the shallowest end, her body would adjust to the change in temperature at a comfortable pace. It wasn't a very big pool, but it was long enough to swim laps.

This was her true nature, one of her life's simplest and most gratifying pleasures: to move through water with a slow, purposeful grace, in ways that were impossible to replicate on dry land. Here she could defy gravity, and lose herself completely in time and space. She found herself wishing, as she often did, that she could breathe water so she could stay submerged for hours, like a happy dolphin or a playful seal. She envied those mammals their ability to do that, and their seemingly effortless speed. How wonderful it must be to travel swiftly for miles and miles without ever touching ground, coming up to the surface only to grab a quick gulp of air, or to squeal and squawk with unfettered delight.

With every lap, she felt her muscles limbering a bit more. Her neck and spine, subjected for much too long to a nearly motionless sitting position, stretched and crackled pleasurably as she moved.

Her thoughts and worries about the trek to the Pacific drifted away with each stroke, and were quietly replaced by random bits of remembered conversation with Jackson.

In the course of their afternoon together, he had awakened long-slumbering feelings, slowly rousing into full wakefulness a part of herself that she had been content enough to let lie dormant. Something about that made her feel guilty, like it was wrong to entertain such thoughts right now. It's not that she had never suffered a moment's loneliness in the past few years; there were many times when the unoccupied spaces of her bed seemed woefully vast. But hers was not a lonely life, not by a longshot. She never allowed herself to believe that it was. She reminded herself often that she had a handful of very dear friends who mostly left her alone—which is what she cherished most about them—but were happy to share a meal with her from time to time, or see a movie or a show on the random Saturday afternoon. What was left of her time and energy she devoted to her work, and caring for Tess.

(tess is dead)

"*Nyaagh!*" she sputtered and shouted loudly to the oldest of her intimates, the sadistic voice inside her own head.

She stood upright in the pool, her toes barely touching bottom, and angrily pushed wet hair back on her head. She looked around, trembling, breathing hard. No one had heard her shout, but the sound seemed to echo for a long time, reverberating off the cold, cinderblock walls.

Sarah put a hand over her chest and concentrated on finding a slower rhythm for her heartbeat. The only sounds now were the rippling of water and her own ragged breathing. She could hear her own pulse pounding in her ears. She could also feel that crushing bubble of rage, guilt, and sadness in her chest, so much a physical, palpable thing. She pushed down on it, willing it to recede.

When the drumbeat in her ears subsided and her breathing was once again closer to normal, she put all of her concentration into reconnecting with the steady, even motion of gliding from one end of the pool to the other. Her earlier ease and grace were gone now, though. The muscles in her arms and legs had turned to cordwood. She pushed herself harder. She would swim to the point of exhaustion, as fast as she could, and then faster. The smiling dolphin of her imagination had deserted her completely. She swam now as a mindless, blood-lusting shark, all razor-sharp teeth and dark, murky eyes, as the bruised and filled-to-bursting thing in her chest throbbed with a pulse of its own.

———

Sarah lay in bed between the plain white sheets, staring straight up at the ceiling. She had finally pulled herself out of the pool, wrung herself out, and trudged up to her room and into a brief, hot shower. Her arms and legs burned accusingly. She didn't care anymore.

Too exhausted to sleep, to bleary to blink, she simply lay on her back and stared at the rough patterns of the tile-like shapes on the ceiling. She wondered if she'd ever move again.

Then, she thought darkly about how that might be better, to never move again.

Twice—no, three times—she had had a life she loved. And three times it had been ripped cruelly from her hands.

If she dared to create yet another life for herself, as she had after Florida and Liliana, after Vincent, and now after losing Tessie, wouldn't it stand to reason that it, too, would be snatched away from her?

She lay on her back and wondered if anyone had ever died in this room.

She imagined that motels by the side of any road in the world had their fair share of such stories. It seemed likely that a great many suicides occurred in places like this, where people like Sarah preferred not to make their loved ones clean up the mess they'd leave behind.

The room was dim, lit only by the street lamps in the parking lot outside, so she couldn't see from here if there was something she could use. She thought about the electrical cords attached to the room's lamps, but couldn't imagine wanting to die of strangulation.

She thought about the pool downstairs, but rejected that as an impossibility; she was a good swimmer, and even with her hands and feet tied with electrical cords, she would float involuntarily to the top with her face above the water line. She would tread water until somebody found her, lying still, but still alive, her body refusing to let her drown.

She thought about her mother's ever-replenishing supply of Xanax, and wished she had had the foresight to sneak a handful of those pills into her pocket before leaving New Jersey.

She thought about the contents of her purse, if there was something in there that she could use. She wondered if she could open the veins in her wrists or the artery in her neck with the jagged edges of her keys, or the pointy end of a ballpoint pen. Maybe. Maybe.

Her body seemed to sink deeper into the mattress as she stared into the darkness, too profoundly weary in her body and in her soul to move a single muscle. In a little while, she'd get up and get her purse. In a little while. In a little while.

Her eyes began to close as her thoughts meandered on their own. Too tired to keep fighting them, she let them wander. Perhaps inevitably, they found Vincent.

_____

Those first couple of years had been happy ones. Their mutual attraction was almost instantaneous, and led to the briefest and wildest courtship of her life. She was twenty-nine when she met Vincent; he was a year and a half older.

They laughed a lot in those early days, and traveled, and sought out unusual culinary experiences that more often than not ended in disaster, but made for great stories when they got together with friends. They had gotten their respective careers off the ground in the most promising ways, and were generally quite happy with their lives, as individuals and as a couple.

The best part was the sex.

They were as uninhibited in bed as they were when they went scavenging for eateries in the lesser-known corners of the city. There were few things they wouldn't try in either venue.

It all seemed to make sense when the subject of marriage came up, a year or so into their relationship. Sarah had been reluctant to give up her little apartment—not to mention the independence and sense of accomplishment it gave her—especially so soon after the transition from renter to owner. Vince wanted a house in the suburbs like the one in which he had grown up, to live like his father had: commuting an hour and a half each way, living a fast-paced business life in the city by day, retiring to quiet and spacious surroundings by night, hiring a neighborhood kid to take care of the lawn on summer Saturdays, and puttering around on Sundays.

The notion of living such a life made Sarah want to blow her own brains out.

But Vince kept applying subtle amounts of pressure over time, nothing too pushy, until she began to protest a little less each time they spoke of it. Eventually, as they were approaching their second anniversary, Sarah acquiesced, but only on the condition that they would keep her apartment in the city. She let him believe it would be "their" pied-à-terre. In her own heart and mind, it would always be her sanctuary. She didn't mind sharing it with him, but it would always be hers to share. For his part, Vince was happy to use the profit from the sale of his own apartment as a down payment for the house on Long Island.

One night, as it happened from time to time, she had to work late to meet a looming deadline that was "life-and-death critical" (as they all were, as far as her boss was concerned). She had called Vince just before six that evening to let him know she'd probably be staying in the city for the night, and so it had occurred. It was past ten o'clock when she finally shut down her computer. She had to be back in the office the next morning by seven-thirty. If she hadn't had the apartment, she would have spent the night in a hotel. She was glad to have her own place to go for rest and comfort, always wishing she had more reasons to go there more often.

The next evening, haggard, exhausted, and glad the project was over, she arrived at their big, comfortable home on Long Island and fell into bed, clothes and all. She closed her eyes and inhaled deeply, gratefully, and found that her pillow was permeated with the scent of another woman's sex.

The next few days were a dark and ugly blur. There was a lot of yelling. There were tears that burned like acid. There was rage. There was hurt. Things flew. Stuff broke. Vince mostly sat in dark corners and was silent. He would neither confess, deny, nor explain anything. Not one thing. This only fueled Sarah's rage and heartbreak to heights she had never before experienced, or imagined herself capable of reaching.

Most of all, she was angry at herself for having ignored all of her old hunches.

Deep down, she knew this was not the first time Vince had cheated. Those nagging suspicions had grown stronger in their last year or so of marriage, but, until the very end, she had not quite been able to make herself to see the signs for what they were: pretty damning—and damnable—proof.

He, of course, either denied her accusations vehemently, or dismissed them as silly and "undignified of their relationship." That pretty silver lighter she once found on the floorboard of his car? *A co-worker must have dropped it when a group of them went out to lunch that day.* The unanswered phone late at night while either one of them was out of town? *The phone must've been charging or in another room; I must've been in the shower; I fell asleep early; no I didn't get that message.* Perfectly plausible excuses. But so many of them. Even that slim silver lighter, as delicate as a piece of jewelry, the closest thing to real proof she had ever found... what if it *had* belonged to a co-worker? If it had belonged to someone he was screwing, then the life she thought she was living would have had to end right then and there. Perhaps she wasn't ready to throw that life away just yet. Denial was so much easier to live with than defeat. But it never silenced the doubt.

There had been many occasions for them to have slept apart, lots of long nights at the office for her that were best spent at the apartment in the city, and not a few out-of-town business trips for both of them. For all Vince knew, Sarah could have been having her own trysts in her old apartment when she said she needed to work late, but the truth was that she had never been unfaithful. Of his fidelity, she could never be one hundred percent certain. But now she knew for sure. This was no accidentally dropped cigarette lighter on the floorboards of his car. This was the unmistakable smell of another woman's cunt in her own bed. On her *pillow.*

She would be a fool to stay. She had been a fool to stay this long. And that was what made her angriest: the willing way in which she had played the fool.

So she left him.

She never saw him again. Her last personal contact with Vince was via e-mail. She told him he could keep the house and its contents if he agreed to an uncontested divorce; it was the fastest and cleanest way out. She only wanted to go back once to collect her clothes and other personal items, and she didn't want him there when that happened. If he didn't trust her not to burn the house down in his absence, he could send his sister over, to supervise. But she did not want to see him.

If he thought about trying to talk her into giving him one more chance, he never mentioned it. His response, via e-mail, consisted only of two sentences: "This sounds fair, under the circumstances. I'm sorry it has to end like this." Not, as Sarah wanted to hear, "I'm sorry I fucked up your life. I deserve to be disemboweled, and then set on fire."

The following weekend, Sarah arrived in a small U-Haul truck. Vince's sister, Patty, was there; Vince was not. Patty tried to hug Sarah, but Sarah wouldn't let her. "It's not you," Sarah explained. "I just can't stand to be touched right now. I think I'll scream—and never stop screaming—if another human being touched me right now."

"I'm so sorry," Patty said, and meant it. "You know, for as smart as he is, he can be so goddamned dumb."

Sarah looked at her questioningly.

"Yeah," Patty said, reading the question on Sarah's face. "He told me everything. I made him tell me."

A bit of the old anger flared up for a second. He confessed everything to his sister, but couldn't say a word to the person who most needed to hear it. Sarah shook it off and went upstairs to gather her things.

It surprised her to see how little she wanted from this place. As it turned out, most of the material things that ever mattered to her, if they mattered at all, had never left her apartment in the city. Those things were, and would always be, only hers.

Once she had emptied the closets and drawers of her clothes, and picked up a few books, old CDs, and a couple of pieces of framed artwork that she had brought to the house from her place in Manhattan, there really wasn't anything else she wanted or needed. She didn't want the dishes or flatware they had both used to share their meals. She didn't want any of the furniture or linens on which they had sat, slept, propped up their feet, or made love. She wanted nothing that looked like him or smelled like him. Even back in the city, she had gotten rid of all her all sheets and pillows, in case Vince had ever used her place for the occasional nooner. She flipped the mattress over, and considered burning it. She found herself sniffing the cushions on the sofa. She re-washed all the dishes, glasses, and cutlery using disinfectant soap. She had never found any evidence of Vince's extramarital escapades in New York, but it wasn't until she had scrubbed every inch of her place and its contents, steam-cleaned the upholstery, and repainted the walls and ceilings that she started to relax in her own home.

Back at the house on Long Island, she picked through the jewelry box he had given her one Christmas, and collected the pieces she had bought for herself or had been given to her as gifts by people other than Vince. She left her wedding band and engagement ring; she had taken those off like they were on fire on the night she returned to the befouled marital bed; it was the only clear memory (besides that smell on her pillow) that she had of that long, bitter night. As far as she was concerned, he could stick everything else up his ass and dance around a maypole at the end of the driveway while whistling show tunes. She was done.

The cut-rate lawyers she had hired to get her through the speedy divorce (the oldest of whom looked to be all of sixteen) assured her that it could all be over in just a couple of months—assuming, of course, that her soon-to-be-ex-husband agreed to play nice and didn't contest any of her demands.

The lawyers had asked her in that initial meeting if the marriage had produced any children. She had answered truthfully: she said no. She did not know at the time that she was pregnant.

She was only vaguely aware that she had missed a period. There was too much going on that week already. By the time she realized that she was approaching a second month since she last menstruated, she attributed the absence to stress. She refused to consider any other possibility. When she passed the eight-week mark, she angrily purchased a home pregnancy test, certain it would come up negative but needing to quell the nagging doubt.

She kept forgetting to save the first urine of the morning for her test, walking sleepily to the toilet for the next three days and voiding her bladder out of habit. Each time, she remembered the EPT kit mid-stream. On the third morning, after missing the opportunity, she set everything up on top of the toilet tank, where she would see it before she sat down and could reach for it quickly, even half-asleep, even mid-stream. Still she refused to worry. It was just a missed period. Or two. Caused by stress.

On the fourth morning, ten minutes after peeing on the stick, she was forced to admit that it was time to worry.

She called in sick and paced her apartment until noon. In the early part of the afternoon, she cried—out of anger, sadness, fear, regret, confusion, shame, and emotional exhaustion. Her hatred of Vince was a seething volcano.

At four that afternoon, she made an appointment.

It would be another week before the clinic could schedule the procedure. In the meantime, she kept as busy as possible. She worked until nine or ten every night, and fell into bed too exhausted to think.

On the weekend in between, she reorganized her closets, ripping out the old boards in the large one in the foyer and putting in entirely new shelving.

On Tuesday night, aching and too spent to do anything more, she sat quietly in her favorite chair by the window. Tomorrow morning, the problem of the missed period would be solved.

She sat in the silence of her little apartment, watching people and traffic go by outside. The evening was quiet and warm. Without realizing it, as if of its own volition, her right hand had come to rest on her abdomen, where it was making small circular motions.

Sarah looked down at that hand, surprised at how natural and irresistible that gesture felt. Something primal or instinctual had taken over. It surprised her even more that she felt no compulsion to stop it.

For weeks, she had been thinking of her situation as a simple case of a missed period. She didn't want to think of it as a baby—or even a zygote—because then she would have to think of it as belonging, at least partially, to Vince, and then she'd have to think of spending the rest of her life looking into the face of a child who would remind her of that bastard every minute of every day. She would never be rid of him, and she would grow to resent a child who deserved nothing of her scorn.

On the heels of that thought, her mind became inundated with memories of Liliana, the whispered stories she had picked up through careful eavesdropping, the half-glimpses Sarah had stolen of the tragic specter of Lily.

Did her grandmother hate Lily because she was the product of some shameful union? Was that justification enough to have heaped all of that violence and venom on that poor girl?

She looked at her hand again, the one caressing the lower part of her belly as if it didn't care what Sarah thought of it.

What if all those little cells dividing in there were turning into someone who would look not like Vince, but like her instead, and, by extension, like Lily? And so what if it was a little boy who looked like a perfect clone of Vince? Could she destroy this child, before or after its birth, as her crazy grandmother had tried to destroy Lily? Did she really want to resemble that monstrous old woman who had lived every day of her life so steeped in incomprehensible hatred?

Would being a single mother be the worst thing in the world? She made a good living, earning more than she ever really needed to spend. Her tastes had never been extravagant, and she was one of the handful of women in America who hated to go shopping. She spent money primarily on what she needed, and socked away the rest.

The logistics would be tricky; from what she had observed at a distance, it was hard work to raise a child and hold down a job, even when there were two parents in the house. But hard work and other obstacles had never succeeded in breaking Sarah's resolve. She had always been able to figure out a way.

She would never begrudge a woman her right to choose, nor judge her for her choices. But she found herself smiling at finally realizing the obvious: one of those choices was to have the baby.

"A baby," she said for the first time, and found that it didn't scare her. "We'll figure this out together," she said to her belly, the first words she spoke to the evolutionary miracle that would someday be known as Tessie.

Sarah didn't cancel her appointment the next morning; she simply didn't show up.

Sarah said nothing to no one until another couple of months had passed, when she could no longer hide the evidence under baggy blouses and big sweaters. She communicated with the divorce lawyers only by phone and e-mail. She stopped seeing the friends she and Vince had once had in common, which was not difficult since they almost never saw any of the old gang after moving to Long Island anyway.

When her parents asked about Vince's planned involvement with the child, Sarah lied; she told them he didn't want to have anything to do with the baby. Her father offered to find him and beat the crap out of him. "What do you want to do," Sarah asked him, "have a shotgun baptism?" Sarah thanked her father, but told him that no beatings would be required at the moment.

She didn't know if what she had done could be classified as criminal. Depriving Vincent of the knowledge that he had fathered a child—and planning never to tell her son or daughter about his or her father—undoubtedly fell under the mantle of moral turpitude, at the very least. Her plan had been to dodge the child's questions until she couldn't anymore. When that time came, she would think of something to tell the kid, but she figured she would have many years to come up with a plausible story, up to and including the truth. She justified her decision not to tell Vince by telling herself that what he had done to her was far more egregious, much more morally turpitudinous. Some part of her wanted to disagree, and had plenty of logical arguments to support that position. That part of her conscience occasionally kept her up at night, but she had done a pretty good job of ignoring it over the years. She hardly ever thought about it anymore.

Her conscience had come back screaming on the day Tessie died.

Now, as she lay naked, physically spent, and immobile between sheets that belonged to everyone and to no one in this soulless room, the nagging voice whispered to her again.

But what would be the point of telling Vince now? Tessie was gone. Did it matter anymore? Did it really? If it had been wrong of her to keep such a secret, wasn't she now paying an unimaginable price for that transgression? Wasn't that enough? No matter how wronged she felt by Vince, would it make *anything* right to give him—and then immediately take away—a child he never knew he had, and may or may not have wanted?

Deservedly or not, she slept a dark, dreamless sleep.

————

Sarah opened her eyes in the darkness at a quarter past two in the morning. It was as if she had only blinked a moment ago. She felt a vague disappointment at discovering she was still alive.

Squinting at the clock on the nightstand, she calculated she had slept four or five hours. She was wide awake now, though, the notion of sleep as far away as the Jersey Shore.

Her mind was still full of roiling dark clouds, but her body was feeling less tired. If she was going to kill herself, she'd find a nicer place than this, and something more efficient than the jagged edge of a key. This gave her some motivation to get out of bed.

Maybe she'd wait until she got to California. What could be more beautiful than to die listening to the sound of the waves at dawn?

There was a coffee maker next to the television on the dresser, but nothing that could pass for real milk or sugar—not unless she pretended really hard that the beige, chalky stuff in the foil-like wrapper was cream, and the tiny bits of white dust in the pink and blue envelopes was not bitter. There was a Lipton teabag next to the pre-measured packet of coffee, but it was already open; the previous guest must have changed his mind about the tea, and the housekeeper either hadn't noticed or didn't care.

It seemed unlikely she'd find a 24-hour coffee shop nearby. A truck stop, maybe, but that didn't sound like the kind of place she should stroll into on purpose in the middle of the night by herself, even on a night when she was feeling particularly self-destructive. She wished she could pick up the phone and have a nice hot bagel delivered, with some good old-fashioned regular coffee in a blue and white paper cup.

For the first time, she realized, she was homesick.

Sarah made her way to the bathroom and almost broke her neck. She slipped on the lump of wet clothing she had dropped onto the floor without a thought when she had come back from the pool. She hadn't worn her pants into the pool, but they were wet now, too, puddled under the things that were soaked. The chlorinated pool water had bleached some spots on the cheap chinos she had purchased at that Target store a million miles ago. "Fine," she said out loud. "They'll go much nicer with the ugly clogs now." She kicked the wet clothes aside and took a nice long pee.

The muscles in her arms and legs were still talking to her, but they weren't screaming anymore. She paced around the room for a while, peeked out the window into the quiet parking lot for another little while, and then paced some more before convincing herself that she was done sleeping for the night. She turned on the TV and let the free HBO chatter in the background while she rinsed the chlorine out of her clothes in the bathroom sink.

When she looked at the clock again, it was still only forty minutes past two.

She downloaded an e-book to her phone, hoping that if she read for a while she would get sleepy again, but she hated reading books this way. She read a few pages and then set the phone aside. If someone had put a gun to her head, she could not have described what she had just read.

The clock said three-ten.

"Fuck it," she muttered. She dressed in the last bits of dry clothing she had, put the wet clothes in a plastic bag from one of the room's waste-paper baskets, and practically ran to the front desk. She was checking out.

———

Something about being in Texas, a state she never thought she'd visit on purpose for any reason, shifted her mood. She wouldn't say she felt better, exactly; she just felt different. Maybe it was Texas, or maybe it was just being back on the road and headed to the ocean with a different purpose in mind, but she felt like she had taken a step back from the edge of an abyss. She could still see it, though.

According to the signs, somewhere up ahead was Amarillo, the only town she had actually heard of since zipping past the tangle of roads near Oklahoma City. There had also been miles and miles of billboards advertising a restaurant there with a giant, waving cowboy out front, a place where your steak was free if you could eat all ten pounds of it in one sitting, or some such horrific thing. If she happened to pass by it, she would take a picture of it and send it to her Dad, the last of the great backyard-grilling carnivores. She'd also try to remember to pick up a bottle of real Texas barbecue sauce for him. At least *he* would get a couple of kicks out of Route 66.

(so you've decided to live?)

She swept a hand in front of her face, as if swatting away a fly.

At a small spot in the distance, there appeared to be a great many flashing lights. She had passed almost no cars and only a few trucks in the two or three hours since she had checked out of the hotel outside of El Reno, Oklahoma, in the dead of the night. It was easy to imagine someone had fallen asleep at the wheel on this long, flat road. There didn't appear to be anything to crash into, except maybe a guardrail or another car.

When she got closer, she could see that a plane had landed on I-40. Not a commercial jet or anything as big as that, but it still looked pretty big and utterly incongruous, sitting as it was on this highway. Such a thing happening near JFK or LaGuardia would result in an absolute massacre at any time of the day or night. Here, it looked like something that probably happened with some regularity. Someone overshot the runway of a nearby county airport, or ran out of gas, or had a little engine trouble, she figured. There were no screaming sirens, no wreckage, no crowds of disbelieving gawkers, no overexcited media people with satellite dishes on top of their vans. All those flashing lights had come from just one cop car, a fire truck, and an ambulance. The officer who was waving his flashlight to divert traffic (what little there was of it) off the highway seemed pretty unruffled by the incident.

When Sarah realized that the little country road she had been directed to take was not heading in the same direction as I-40, a brief moment of panic bubbled up inside her. She had a terrible sense of direction in broad daylight and under the best of circumstances; by night, she was hopelessly clueless on streets that weren't consecutively numbered. If she had to make more than two turns after the exit ramp or lost sight of the highway, she'd become completely disoriented in the dark. She didn't entirely trust that the GPS service on her phone worked out here in the middle of nowhere; and it was hard to see or hear it without the ear buds, which may or may not be buried somewhere inside her purse.

She drove straight ahead for a mile or two, then began to zigzag down nameless two-lane country roads, hoping she was heading in a more-or-less Amarillo-bound direction. Most of all, she hoped she'd chance upon something that looked more like an alternate highway going west.

There wasn't a building in sight; she felt like she was driving on the moon. Once again, the lunacy of this adventure laughed cruelly in her ears. The more she tried to ignore it, the more foolish and tired she felt.

She rolled down the window for a blast of fresh air, turning her face toward it for a moment, and saw something that had been completely hidden to her all this time by the dark tint of the upper portion of the windshield, the glare of her own headlights, and the distraction of the endless white lines of the road immediately before her.

She saw stars. Billions of stars.

The sight took her breath away.

She slowed to less than thirty miles per hour, then to fifteen. Foolish, crazy, or suicidal, she no longer cared. She needed to stop the car and get out to look at this spectacular sight.

Sarah had never before seen anything like this. City lights dimmed all but the most brilliant stars. You were lucky to see just a couple of them every now and then. She had seen starry nights in the suburbs, and on brief junkets Upstate, but never anything like this Texas sky. All those other vistas had been mere glimpses through a peephole compared to this.

She pulled over and parked on the soft shoulder of the road. She thought for a moment about the small canister of pepper spray that had never been discharged and that had occupied space at the bottom of every purse she had owned in the past seven or eight years. She decided it could stay there forever in exactly the same state. If someone meant to do her harm out here in the middle of nowhere, he would likely be armed with something more deadly than an ancient and probably defunct can of mace. She was prepared to take the risk.

A clean, cool wind enveloped in velvety darkness blew against her skin and through her hair. She circled the minivan, looking straight up at the sky. What constellations were looking back down on her, she wondered. What spellbinding secrets had they whispered to ancient mariners and other voyagers? What would they say to her now if she knew how to read them?

She opened the passenger side door and, planting a foot on the seat, hoisted herself up to the roof. She lay flat on her back, listening to the clicks of the cooling engine playing out a syncopated rhythm against the night songs and muted chatter of the invisible creatures that inhabited this incredible place.

Then something off to her left caught the corner of her eye. A long, thin line of deep purples and reds had begun to trace the outline of the horizon. She sat up and faced it, legs crossed beneath her. She braced her hands by her hips, against the roof of the car. She held her breath and watched. Something miraculous was about to begin; she could feel it.

By tiny increments, the edges of the world revealed themselves to her. Morning rose like a goddess from a profound and restful sleep, stretching slowly, with a power and a grace that was utterly beyond the clumsy imitations of even the most gifted mortals.

As the first edges of the sun's crown lifted above the horizon, and the goddess stretched her arms for miles and miles in either direction, layers of pink and gold were added to her vestments, revealing to Sarah's weary, wondering eyes the actual curvature of the earth.

The silhouette of a solitary tree in the distance was backlit by the dawn. The old tree had grown at an angle, as if pushed all its life by a persistent wind. Its long branches waved minutely, reaching out in a gesture of yearning, of praise, its own size dwarfed by the majesty of the rising sun.

Tears began to roll down Sarah's cheeks, so moving was this sight. Then tiny gasps became soft sobs. As the sun rose higher, transforming itself from sleepy nymph to conquering warrior, Sarah lay on her side, resting her cheek into the crook of one arm.

She had found the bigness of the world on dry land, not by the sea.

But would this be enough? Would it ever be enough?

She wept, at long last, for her beloved lost child, for her lost loves, for every one of her lost dreams. Her cries filled the massive morning, sounds dissipating to nothing in the distance. She curled up into a ball, whimpering, keening. That dark and bruised thing in the center of her chest began to tear open, that place where she had imprisoned all of her horror, shame, guilt, and sadness. The sound transformed itself into the soul-shattering howl of a mortally wounded animal.

She wept like this for a long time, in the way that babies and very small children do, before they're trained to hush, before their cries are stifled either by threat or through comfort, before they learn that no one likes to hear that noise, before they understand that they're not supposed to cry. They cry out their rage, their need, their boredom, their hunger, their loneliness, their disappointment, their hurt, their discomfort, and someone is supposed to come and make everything right. She cried like that now, full-throated and screaming, knowing deep in her heart that no one would ever make this right, and she cried for that, too.

———

After some unknowable time, Sarah's whimpering dissolved into a low, tuneless hum, she rocked herself slowly, hugging her knees against herself.

In the end, she found there was no anger left inside her; only a cavernous space in which the residues of sorrow would echo forever. Someday she might learn to live with those echoes. But that pounding, suffocating bubble that had been pressing down on her heart and lungs for so long had finally broken apart. Whatever had been in there had, at last, found a way out.

Still lying on her side, Sarah closed her eyes. The horizon had become too bright to look at. She could still see red light through her closed eyelids. Warming sunlight enveloped her body gently. A soft breeze kissed her cheeks and dried her tears. She accepted this comfort quietly, having gratefully surrendered to it the crushing burden of her grief, by inches, by grams, and, finally, in a tidal wave of sorrow.

Once or twice she heard passing vehicles. One of them had slowed down a bit, but didn't stop. She would stay here until she no longer could, until she was ready to rise, until someone made her leave.

No one made her move. The ever warmer morning breezes continued to stroke her hair.

It is possible she slept.

———————

When Sarah opened her eyes again, the massive plains all around her had turned into a giant game of Whack-A-Mole.

Little brown creatures, as far as the eye could see, popped up out of the ground and quickly ducked back down. They didn't move like squirrels or rats, or hop like rabbits, but she didn't know what they could be. Whatever they were, they were cute and very funny, and—she hoped—perfectly harmless. Thankfully, they were far enough from the road so as not to make her feel trapped on the roof of her car.

She wasn't sure what she wanted to do next. She kind of liked it here. And she wanted to see those stars again, in this exact place. Maybe she'd stay a while.

She stood up on the roof of the car, carefully, not wanting to fall or dent the metal, and took a good look around. She saw not a single dwelling, except for something that looked like a barn not far from the big leaning tree.

She tried to get her bearings, to remember how far behind she had left I-40. She looked to the place where she had seen the sun rise. She stuck both arms straight out for balance and turned her back to that spot in the east. The highway must be someplace to her left, running perpendicular to the sunlit horizon. The big leaning tree was roughly north of here. "I am the compass," she said immodestly. "I believe I have figured this out." It gave her a great sense of self-reliance not to have to depend entirely on maps or technology to know where she stood in the world.

If she took a left at that crossroads just ahead and stopped trying to zigzag all over creation, she was bound to run into some little town, or at the very least, the north side of Amarillo. Also, she might be able to find her way back to exactly this spot for a little more star-gazing tonight, if that still felt like a good idea after she got something to eat. She climbed down from the roof of the car.

As she turned the key in the ignition, that old barn caught her eye again. Maybe it was a house, or a little general store.

Or a meth lab. Or some psycho's digs.

"Shut up," she said, and drove.

————

A narrow and very bumpy dirt path led up to the structure she had spied in the distance. It wasn't as close to the tree as it had seemed from farther away, but easy enough to locate given that the only other thing sprouting up from the ground was another tree, a mile or ten or twenty away. Her sense of distance had become completely distorted here. They weren't kidding when they said everything in Texas was bigger.

The building looked abandoned. She drove all the way around it in a wide circle, just in case there was someone inside, but there were no signs of life here. She parked closer to the barn, on the shady side.

On that side, a tall wide door with wheels on the bottom was partially open on a metal track. "Hello?" she said timidly into the barn. The sound echoed up to the rafters. She kept both hands on the edge of the door, ready to jump back into the car if something or someone answered menacingly.

She heard some clicking sounds, and then something that sounded like a purr. "I'm a dog person, myself," she said in the direction from which the sounds had come, "but I promise not to hurt you if you don't hurt me." She waited for a response, but none came. "Is that okay with you?"

Something clicked again, but she couldn't decide if it was dangerous. She waited a moment longer. "Kitty, kitty?" she offered shyly, hoping for another purr. Maybe the clicking sounds were crickets.

She tried pushing the door open a little further on its track, but the wheels wouldn't budge. She took one cautious step inside, keeping one hand on the door.

Enough sunlight poured in through the two grimy windows and an open doorway on the other side, so she could see everything in here pretty clearly. Piled up against the back wall like giant Lincoln Logs were a number of long wooden benches with their metal legs folded flat. A rickety ladder was propped up crookedly near one of the corners, leading up to a loft. There were things up there, too, but in the shadows. She was not curious enough to find out what those things might be, and that ladder looked like it would turn to dust the second anyone touched it.

At the opposite end were a few old and rusty metal folding chairs, and something that looked like a cross between a music stand and a lectern. Whatever this place was in its first incarnation—house, barn, or something else—it was last used as some kind of gathering place.

"A church?" she heard herself say.

The clicking thing in the loft seemed to agree.

"Mm-hmm," she said softly, and stepped gingerly back outside.

She walked around the north side of the barn-church and saw something that looked like a spigot with a big lever. Underneath the spigot was a big wooden tub, perhaps made from the bottom half of a barrel. There was a little water puddled at the bottom. She pumped the lever, expecting it to be as rusted as the wheels on the big door. It moved, to her surprise, but with a loud screech. She pumped it a few more times. She was about to give up when the first trickles of water began to pour from the spout. She pumped the handle a few more times. The trickle became a gush.

The water was cool, almost icy, under her fingers. It looked clean, but she didn't trust that it was safe to drink. She wet both of her hands and held them close to her nose. She could discern no ominous smells, except for a slight metallic quality to the scent. She brought her wet hands to her face and relished the clean feeling.

She walked the rest of the way around the barn, but found nothing much of interest, except something that looked like a trap door set at an angle between the outer wall of the barn and the ground. Nothing in the world would make her open that door and explore whatever might be behind it or under the barn.

Back by the car, Sarah stood with her hands on her hips and looked out over the big flat fields. Patches of bright yellow adorned the landscape. The same little flowers grew wild all around this barn as well.

If the clicking, purring things in the loft would let her, maybe she would stay for a while.

———

Sarah gave up trying to figure out how to make the middle row of seats disappear into the floorboards of the minivan. She had seen her father do it once—or, more accurately, she had once seen the aftermath of the configuration after her father had put the seats down. She knew it could be done, but could not make it happen without instructions. The Owner's Manual had long disappeared from the glove compartment, if it had ever been kept there.

Instead, she lowered the back of the middle seat on the right as far as it would go, and in a flash of inspiration, lowered the front passenger seat as well. She found that if she removed the head rest on that front seat, she ended up with something that looked like an extra-long dentist's chair. It might be comfortable enough to sleep, if she didn't mind sleeping on her back, or dreaming of root canals.

The temperature had quickly gone from fairly cool to goddamned hot. She left the back door open and rolled down the windows at the front of the car. A hot but almost pleasant breeze blew through the minivan, made more tolerable by the shade of the barn. She fell asleep almost as soon as she lay down.

———————

Sarah didn't hear the truck that had pulled into the yard near her car, and didn't stir at all when the driver's door slammed shut. It was the loud bark of a dog that nearly gave her a heart attack.

She jumped straight up and came back down, turning toward the open rear door in a single spinning motion. Leaning on her elbows, she looked into the face of a big, goofy, red-haired dog. It looked to be an Irish Setter.

The dog was smiling at Sarah, panting heavily, tongue lolling. Next to the dog was a tall, thin woman with wild curly hair that had turned mostly gray. The woman was peering inside the minivan. She held a long, skinny rifle, crossed casually across her belly, the barrel nestled loosely in the crook of her left elbow.

"Howdy," the woman said to Sarah.

Howdy?

Sarah raised herself a little higher, still on her elbows, not taking her eyes off the woman. "Holy cow... you're not going to shoot me, are you?"

"That depends," the woman replied, still peering, not smiling.

Sarah was too afraid to ask, but felt that she must. "On what?"

"On you, Miss New Jersey. This is Texas. And, technically, you're trespassin'. Shootin' trespassers is practically required by law around here."

Sarah held up both hands as well as she could from her position in the folded-back seat. "Look... I'll leave. I'm sorry. I didn't mean any harm. I... I just stopped for a little nap. I'm sorry. I'll leave right now. Please don't shoot me."

The woman smiled at last, just a little bit. "Put your hands down, girl. I ain't hardly as mean or as crazy as I look."

Sarah tried to get up on her knees without taking her eyes off the woman. She felt for the door handle and opened it, still holding up her free hand. She crawled backwards out of the car, and walked slowly toward the back, still looking at the woman.

"My name's Linda," she said to Sarah, "This here's Lucy," she said scratching the top of the Setter's head. Another dog ambled up from the other side of the minivan, a beautiful Golden Retriever. "And here comes Ethel."

At this, Sarah had to laugh, a nervous cackle that was dripping in relief.

"Lucy here's not much use on a ranch. We keep her mostly for entertainment. Ethel's the real brains of the operation."

Lucy bounced over to Sarah, then took a step back, looking over her shoulder and then back at Sarah. She was inviting Sarah to play. "Hey there, Lucy," she said, holding out the back side of her hand for the dog to sniff. Lucy responded by jumping up and putting both paws on Sarah's chest, panting wetly into her face. Ethel looked humiliated by her companion's inelegant display of affection.

"Down, girl!" Linda commanded. Lucy ignored her and gave Sarah a big, sloppy kiss, then took off without warning in a happy, aimless gallop. Her back legs seemed to be operating independently of the ones in front. Ethel decided that looked like a good idea—or that

Lucy shouldn't be allowed to run wild without adult supervision—and followed her off into the field. "Sorry about that," Linda told Sarah.

"It's okay." She watched them run for a moment. "Those are some great dogs." She turned to face Linda. She held out her hand. "My name is Sarah."

Linda shook Sarah's hand, not exactly warmly. It was a gesture Linda did not often practice. It felt awkward to them both. "Nice to meet'cha, Sarah."

They faced each other self-consciously for a moment, both women guarding questions behind their eyes. Linda spoke first. "Did you spend the night out here like that, with all the windas and doors open?"

"No, no," Sarah said, but then was unsure how to explain. "I... well... I was driving through on I-40. Or Route 66. I'm not sure anymore. It seems to keep changing. But I got veered off the road last night. There was an airplane on the highway." The idea sounded so absurd to Sarah once she heard the words coming from her mouth that she felt no sane person would believe such a story. "For real." Linda's expression did not change, so Sarah kept talking. "I wandered around a bit after the police directed me off the highway, and I ended up here." Then, a bit more uncomfortably but full of the desire to talk about it, she said, "I saw the most beautiful sunrise."

Linda nodded, still sizing up Sarah. "Yeah, we do get some good ones out here. Even the duds are pretty, in their own way."

"Wow..." Sara said wonderingly and looked toward the place on the horizon where she had witnessed this morning's spectacular awakening. "Anyway... I saw this old barn out here. It looked aban–...it looked like it didn't belong to anyone. I thought... I thought maybe I'd spend the night. And see it again. That sunrise."

Linda nodded again, understanding, appearing to be making some kind of decision.

"What if I paid you?" Sarah said.

"Do what now?" Linda looked at Sarah like she had sprouted antennae.

Sarah tried again, hoping she wasn't being insulting. "If I paid you to use your barn for the night, would I still be trespassing?"

"Oh, good Lord, girl," Linda said, flapping a hand in the air. She gave Sarah that curious look again. "How many sunrises were you planning on watching?"

Sarah shrugged. "Maybe just one more?" Sarah offered, although, truth be told, she could set up camp here indefinitely. "No more than two?"

Linda considered this a moment. "If you're gonna sleep in your car, technically, I s'pose, I should only charge you for parking." Linda gave Sarah the smallest smile and started to walk away. Sarah had no idea whether Linda was kidding or serious. "Keep an eye out for coyotes," Linda said over her shoulder.

"Coyotes?" Sarah looked all around, though she would not have recognized one if it came right up and kissed her on the nose the way Lucy had. She scanned the ground all around her, even lifting her feet, as if she might have accidentally stepped on one.

"You know. Coyotes. Like dogs. Only meaner. And wilder. I thought I heard one out this way this morning." She lifted the crook of her elbow a bit, raising the barrel of the rifle a few inches and then letting it fall back onto the crook of her arm. "You got a gun?"

"No," Sarah said. "I have a can of mace...?"

Linda laughed out loud, and a wonderful, deep-bellied thing it was. "Well, good for you." She brushed a lock of hair away from her forehead. "It's not likely a coyote's gonna wanna mug you, but... Maybe it's best you just stay in your car."

Then Linda did something that Sarah found astonishing: She curled her tongue behind her bottom teeth and emitted an ear-piercing whistle. "Come on, girls!" she shouted to the dogs.

Ethel perked her ears up for a second or two, then came running obediently toward Linda. Lucy was pretending to be deaf, dumb, and possibly demented. Linda whistled again. Lucy looked at her with her head cocked and her mouth shut tight. A thought-bubble over her head might have read, "Aww, really? Already?" But then she put the big goofball grin on her face again and ran, trailing about a yard of tongue behind her until she reached her adored best friend, and the nice lady who fed them.

Linda walked toward the water pump. Sarah followed at a humble distance. Linda put a hand on the lever, but realized the bucket was already half-full. "Looks like you figured out how to work this contraption."

"Yeah. I hope that was okay."

"Oh, sure."

"Is that water safe to drink?"

Lucy and Ethel had reached them and, as if in response to Sarah's question, began lapping noisily at the water in the bucket. "It's never hurt the dogs. You might find it has a funny taste, though. That's what visitors tell us, anyway." She looked over her shoulder and peered at Sarah. "Where were you planning on using the facilities? There's no ladies' room in that barn, you know."

Sarah looked down at her shoes. "I have a little camping gear with me."

"Hmm," Linda said, still peering. "In that big Target bag?"

"Uh-huh."

"You ever been camping before?"

"Well... I've seen pictures."

"Hmmph," Linda said, shaking her head. "Tell you what: If you don't start no campfires—like in the pictures—I don't see any harm in you spending the night. Don't pee too close to the barn, though. And if you do anything else, bury it."

"Thank you," Sarah said, relieved and embarrassed all at the same time, and hoped one more day would be enough.

"But there are critters," Linda continued. "Don't sleep out in the open if you don't know what you're doing or what you're in for."

"I won't. I'll leave everything as I found it. I promise."

"You got food in that picnic basket?"

What Sarah had in the basket was a plastic garbage bag full of wet clothes. "Yes," she lied.

"All right then," Linda said, nodding slightly, satisfied. She turned to the dogs. "Let's go for a ride, ladies." The dogs immediately ran to the dusty old pick-up truck and leapt into the back of it.

Sarah watched them drive away. The truck went quite some distance before disappearing down a road that veered to the left.

"Coyotes," Sarah whispered to herself and scanned the plains all around her. "I should've asked what kind of 'critters' click and purr."

Mountain lions?

"Stop it."

———

Sarah spent the next few hours doing what came naturally to her: sorting things into categories. She even considered alphabetizing them.

She started by taking inventory of everything in the car. She emptied the Target bag, the entire contents of her purse, the cooler, the picnic basket, everything she could find in the glove box and side door pockets, and the console compartment between the driver's and passenger seats.

First she propped Jilly's doll against the back of one of the middle seats, facing her, to keep her company. She wondered what Tessie might have thought of this little doll. Despite the ache that filled her chest once again at this thought, she allowed herself to imagine Tessie sitting cross-legged in that spot, cradling the doll. She could almost see her little girl. She could almost smell her. "It's all right," Sarah said. Meager words of comfort, but comfort nonetheless.

She took the wet clothes out and, after deciding the leaning tree with the bowing branches was too far away, she hung them from the slightly opened windows of the car. The hot, dry air would make quick work of making these things wearable again. She found, to her surprise, that in her haste to gather up the wet clothes the night before, she had inadvertently grabbed a small white washcloth from the bathroom floor along with her own things. Maybe the housekeeper wouldn't notice. And if she did and the hotel charged her credit card another twenty bucks for it, she would be happy to pay it.

Next she began to organize the rest of the items that were scattered in the cargo area of the minivan. She put the boxes with the air mattress, foot pump, and collapsible toilet in a neat pile on the ground outside the car. She folded the assortment of plastic store bags she had gathered along the way and tucked them neatly into the mesh pocket behind the driver's seat.

She made a pile of anything edible on the left side of her workspace: half a bag of pretzels; an almost new pack of Tic-Tacs; most of a package of oatmeal raisin cookies; a half-gallon juice bottle she had been refilling with water at various stops along the way; an almost empty bottle of Diet Coke, probably flat; a handful of dusty, individually-wrapped cough drops from the bottom of her purse; two unopened cans of ginger ale from her mother's original stash of beach snacks. Not the most nutritious assortment of items, but at least she wouldn't starve today, or have to leave her spot and risk never finding it again if she ventured out in search of a town or a grocery store. She put all the food-related items into the picnic basket, and the two plastic bottles in the cooler.

The next pile was made up of personal products: four tiny bottles each of shampoo, conditioner, and body lotion; two small bars of hotel soap; a small bottle of Scope mouthwash, half-empty; a toothbrush; a tube of toothpaste; a hairbrush; a small compact with two mirrors inside, which she remembered putting in her purse about a thousand years ago but never remembered to use; a small packet of moist towelettes; and a tub of baby wipes. So now she would neither starve nor die stinky or terribly unkempt. At least not today.

The beach blanket was still neatly folded in a corner of the trunk space. She put it on top of the air mattress box.

She made a pile of things that could be used as tools: a nail file; a sewing kit that included a tiny pair of folding scissors; an assortment of pens; a huge golf umbrella; the phone charger; a rubber band; the ancient canister of mace; three promotional eyeglass repair kits that included two miniature screwdrivers, a pair of tweezers, a couple of tiny screws, and a magnifying glass about the size of a quarter attached to a red plastic inch-long handle. This last set of items reminded her of her father's old optometry practice; that made her smile with a touch of melancholy. But when she looked at the sharp, pointy objects, that smile slowly faded. She made a mental note of these objects, then filed it away with the other things she was trying not to think about. She put all of the "tools" into another one of the plastic bags.

What was left was a pile of envelopes and papers of various sizes. She crumpled up a dozen or so cash register receipts from gas stations, stores, and diners across America. She saved the hotel receipts. She folded them neatly and put them back inside her purse.

She stared for a long time at the collection of larger sheets of papers. There was a flyer from Tessie's school, printed on bright red paper. There were also documents from the hospital and funeral home. Most of the sheets were folded in three places, to envelope size. Some were stapled together and folded in half. They lay on the floor of the trunk space in various stages of openness. She could see the hospital name and logo on one set.

She retrieved another one of the plastic bags. She put the folded papers inside without looking at them. She packed them tightly, flattening them as much as possible, and wrapped the empty part of the bag around the stack. When she put the bag down, she wiped her hands against the sides of her pants.

The papers inside began to unfold themselves, as if trying to push their way out of the bag. She pulled the rubber band out of her "tools" stash and wrapped it around the package. The ends flared out a little, like a bow-tie. She put the package into the bottom of her purse, and lay her wallet, checkbook, and house keys on top of it to hold it down.

She put her hands into her pockets and realized she was hyperventilating.

Then her fingers found another couple of items: her phone in one pocket, and the ring with the car keys in the other.

On that key ring, there was a tiny pocket knife with two blades: one was a file with a quarter-moon cut-out at the end; the other was a dull little knife with a pointy end. Sarah flicked the tip with her thumb, then folded both blades back into the handle.

The key ring also held a miniature Maglite. She twisted the top and saw that it worked. It emitted just enough light to find a keyhole in the dark, but would probably be generally useless otherwise. She turned it off and put the key ring back into her pocket.

She took her phone out and found she had a signal. She must not be too far from the highway, where she had seen a few cell phone towers along the way.

When she put her phone back into her pocket, her knuckles brushed against a small folded piece of paper. It was the note Jackson had given her outside the diner in Oklahoma. He had scrawled his phone number and e-mail address across the top, and a note below that read:

Here's hoping the ocean is big enough. Send
pics when you get there.

Jax^2

She found herself smiling like a silly schoolgirl, feeling simultaneously giggly and ridiculous. The cute funny boy had passed her a note. No one had ever done that before.

———————

Sarah spent about half an hour trying once again to figure out the mechanism to make that middle row of seats fold down before giving up for good. She thought about taking a walk to the big leaning tree, but the sun was too hot. At high noon, the only shade was inside the barn or inside the car, and the car had become an oven, even with all the doors and windows open.

The heat gave her an idea, though. She took the two plastic bottles to the water pump, and rinsed and filled them both. She splashed water on her face and wrists, instantly cooling off. She then put the half-gallon bottle on the roof of the car; the sun would warm it up and she'd be able to use it for a more serious washing-up later. She used the smaller Diet Coke bottle to carry cool drinking water.

The barn beckoned to her. She looked at it, debating whether or not to accept its invitation. Old and creaky as it was, it looked fairly harmless from the outside. She decided to take a closer look inside. But she took the umbrella and the can of mace with her, just in case.

Standing at the threshold of the half-open rolling door, she looked up at the loft, where the purring, clicking noises had come earlier that morning. All was quiet there now.

The open doorway on the wall opposite to where she was standing created a kind of breezeway through the barn. She figured that whoever built this place knew from experience that yielding to the wind rather than resisting it would be the key to this structure's ability to remain standing; it might otherwise have been flattened by the persistent winds a long time ago. The barn still leaned a little, but mostly it let the winds blow right through it.

She looked to the stack of rusty metal folding chairs and wondered, if she took one outside and sat on it, if she'd be killed first from the fall or from tetanus poisoning. She decided to take a closer look.

She used the umbrella's metal tip to move one of the chairs away from the stack a little bit. The cluster was cobwebby, but she didn't see any spiders on that chair at the front of the stack. She tipped it the rest of the way down until it fell noisily to the floor, hoping the clatter would scare anything living in or near the chairs out of hiding, and got ready to run for the door in case something did emerge to fight her.

The blood-curdling scream she heard instead came from the loft.

She turned her head and crouched instinctively, her feet frozen to the ground. She held the umbrella like a sword. She clutched the can of mace in her other hand, fingers curled around it as if it were a small club.

High up, near the rafters, she saw a face that looked so much like her night visitors that, had she been able to find her voice, she might have screamed.

Instead, she stood immobile in that crouched position, too afraid to look away from that creature with its huge round eyes and brilliant white face. She could hear her heart pounding wildly in her ears.

The creature all of a sudden became bigger, spreading its brownish-gray mottled wings wide, like Dracula unfurling his cape. It made some loud, clicking sounds.

It was an owl.

She had never before seen an owl in person. She knew nothing about owls, whether they killed people for food or out of spite, or if they only ate smaller things. She had no doubt that if the owl saw her as an enemy, it would attack and it would win.

Without taking her eyes off it, she rose, very slowly, from her crouched position. In her mind, she willed it to see her as a friend, or at least as someone who would never do it harm. She stood stock-still, ready to run if it came after her.

The owl lowered its wings, wrapping them around itself, like an actor about to take a bow. Tall and skinny now, it looked at her curiously over its shoulder. It did not seem menacing at all this way. It was actually quite beautiful. Its heart-shaped face seemed to glow in the dimness of the loft.

"Hello," she whispered in a shaky voice, and began to inch her way toward the door. The owl kept its large eyes on her. "Nice little owly," she crooned to it.

She was mere inches from the door when the owl suddenly descended, in absolute silence, but not toward her. It landed on the lectern on the other side of the barn.

"Okay... Nice owly," she whispered again, and took another step toward the door. The next step had her left foot planted securely outside. Still she watched.

The owl had made it clear whose home this was, and Sarah had no intention of challenging him for it. Still, much less afraid of it now, she was fascinated by the sight. She wanted to stay and look at it.

They watched each other for a long while, the owl losing interest first. Apparently it had decided that Sarah was no threat. It wasn't until the owl looked away that she dared to take a deep breath and relax the tension in her shoulders.

She wondered how she could make friends with it. Then she got an idea.

She went to the food stash and got a couple of pretzels out of the bag. She crumpled them into small pieces as she walked back to the barn door. From the threshold, she looked at the owl, still perched on the lectern, and said in a soft voice, "Polly want a cracker?" She tossed a few of the crumbs toward the center of the barn and took a step back.

The owl cocked its head once or twice, examining the offering from its perch. Moments later, it glided to a spot near the pretzel pieces and nudged them with a sharp, pointy talon. It ate one, and looked at Sarah. "Nice owly," she said with a little more confidence. She tossed a few more crumbs, but closer to the door. The owl ate from the first little pile of pretzel pieces, but stayed away from the second. When those first morsels were gone, it went back to the lectern. It seemed they had made a cautious peace with one another.

Sarah pulled her phone out of her pocket as discretely as possible, aimed the camera lens at the beautiful bird, and snapped a picture. It came out blurry because her hand was a little shaky and she hadn't aimed carefully enough, so she tried again. The second one was almost good enough to frame.

She watched the owl until it flew back up to its loft, presumably to sleep the rest of the day away.

Sarah laid the blanket out on the ground near the car. She made a hole in the dirt and wedged the handle of the open umbrella into it, creating a shady spot for herself. She settled in and looked again at the picture of the owl. On a whim, she decided to send it to Jackson with a text:

My new friend - Rev. Owl (say it out loud)

Before she could change her mind, she hit SEND.

————————

At a little after six that evening, Sarah saw Linda's pick-up truck coming up the road. Lucy and Ethel were in the truck bed. Someone else was driving.

A very tall man in sun-bleached but clean jeans, a big white hat, and a plaid shirt got out from the driver's side. He looked like a cowboy straight out of Central Casting. Linda came out of the passenger side, and walked over to where Sarah was shaking the dust and dirt off her blanket.

"Hey there," Linda said when she got closer. "I thought if you were still out here, you might be hungry." She handed Sarah a warm, square, Tupperware container topped with a rolled-up white napkin. Inside the napkin were a fork and knife.

"Oh, my goodness… you didn't have to do this."

"This's my husband, Ed," Linda said, gesturing behind her.

The cowboy touched the brim of his hat and gave Sarah a tiny nod.

"Nice to meet you," Sarah said to him.

Lucy and Ethel came bounding up to say hello and possibly beg for some scraps, but Ed stopped them with a short, loud whistle. The dogs immediately stopped at his heel and sat obediently. Lucy looked miserable in this forced attitude of restraint.

Sarah looked around, wondering where to put down her dinner or sit. Linda was one step ahead of her. "Why don't you bring out one of those old benches, Ed," she said to her husband. "If they're still sit-able, that is."

Ed disappeared into the barn and began rummaging noisily. A moment later, he was unfolding the legs of one of the benches. He tested it out by leaning into it with his big hands. "This'll hold fine." He went inside to get another.

Sarah peeled off the plastic lid to find two large pieces of fried chicken, a baked potato with generous dollops of butter and sour cream, and corn on the cob. The aroma was heavenly.

Linda handed her the slim, silver-colored thermos she had been carrying under her arm. "I hope you like milk," she said, handing it to Sarah.

Sarah was overwhelmed almost to the point of tears. Absurdly, perhaps, she felt she should be offering them something.

Ed set up the other bench across from hers. He and Linda then sat facing her, which made Sarah intensely self-conscious about eating in front of people who were sitting empty-handed, just looking at her. But she was starving. The aromas alone had opened her appetite to a gaping maw.

She couldn't remember the last time she had drunk milk, but nothing in her experience compared to the rich, delicious flavor of the large sip she had just taken. She closed her eyes and moaned. "Oh, my God... this is incredible."

"It's from one of our own cows. You can't get any fresher."

"Unbelievable," she said through a mouthful of chicken, astounded at how hungry she felt all of a sudden.

The dogs were whining, so Ed got up to distract them. All three headed out into the field behind the barn.

"You find enough to do out here all day?" Linda asked.

Sarah swallowed and smiled. "I gave myself a headache trying to read a book on my phone. Got a little laundry done, though," and motioned with her head toward the car windows. "Tried to get organized before I get back on the road."

"Where're you headed?"

"California, I think."

"You *think?*"

"Well, it was kind of a spur-of-the-moment decision. Not really a plan." She looked into her Tupperware bowl and poked the mashed potatoes with her fork. "It seemed like a good idea at the time. But it wasn't until I got here that I was really glad I did it. Do you know there's an owl living in your barn?"

"I wouldn't be surprised. Seems like there's always been one there. Sometimes a whole family of 'em."

"Why is your barn so far away from your house?" What Sarah really wanted to know was why it was so dilapidated.

"We've never really used it as a barn. I mean, my Grandpa did, but not us. There used to be a house right over there," Linda said, pointing to a spot just beyond the water pump. "It belonged to my great-granddaddy. He built it with his own two hands. Him and his sons. This barn, too. My Grandpa was born in that house, and so was my Daddy."

"Wow."

"Wow is right," Linda said gazing toward the spot where there used to be a house. "I remember visiting my Granny and Grandpa there when I was little." Linda cocked her head and looked at Sarah. "That was a looooong time ago."

"What happened to it? The house?" Sarah asked, polishing off the last of the drumstick.

"Tornado blew through here one summer. Flattened the whole place down in about ten seconds. Didn't even breathe on the barn.

"Granny was ailing, and bedridden that particular day. Grandpa carried her here to the barn. There's a storm cellar down around the other side, but he was getting on in years himself, so he didn't quite make it to the cellar. He laid Granny down by some bales of hay inside the barn and covered her with his own body, and prayed like there was no tomorrow. He was pretty sure there wouldn't *be* no tomorrow. God spared them both, but took their house in the swap.

"Grandpa saw this as some kind of sign, and this barn as a place of holy refuge. And that's what he called it: The Church of Holy Refuge. He took up preaching in the last years of his life, but not about fire and brimstone. His favorite sermons were about enduring love—love of family, love of a good woman, love of the land, love of horses, love of cows, love of chickens, love of cornbread, love of bright yellow flowers that grew wild... even the love of a good wind that keeps the land clean, even if it takes your house right along with it. If you could name it, he could love it. And he preached, of course, of the love of a merciful God that ran through all things, most especially and gratefully through him.

"He had another house built—the one me and Ed live in now—down by where the land dips a little. The wind blows mostly over the roof shingles now. But this old barn, God bless it, got a new lease on life, just like Grandpa, and he dedicated it—and himself—to serving the Lord.

"Grandpa was a hundred 'n one when he preached his last sermon here. He died a peaceful, happy man, in his sleep, more than twenty years after Granny passed. Nineteen-ninety-two, that was."

Sarah sat in wonderment, listening to Linda's story. It sounded like something out of a movie, an old western maybe, when in fact Linda's grandpa had been a real-live country preacher in Sarah's lifetime, probably while she was skipping rope and playing hopscotch with Shirley on the sidewalks of Brooklyn, and the only tornado she had ever heard of was the one that landed Dorothy in Munchkinland. "Wow," she said again in almost a whisper.

"We don't use the old barn for much of anything anymore. Sometimes I feel bad that we don't keep it up better, but it always feels like to me we should leave it the way Grandpa left it. It feels wrong to use it as a barn, and me and Ed, we're no preachers. But we do have family reunions here every summer. Our people come from all over the place. Seems like hundreds of 'em. We set up picnic tables and a couple of tents out here around the barn, rent a few Port-o-Potties, and make us some damned fine barbecue. And bake every kind of pie there is. We even have our own chili contest!"

At this, Sarah laughed. She looked around and could almost see the place swarming with cousins, aunts, uncles, in-laws, and anyone else who could pass himself off as family. Generations of them, in all shapes and sizes.

"It seems right to have it here, where the homestead began, where Grandpa was happiest. You can almost feel him smiling when we're all gathered here.

"So you can see why I was a bit concerned about seeing a van parked out here this morning. I don't mind the occasional tourist stopping to take a picture or getting a drink of water from the old pump, but you can't be too careful these days."

Ed and the dogs were coming back from their walk, Lucy literally running circles around him and Ethel, and Ethel heeling obediently by her master.

"Where were you planning on sleeping tonight?" Linda asked Sarah.

Sarah scratched her head and looked at the unopened air mattress box, and then at the minivan. "I was hoping I could make that middle row of seats fold down. I know it can be done, but I can't figure it out. I think the air mattress will fit in there. If it's too big, I can let some of the air out to make it fit. But there's some trick to those seats that I don't know."

"Oh, I bet I can fix that," Ed said, looking into the car from the side window.

"You can?" Sarah asked hopefully.

Ed responded by immediately going to work.

"That reminds me," Linda said, and walked over to her truck. She came back with a couple of garden lamps. They looked like spotlights with spikes on the bottom. "Solar powered," she said to Sarah.

"Yeah, I've seen those," Sarah said. "My mom has some around her little flower bed in New Jersey. I never would have thought of that. Thank you again."

Linda planted the spotlights near the benches where they were sitting. "You can move 'em later if you want, of course. I would like to have them back when you're done, though."

"Of course."

"They're not powerful, but they're a damn sight better than pitch-darkness. These'll at least give you some light through the night."

"I don't know how I'll repay you for your kindness."

"Oh, you'll think of something," Linda said good-naturedly.

The giant Whack-a-Mole game had started up again in the distance. Sarah asked Linda, "What are those?"

Linda looked over her shoulder and said, "Uggh... damn prairie dogs."

"They're kind of cute," Sarah said. "Should I be scared of them?"

"Only if you're a horse."

"They eat horses?!"

Linda chuckled. "No, silly girl, their holes. A horse can break a leg if it steps in one of them holes."

"Oh. So this is a horse ranch."

"Horse 'n cattle. Mostly cattle. And a few chickens."

Sarah looked dubiously at the Tupperware bowl she had practically licked clean. She looked up, wide-eyed, at Linda.

"Yep," Linda said, and smiled.

"Well... I'm glad you told me *after* I ate it. I'm sorry for the chicken, but it was delicious."

Linda was looking at her curiously, and after a moment said, "So you drove all the way out here from New Jersey, all by yourself, with no luggage or nothing, and somewhere along the way you stopped at a Target and bought you some camping stuff."

Sarah nodded, and gave Linda a half-sheepish smile. "Mm-hmm."

Linda shook her head slowly. "There's a story there. And I'd like to hear it."

Sarah put her napkin and utensils into the bowl and put the lid back on it. She set it down beside her on the bench. She leaned forward a bit with her fingers curled under the edges of the seat, her head bowed and looking off to the side. She searched inside herself for the big bruised thing that had been crushing the air out of her for days and days, and found that it was quiet, no longer full to bursting. Not completely gone; more like it had made itself smaller and gone to sleep for a little while. Perhaps the combination of a serene and sunny day in the wide open spaces, the early morning catharsis, and the kindness of these good people had all served to break it down. She felt a calmness like she hadn't felt in eons. She breathed in deeply the day's-end aromas of rich earth and pasture.

"I think I've been trying to outrun myself," she began.

She told her story softly, infused with gentle pauses. It was a little like confession, but with none of the old shame or fears.

"My little girl, Tessie," she began. "She's five. ...Was five."

Linda sucked in a breath, but did not interrupt.

"I came home from work one night, about a month ago, I think. Maybe a little more. It was one of those days full of noise coming at me from every corner. Crazy-busy at work. The trains were delayed, and that made them more crowded than usual, which made me late picking Tessie up from the daycare center. The grocery store was packed, I was starving, I hadn't had lunch that day, Tessie was cranky... and as soon as I get home, the phone starts ringing again. My boss asking me a billion questions about this stupid project we were working on. Nothing that couldn't have waited until morning.

"I plopped Tess in front of the TV with a bowl of grapes while I tried to make us dinner and keep my boss from losing her mind. I dropped a glass and cut my foot. The TV was too loud, I had a pounding headache, Tessie needed a bath, I needed a bath, sirens were blaring outside... too many things going on at once.

"I finally got my boss off the phone, stuck a frozen mac & cheese dinner for Tess in the microwave, and started tending to my foot. I went to get a Band-Aid, and that's when I saw Tessie. She was unconscious on the floor. She was blue."

(you let your work *get in the way of your* job*)*

Sarah squeezed her eyes shut. She wanted to silence that maddening voice in her head, but deep down she knew it was right this time. Her job had been to take care of her little girl, to be vigilant, to protect her from all harm, accidental or deliberate. Her boss was a grown woman who was happy only when she was dancing on the ledges of her own hysteria, inventing crises if none arose on their own. When she called, Sarah should have just told her to jump, or pushed the inept woman off the ledge herself.

Sarah pressed the heels of her hands into her eyes and breathed deeply again. After a moment, she continued. "I picked Tessie up by the shoulders and shook her. There were grapes in both of her hands, and they rolled all over the floor when I tried to sit her up. She had aspirated one of them. I stuck my fingers in her throat—I could feel a grape lodged in there, but I couldn't pull it out. I tried pushing it in, but I think that only made it worse. I grabbed her by the ankles and shook her upside down, but that damned thing wouldn't come out. I tried doing the Heimlich maneuver, but I had never done that before. I didn't know if I was doing it right, or if I would break her ribs or rupture an organ trying to save her life, but I did it anyway. I knelt on the floor beside her and pulled her into my lap, and squeezed my fist into her belly a whole bunch of times. The grape finally popped out. Tessie let out a long breath. But she didn't take another one in. I started screaming at her, shaking her. I breathed into her mouth, blowing air into her. It just came back out. She wouldn't breathe on her own.

"I picked Tessie up and ran for the door. I grabbed my purse from the little table in the foyer where I had dropped it on the way in. …Funny the things you remember to do, the things you do out of habit." Sarah paused again, but this time, she didn't close her eyes or look at Linda. Ed was now standing by the minivan, listening quietly. Sarah didn't notice him. She went on.

"My shoes were by the door, where I had kicked them off when I came in. I jumped into them and ran down the stairs with my little girl in my arms. I ran to the end of the block and into the street, and crossed without looking. Cars honked and tires screeched all around me, but I kept going. There's a hospital on the other side of Central Park, a half mile away if you cut right through in a straight line. I thought I could get there faster if I ran instead of waiting for a cab. A taxi would've had to loop around too many one-way streets to get us there. I could run straight across, I thought. I had my little girl in my arms, clutching her, talking to her, begging her to wake up and breathe. I must've looked like a maniac. A cop would've stopped me if there had been one around, and I would have knocked him down and kept running, like a linebacker. He would've had to shoot me."

(but there had been a cop. two of them. back at the apartment. a man and a woman. had tessie ever eaten grapes before? how many did you give her? who else was in the apartment when it happened? what's your boss's name? why didn't you call 911? where did you buy the grapes?

(why are they bagging the grapes? where are they taking tessie's bowl? seriously? 'where did i buy the grapes?' *that couldn't have been a real question)*

how long were you on the phone? how did you get to the hospital?

"I ran," Sarah continued. "I ran so fast. Faster than I've ever run in my life."

(not fast enough)

"But not fast enough. Not fast enough."

Sarah squeezed her eyes shut again. A small, strangled sound escaped from deep in her throat.

When she opened her eyes and looked up, she saw that Linda was sitting with both hands pressed against her lips, her eyes shining. Sarah looked over at Ed, who stood looking at her with deep furrows in his leathery forehead, his thin lips pressed together tightly. "She died," she said simply to him. She looked back to Linda. "She died." And that's when Sarah cried. She didn't make a sound. She just cried.

Linda blinked a few times, which made the tears she was trying to hold back spill down her cheeks and through her fingers. Ed bowed his head, hiding his face under the brim of his hat. Sarah wiped tears from her own cheeks. They were all quiet for a very long time.

It was Linda who spoke first. She inhaled loudly, slapped her hands on her lap, and sat up straight. "Well, that settles it. You're coming home with us tonight."

"Oh, no. No," Sarah said. "Thank you, but no. You've done so much for me already. You have no idea—"

"Nonsense. We can't let you sleep out here like a hobo. Isn't that right, Ed." She did not wait for Ed to reply. "Plenty of room up at the house." She stood up.

Sarah stood up and touched Linda's arm briefly, lightly. "Really. I'll be fine. Besides, I never get to see stars like the ones I saw last night, or a sunrise like the one I saw this morning. Once I leave here, I'll probably never see one like it again. But thank you. From the bottom of my heart. Thank you."

Linda considered this for a long moment, looking deep into Sarah's eyes. "All right then. Hand me that thermos. I'll come back with it full of coffee in the morning. And maybe I'll try to talk you into coming back with me and drinking it at my kitchen table."

"That would be nice," Sarah said with a smile caught somewhere between sadness and gratitude.

"All right then."

As they walked back to their pick-up truck, trailing happy dogs behind them, Sarah heard Linda say to her husband through sobs, "That wasn't no goddamned coyote I heard this morning."

———

Sarah wore all three of her tee-shirts and the blouse under her jacket, and the athletic socks pulled all the way up to her knees. She wished she hadn't put the blanket on the ground earlier that day, but there was nothing to be done about that now. She shook it out one more time before bringing it inside the car and tried not to think about it being dirty. She wished she had thought about buying sheets for the airbed when she had the chance.

The mattress fit snugly inside the minivan, now that the middle row of seats was down and the two front seats were pushed forward as far as they would go. Ed had cut open the cardboard box it had come in, and laid it flat on the floorboards, serving as a layer of protection between the mattress and anything that might poke a hole through it.

Sarah wrapped herself in the blanket like a cocoon. There would be no star show tonight. Clouds had begun to gather shortly after Linda and Ed went home. Now the darkening sky was mottled and drab, and the air was full of the evening chill.

Sarah had wedged the garden lamps between the dashboard and the windshield. It was quite the cozy little nest she had managed to create for herself, if a bit like trying to sleep in the crisper drawer of a refrigerator. The only thing missing was a good book—a real one, with paper pages, printed in ink—or one of those little television sets, like the one she had in college. Add a glass of wine, and it would have been her idea of a perfect night in.

She dug her phone out of her pocket to try to read again for a little while before going to sleep, and saw that she had a text message waiting. It must've come in during the warmer part of the day, when her jacket and the contents of its pockets were in the car.

The message was from Jackson.

Terrible joke. I LOL'd anyway.

She replied:

> Thought about calling him Owl O'Bama,
> but he looked more like a preacher than
> the prez. Also, wrong state.

Given the cloud cover and the remoteness of her location, she wasn't sure she should expect a response. But a few seconds later, she did get one:

> Where R U?

Grinning like a dumb girl, but also feeling happy for the first time in a long time, she texted back:

> TX

Several minutes passed and the rain began to fall. She thought that would be it for tonight. She was about to roll over and try to sleep when the phone chimed again:

> May I call you?

Say yes. No, don't. Thumbs hovering over the letters for a minute or so while the voice in her head argued with itself, finally she typed:

> Sure.

The phone rang almost immediately.

"I thought by now you'd be hollering into the Grand Canyon," said a voice she was beginning to find very sexy.

"Really? That's what comes after Texas?"

"Well, eventually. Where in Texas are you?"

"The flat part."

"Well, *that* narrows it down…"

"I don't know what it's called. Somewhere east of Amarillo. It's the flattest place on Earth. So I decided to stop and look at it."

"Does that mean you gave up trying to find a big enough ocean?"

"Well," she began, "I've come this far. I might as well keep going. And now that I know the Grand Canyon is out there, I might as well see that, too."

"It's pretty damn big. But if *big* is what you're after…"

"Ohhh…" Sarah moaned. *Don't ruin it,* she wanted to say to him.

"No, no, no. Pull that dirty mind out of the gutter. I would never be so vulgar. Not this early in our relationship."

"Okay, good." *Did he say 'relationship'?* "So how are things in Unka-hunka-nopolis?"

"Ah, you daggone New Yorkers. If you can't see it from the Brooklyn Bridge, it's not worth noting. Right?"

"You know what? You might be right. No wonder the whole world thinks we're rude. I always thought it was because we hate tourists."

"What's wrong with tourists?"

"It's the slow-moving herds of them who make us crazy, the ones who walk six-abreast on the sidewalk, like a wall, and then get offended when we yell, 'Excuse me!' at them."

"Damned tourists."

"Damned right."

"Thank goodness you're not one of those elitist liberal snobs."

"What's wrong with elitist liberals?"

"Yikes…"

Sarah chuckled at this. "Don't worry. I do a pretty good job of dialing back the bitchy now and then. You know, to be a nice, normal neurotic who's just trying to get from one side of town to the other without killing anyone. But the tourists sometimes make me wish we could bring the hookers back to Times Square."

"When that happens, can I come visit? I promise not to gawk at the ones with six breasts."

It felt good to laugh, to have a regular conversation about nothing important, with someone who was probably not a serial killer after all. She would still Google him, though. Maybe tomorrow.

"You know what?" Jackson asked.

"What?"

"This is the most you've ever told me about yourself. And the happiest you've sounded."

"Is it?"

"Maybe I should shut up more often. God knows how many interesting people I've missed getting to know. I'm just so darned engaging sometimes, you know?"

"And humble. Don't forget humble."

"Well, that goes without saying."

A moment of silence came between them, but it was not at all uncomfortable. After a bit, he asked, "So how long do you plan to wander the prairie?"

"Maybe just until tomorrow. And then back on the road, headed west."

"So I won't see you at our diner tomorrow night."

Sarah smiled ruefully. "No," she said with a touch of regret. "Not likely."

"Good."

"Good?"

"Now I can drive back on the Interstate. Cut my trip-time almost in half."

"Why weren't you on the Interstate on your way up to... you know... Kansas?"

"I had to make a stop, way west of I-35. It's a long story. Not about me, therefore, not fascinating."

"Tell me anyway."

Jackson made some hemming and hawing noises, and then decided to tell her a little bit of it. "It's kind of a sad story. A kid on our school's football team. Eddie Alvarez. Promising athlete. Good student. Great kid. He was in a car accident a few months ago. Spinal cord injury. He's in a wheelchair now."

"Oh. That is sad."

"His mom is one of the sweetest people I've ever met. Works like an animal, two or three jobs, just to scrape together enough money to keep a roof over their heads and her son fed. She couldn't afford not to work, couldn't afford a caretaker, and she couldn't leave Eddie alone all day, so they ended up having to move in with her brother and his family, just outside a town called Bowie.

"I go up and visit them once in a while. I usually take a few kids from school with me, two or three of Eddie's classmates and team buddies. This time I went alone because I wasn't going right back to Fort Worth."

"That's really nice of you to do that."

"Yeah, well… If you knew this kid and his mom, you'd do the same."

"Maybe… Not a lot of people would."

"Don't get the wrong idea about me. I'm a lot more selfish than I let on."

"Really? How so?"

"Well," he began in a playful tone, "if not for that detour, I never would've stopped at that diner in Oklahoma. And I'm kind of liking how things are turning out for me."

"Oh, tell the truth. You just couldn't stay away from Betty and her apple pie."

"I'd never been there before!"

"Really? Me neither."

"We'll have to go back. How about if, on your way back east, we meet there again? What do you say? Can we call it a date?"

A date? Seriously? She couldn't remember the last time she had been on one of those.

Jackson continued. "Of course, now that we know which one of us is a greedy little pie-stealing bugger, we'll have to order two pieces, so *somebody* won't be left out."

"Of course."

"So you'll meet me there? Really?"

Why the hell not? "Sure," Sarah said, not really believing it would happen. "That would be nice. I don't know when that'll be, though. It could be a while."

"I can wait. Sometimes." Then he had a thought. "You know, it's still a few weeks until school lets out. We'll either have to time it for a weekend... or maybe you can come back by way of Fort Worth? I'd love to show you the town. Our tourists are much better behaved. And hardly any of them have six boobs."

"Heh-heh," she chuckled. "We'll see."

"Well, think about it. You already know I'm a great date. It could be pretty wonderful... Sarah."

There. He said it again, like he did the first time. She felt her knees go weak, even lying down under the blanket.

"Still there?" he asked.

"Yes," she answered quickly, a little out of breath. "Still here."

"I'm really glad you decided to get in touch."

"Yeah. Me, too. Oh, and Jackson?"

"Yes?"

"You're not a serial killer or anything, are you?"

"Not since 1997. Gave it up cold turkey."

"Okay. Just checking."

"Have a good night, Sarah."

"You, too. Jackson Jackson."

————

At first, Linda thought Sarah had vanished in the night. Her car was no longer parked by the barn. She drove around to the other side and was both relieved and amused to find Sarah sitting on the roof of the minivan, cross-legged, her back perfectly erect, and with a blanket draped over her shoulders. To Linda, she looked like Tecumseh surveying the land for buffalo.

"Mornin'," she said to Sarah.

Sarah looked at her only long enough to say, "Hey, Linda." She turned her gaze back to the horizon.

"You'll go blind staring at the sun," Linda said.

"Nah. I'm not looking straight at it. Look at that," Sarah said, spreading her arms slowly. "It's the actual curvature of the earth. I've never seen it so clearly. Maybe I should listen to my parents more often. They're always trying to talk me into going with them on one of their cruises. I love the water, but only from the shore. That's probably why I've never seen this. There's always something in the way, a cove, the curve of the shore, the crooked way bits of land jut out into the water... But I've never wanted to go way far out into the sea on a ship." She looked at Linda. "Crazy, huh?"

"Makes sense to me. *I* saw *Jaws*."

"I love that movie. Terrible book. Great movie."

"Well, come on down from there before you finish burning your retinas or break your neck." Then, as a terrible afterthought, "Hey, I didn't interrupt your morning prayers or meditations or something, did I?"

Sarah chuckled. "Nah. I don't do any of that." She unwrapped herself and started to climb down. Linda lent her a hand.

"Never?"

"Nope."

"But you believe in God, don't you?"

Ah. The ultimate loaded question, a bullet in every chamber. There was no way for Sarah to answer it truthfully without pissing somebody off. And the more religious the person asking it, the more angry and violent the reaction tended to be.

But she wasn't going to lie to Linda. This good woman had been a straight shooter with Sarah from the very first. And if she was wrong about her new friend, well, them's the breaks. "No. Not anymore." She started to fold the blanket. Linda helped her.

"But you used to," Linda pressed.

"Yes. A long time ago."

"So what do you believe in now? What do you consider yourself to be?"

Sarah didn't know if there was a word for what she was. She saw things that weren't supposed to be there. She didn't see or feel the ones most everyone else claimed were real, the ones for whom the most magnificent temples and cathedrals had been erected, and in whose name countless millions had been slaughtered and forsaken. "I guess 'atheist' would be the closest thing."

"Huh." Linda thought about this for a moment. "Well, you don't *look* like an atheist."

Sarah smiled. "What do atheists look like?"

"Oh, I don't know... nekkid hippie cannibals? Something like that?"

The mental image this conjured made Sarah laugh. Linda, too. "Wow, that's vivid, Linda."

"Yeah. I think I outdid myself on that one." Linda handed Sarah her end of the blanket.

Sarah folded it a couple more times, and then hugged it against herself. "Well, we're not always that easy to spot. Like, not all Jews wear a beanie, and not all nuns are bald under their veils." Something about that last thing bothered Sarah, but she couldn't put her finger on it. She shrugged it off. "Not all atheists are immoral. Not all Christians are kind."

"Well, I know *that's* right," Linda said quietly. "Some people are moral because of their religion. Some people are immoral in spite of it."

Sarah smiled. "See? We probably agree on more than we don't."

Linda watched Sarah for a moment, ruminating. "But just because there's good people and bad, that don't mean there's no God."

"It doesn't mean there is."

Linda turned toward the horizon and looked out over the fields and the wildflowers in bloom. All of that couldn't have come from nothing. "So who do you think made that big ol' sunrise you've so fallen in love with? And all them millions of little bitty stars?"

Sarah looked again at the place where she had discovered this new wonder. "I don't know the answer to that, Linda. All I know for sure is that nobody knows for sure." Who made the universe wasn't the kind of question that kept Sarah awake at night. But no matter who or what made that sunrise, she was grateful beyond words that she got to see it. Awestruck beyond imagination that there could be anything so beautiful. She turned to Linda, and took a step closer. "I'm really glad I ended up here, on your ranch, Linda. And that you let me stay to see that sunrise again." She wanted to embrace Linda, but held back.

Linda nodded.

"And I'm thrilled to bits that you didn't shoot me for trespassing yesterday."

"I would've, you know."

"I believe you."

Linda was examining Sarah in that curious way again, head slightly cocked, eyes full of questions. "What if I told you that I think maybe God led you here," she said softly.

Sarah could feel the hackles on the back of her neck rising. Why the hell would God lead her here, to this place? As a consolation prize for letting her baby die? Why didn't he lead her stupid boss to a couple of Xanax that night, and saved them all a lot of trouble? Why didn't he lead Sarah to the freezer instead of the fruit bowl, and make her fill Tessie's dish with ice cream instead of grapes? Why didn't he lead her into the living room ten or twenty minutes sooner, or however many minutes it would have taken to keep her child from choking to death in the first place?

Sarah clenched her jaw and looked away, her hands trembling. She turned her back to Linda on the pretext of putting the blanket back in the car. She didn't want to take her rage at the concept of God out on Linda, or let loose a barrage of arguments against the idiotic notion that he was some kind of beneficent puppet master, that after he crushes every bone in your body, he offers you a Band-Aid, and then, in your gratitude, you should thank him for only dropping one boulder on you at a time.

She mustered up as much restraint as she could and said simply, "Who's to say, Linda. Life is full of questions. And real short on answers."

But Linda wouldn't let it go. "Didn't you ever think to ask God? Talk to him in whatever way made sense to you?"

"I was raised Catholic. I wasn't taught to ask questions. I was taught to fall on my knees and beg for mercy."

"Well, no wonder—!"

"Let it go, Linda. Please."

"But—"

"God doesn't talk to me, Linda," Sarah said through her teeth. The edge in her voice made Linda flinch. "He doesn't answer questions, he doesn't show his face, he doesn't lead, he doesn't follow, he doesn't do anything because he isn't there. He's a myth. And if he isn't... well, then, we're more fucked than we know."

Linda's mouth hung open in astonishment. "God doesn't *talk* to you?" She held an arm out toward the horizon without taking her eyes off Sarah. "Well, what do you think *that* was? I'll *tell* you what it was: That was God saying, 'Good got-dang-spangled morning to *you,* Sarah! Look! Looky here! Another beautiful day! Can you believe it? Just for you!' " Linda was hopping around as she spoke, skinny legs poking out from under her skirt, looking a lot like Olive Oyl welcoming Popeye back home. Her arms were spread wide, as if wanting to embrace the planet. Her springy gray hair was flying all around her. She looked like she was about to do cartwheels. " 'Look—*look* at this big, beautiful world I'm giving you. For nothing! For free! All you gotta do is love it! That's all, little girl! It's all for you! No more, no less! Yes, it's a tough old world sometimes, yes, but ain't she a beauty? Look at it, *look* at it, Sarah! Did you see how I didn't let the darkness go on forever? Every mornin' I do this! I fire up that great big old ball of a sun and give it to you again. Every day. —Oh, and, by the way? You're welcome!' "

Sarah watched, stunned, almost not noticing how her anger was being doused by the comical spectacle of Linda playing the role of God's carnival barker. She had to press a hand to her mouth to keep from laughing.

But when Linda starting laughing, they both collapsed in gales of gleeful cackling, into each other's arms.

Linda hugged Sarah in the most wonderful way. Sarah let her. "Not a preacher, my naked hippie ass," Sarah told her.

"Oh, sweet baby Jesus... I think I just got possessed by my old Grandpa, God rest his crazy soul. That's *exactly* the kind of sermon he used to give."

Sarah wiped tears from her eyes, not sure if they were from laughter or the exasperation of having all of her God issues stirred up again. "Oh, Linda."

Linda held Sarah out by the shoulders. "I'm gonna tell you a secret: I never go looking for God in no church. Not unless you count me coming to this old barn every now and then, when I need a quiet moment, when I need to remember that it really is all about love, like Grandpa used to say. God—or love, or whatever you want to call it— is mostly about what we keep in here." Linda patted a hand lightly over her heart. "That sun is gonna rise every mornin' whether we see it or not. But it's better when we get to see it." Linda hooked an arm around Sarah's elbow. "C'mon with me. I got warm biscuits on the stove and a big-ol' pot of coffee waiting for us."

―――――――――

At about mid-morning, Sarah made the acquaintance of Ed and Linda's sons, Tim and Will, both in their late-teens. Tim was all cowboy: soft-spoken like his father, but more open and engaging in conversation, like his mother. Will was polite, but a bit standoffish; he seemed restless, like he was late for something important. Sarah would soon learn he was a young man just dressing the part and biding his time. He wasn't long for this ranch.

Tim invited Sarah to come meet their horses. He introduced her to his favorite, a beautiful red mare named Sapphire Rose. "I raised her up from a foal," Tim told Sarah. "I watched her be born when I was eleven. I named her and everything. My Dad said there was nothing blue or rosy about her, but I knew that would be her name even before she was finished coming out."

"It's a beautiful name," Sarah said. "She's a beautiful horse."

Sarah had never been this close to an animal this size, and she was a little afraid of it. But the mare was a gentle and placid creature who welcomed the touch of a kind human.

Tim showed Sarah how to brush Sapphire's long neck and powerful shoulders. The mare seemed to appreciate Sarah's attentions, nodding and snorting whenever Sarah brushed a spot that felt particularly good. Soon, Sarah became accustomed to the smell of fresh manure, and arrived almost hypnotically to a place of mutual contentedness with the horse. The act of grooming this magnificently benign creature was a meditation in tranquility.

"You ever ride?" Tim asked Sarah, bringing her out of her reverie.

"Only the ponies at the Bronx Zoo, when I was a kid."

"They let you ride the animals there?" Tim asked, incredulous.

"Just the ponies. And a bored old camel. Once or twice around a circle inside the Kiddie Zoo, on a saddle with a seatbelt, and a man who was taller than the horse walking beside us. If you wanted to ride the camel, you sat with a bunch of other kids in this big box-like thing strapped to the camel's hump, and they'd walk us around another little path. The camel ride jostled us around a lot, and it was really high up in the air. I was always afraid I'd fall out of the box, but I held on tight, pretending I was having a good time because it made my Dad smile. But I always liked the pony better."

"Well, I never rode no camel, but I can teach you to ride Sapphire."

"Oh, no, that's okay. I'd rather she remember me as the nice lady who brushed her, and not the crazy woman who clung to her neck screaming."

"Don't you boys have some important business to take care of?" Linda asked as she approached them, a big close-lipped smile across her face.

"Yes, ma'am!" Tim said agreeably, and began leading Sapphire back to her stable.

Will had been sitting on a bench outside the stables, reading a tattered old paperback novel. He dog-eared the page where he left off and put it in the back pocket of his jeans as he walked past, peering shyly at Sarah.

"What'cha reading?" Sarah asked him.

Will pulled the book back out of his pocket and showed her the cover. It was *Carlito's Way*.

"Whoa," Sarah said. "That's intense, isn't it?"

"This is my third time reading it," Will said. He ambled a little closer to her. "You know it?"

"I saw the movie."

"Is New York really like this?" he said, raising the book slightly in her direction before putting it back in his pocket. "I mean, the *real* New York. Not the one they show in the Christmas movies."

"They say it was during the Seventies. It's not really like that anymore. Not since they sold Manhattan to Disney."

Tim smiled at Sarah for the first time. "I want to go there someday. Be a lawyer. But not like Kleinfeld."

"I would hope not!" Sarah said. "Wasn't he a coke-head? And involved with all the wrong people?"

"Good Lord, Will," Linda said. "Why'nt you just kill me now and get it over with."

"Oh, Momma," he said and ruffled her hair.

"Life ain't like books and the movies, son," Linda said, ruffling his hair back. "Now go on and get cleaned up. I've been looking forward to this all week."

Linda walked over to Sarah and hooked an arm through her elbow again, a gesture Sarah was coming to love about her. Linda strolled her out a little way into the yard. "Ed and the boys and me are fixin' to go out for Sunday dinner," she said, as she had carefully rehearsed in her head. "We'd love for you to come with us."

Sarah knew exactly what the special Sunday dinner was about, as she also knew that "dinner" was "lunch" in this part of the world. "Thank you, Linda. But I need to get going."

Linda expected as much, but she needed to make the offer anyway. "All right then. Will you stop in and see us on your way back?"

"I'd love to."

"Good girl," Linda said, and pressed Sarah's arm to herself with her elbow.

Seven

I F WILL HADN'T MENTIONED there was another giant cross just a few miles up the road on I-40—"The biggest one in the northern hemisphere," he had said—Sarah might have ended up at the Santa Monica Pier, where Route 66 came to its much ballyhooed end. Instead, she drove south, cutting straight across I-40, on a road the GPS app told her was TX-70.

Before leaving the ranch, she had filled up her juice and soda bottles with water from the well when she went to say goodbye to Reverend Owl. He had been perched on the lectern when she peered into the barn one last time, as if waiting for her to drop in. "So long, old buddy, old pal, old Owl," she had said to him.

Click-click, he responded.

"Yeah. You, too."

She was well into New Mexico before she started seeing something other than extreme flatness and red dirt. She had seen natural monoliths and cliffs in shapes that might have terrified her if she had been driving through there alone at night, but by the light of day looked like beautiful castle turrets and the remains of cliffs where waterfalls might once have drenched the earth. This, she could love. Giant crosses, she could not.

The shadow of a mountain range in the distance broke up the monotony of the arid New Mexico landscape and gave her something to aim for. Afraid of running out of gas or water in the middle of the desert, and not entirely sure that this was the actual desert—as opposed to a particularly dry and dusty part of the country—she stopped as often as she could to top off both supplies.

She drove until well past dark, wanting more than anything to get this day behind her. She kept the radio off so she wouldn't be accidentally reminded of it, even though all she could do was think about it. She would call her mother tomorrow, not today, and have an ordinary conversation with her—or as close to ordinary a conversation as was possible with Ana. Such a thing would not be an option for either of them today. Ana would say something that, despite her good intentions, would push Sarah over the edge.

The next morning at breakfast, after a long soak in a hot tub and a restful night at a hotel near Las Cruces, she checked the GPS navigator to see if she could make it the rest of the way to the coast in just one day. It was still early, not quite seven-thirty in the morning. She estimated that, if she left in the next half-hour, she could make some serious headway, even if it meant arriving at the coast late at night.

There were two messages waiting: one a voice mail, the other a text. The voice message was from her parents' number. She deleted it without listening to it.

The text message was from Jackson. He sent it at one-thirty in the morning.

> Missed talking to you tonight. Free tomorrow?

She texted back:

> Back on the road today. May make it to CA by
> tonite. Will txt @ FGPS.

She paid for her breakfast and headed into the parking lot. As she was getting into the car, the phone vibrated in her jacket pocket.

> FGPS not on my texting cheat sheet. DMRWO

She responded:

> FGPS = food gas pee stops DMRWO?

She put the keys in the ignition and waited for his reply.

> Dirty Mind Reeling With Obscenities. TTYL.
> L8 4 work. ☺

She sent one last message:

> Emoticons are out, grandpa. ;-)
> Call me when you break for lunch.

Jackson's response:

> I love it when you spell.

She smiled at the text for a long time.

Sarah was sitting in an urban park, or something like it, situated among some modern office buildings in downtown Tucson. When she had glimpsed the city skyline from I-10, her heart had skipped a beat. Maybe now she could satisfy the desire to take a long walk on a real sidewalk.

Tucson's business district had plenty of sidewalks, but eerily few pedestrians. They probably knew better than to do such a thing as take a walk on a sunbaked street in the middle of the desert at midday. This was probably one of those places where people simply ran from their air conditioned houses to their air conditioned cars to their air conditioned offices, or sought refuge in gigantic air conditioned shopping malls. Sarah could feel the skin on her cheeks pulling tight, baking in the arid heat. *They must spend as much money on moisturizer as on food*, she thought.

The phone rang.

"Grab a sandwich," Jackson said. "I'm taking you to lunch."

"One step ahead of you." Sarah took a sip from a can of rapidly warming Diet Coke to wash down a bite of her sandwich.

"Where are you now?"

"Downtown Tucson."

"What's it like?"

"Kind of empty. Pretty, but not what you might call bustling."

"What are the people like?"

"Haven't talked to any. The few I've seen look hot."

"Hot, as in sexy?"

"Hot, as in fresh out of the oven."

"So you're the hottest thing there," Jackson ventured.

Sarah blushed a little. "I'm the *only* thing here."

"Well… I wish you were here."

Sarah didn't know what to say to that. She made a soft sound that almost sounded like a chuckle.

"Too much?"

"No. Just right."

"Aha! Okay. I think I'm dialing into the right speed now." He took a bite of whatever he was eating. After a moment, he asked, "What are you having for lunch?"

"Some kind of vegetarian wrap—bean sprouts, green stuff, crumbly cheese bits, brown things... It looks like a house plant wrapped in a tortilla. Everything else in the sandwich shop had jalapeños in it."

"You don't like hot peppers?"

"No. Food is not supposed to hurt. And jalapeños hurt twice."

This made Jackson laugh. Sarah loved the sound of it, how completely uninhibited it was.

"What's the plan for today?" he asked.

"I think I can make it to San Diego by this evening. I found out there's a beach with a camping area. If I can pass this minivan off as a teeny-tiny RV, or pay somebody to let me hitch it to a real RV, I might just set up camp there for a while. If not, I'm sure there are plenty of normal places to stay."

"Camping isn't normal?"

"Not to me, it isn't. Not without an instruction manual, a Sherpa, and a high-rise condo with running water and electricity. The only reason the RV place appeals to me is that I can park right next to the water, and have a place to sleep that I can walk back to. I'm sure ocean-front hotels will cost a fortune."

"Hmm," he agreed. "How long do you plan to be there?"

"Don't know. I guess I'll have to see how it feels when I get there."

"And you don't know anybody there."

"Nope."

"Wow. I'm jealous. I admire your courage."

It was an odd thing to say, Sarah thought.

"Still there?" Jackson asked.

"Yes," she said. "That word just threw me, I guess."

"Which word?"

" 'Courage,' " she repeated.

"You don't think what you're doing is brave? Traveling cross-country by yourself just because the water didn't look right on your side of the world?"

"Not really. Foolish, maybe. Impulsive. But certainly not brave. Courage is running into a burning building with sixty pounds of gear on your back, not knowing if you're going to make it out alive but doing it anyway because you might save somebody's life. All I did was get in a car and drive away. It isn't even my car."

"You stole it?!"

"No! Well, I borrowed it for longer than I said I'd need it. It's my parents' car. My mother's friends are probably pissed off at me for throwing off their carpool schedule. I'm sure they'll figure out some other way to drive the herd to St. Anthony's for Bingo, though."

Ah, so her mother isn't dead, Jackson thought. The mention of Mother's Day had clearly rattled her at the diner the other day, but maybe there was someone else she was missing. "So you got in the car and drove away... from what?"

The searing silence of a place that was once a refuge and is now a tomb.

Could she ever go back there? Would she?

"Sorry," Jackson said. "But if you ever want to talk about it…"

"Thanks, Jackson."

"Good enough," he said. Sarah heard the satisfied, no-nonsense crumpling of paper and cellophane on Jackson's side of the connection. "Well, I need to get ready for another round of Iambic Pentathlon. I have the jocks next period."

"Which play are you reading?"

"Not a play. The sonnets. I'm trying to convince these guys that what Shakespeare really wrote was Elizabethan porn." Sarah laughed at that. He loved that sound. "Do you know the sonnets?"

"I remember reading one or two in school. I don't think I've read any since then. And I certainly don't remember them being pornographic."

"Well, yeah. That is stretching it a bit. What our buddy Bill wrote was stuff that made women swoon, and once you make a woman swoon, that almost always leads to sex. And if it doesn't, well, there's always porn."

"Hmm," Sarah said. "Maybe I should give Billy another chance."

"Tell you what: I'll have a nice treat for you later today. I'll send you one of my favorites."

"That sounds nice. But now I know your trick."

"Ah. Dammit. Me and my big mouth."

"Send it anyway."

"Okay, I will. Drive carefully, Sarah."

"I will."

San Diego welcomed her with a twinkling of distant lights in a gently darkening sky still glowing in gorgeous purples and gold. She felt tears gathering at the edges of her eyes, tears of relief, of sadness, of weariness, of regret, of hope, of things coming to an end.

Suddenly, though, she wasn't sure she was ready to see the ocean, not just yet, not at night. She drove around instead, trying to get a sense of the city.

After a while, she found a small motel that was really a collection of tiny old cabanas, in an area of town that didn't tweak her danger radar, and, as far as she could tell, was within a reasonably short drive of nearby beaches. She had nothing but time on her hands now, and had long ago stopped caring about how she was going to fund her retirement. Perhaps tomorrow she would look into short-term rentals in the vicinity. It would be nice to have access to a microwave and a fridge, maybe even a little stove. She was sick to death of road food, and of not being able to have her morning cup of coffee in private, in her underwear.

She spoke to her parents for a while after settling in, letting them know she had arrived in more or less one piece, and was actually feeling better than she had in a long while. She told them about Ed and Linda, and their sons, Tim and Will. She told them about Lucy and Ethel, dogs her father would have loved. She told them about the beautiful and gentle Sapphire Rose, and about quirky old Reverend Owl. She told them these stories as much to reassure them about her own wellbeing and state of mind, as to affirm for herself her own beliefs—windblown and ripped to shreds though they felt—that there was more to love about the world than not, and more good people in it than bad. And that, maybe, that might be enough motivation to keep putting one foot in front of the other, at least for one more day. She thought of all she would have missed in the hours that followed that dark night when she had hit rock bottom in that Oklahoma motel.

She did not tell Ana and Dan about sleeping in the van, or the soul-cleansing catharsis inspired by the Texas dawn. She didn't mention Jackson. Maybe she'd tell them about all those other things someday, about Jilly and the storm, about Edna the tongue-speaker who may or may not have died demanding that God keep her house and car safe, or about the black-haired little girl she held in the dark. Someday. Maybe. A long, long time from now.

Before she hung up, she thanked her parents again for letting her abscond with their car.

While she was washing away the desert dust and grit from her skin and hair and the weariness from her bones, a text message from Jackson arrived.

Feeling renewed and pleasantly fragrant in every drop of lotion she had collected in her travels, she slipped between the linens and read his latest missive.

It was the sonnet he had promised.

> When, in disgrace with Fortune and men's eyes,
> I all alone beweep my outcast state,
> And trouble deaf heaven with my bootless cries,
> And look upon myself, and curse my fate,
> Wishing me like to one more rich in hope,
> Featured like him, like him with friends possessed,
> Desiring this man's art, and that man's scope,
> With what I most enjoy contented least.
> Yet in these thoughts, myself almost despising,
> Haply I think on thee, and then my state,
> Like to the lark at break of day arising
> From sullen earth, sings hymns at heaven's gate
>
> For thy sweet love remembered such wealth brings,
> That then I scorn to change my state with kings.

Those last two lines knocked the wind out of her.

She had to read the sonnet several times to fully understand it, stumbling a bit on some of the more archaic turns of a phrase, but then finally able to drink it all in. With each reading, words became living, breathing, pulsing imagery of nearly heartbreaking beauty. She would never again dismiss Shakespeare as "inaccessible."

There was so much of the sonnet that spoke to her, and for her. She couldn't help wonder how much of it belied Jackson's warm and cheerful manner. Down what dark alleys did his own soul wander in the indifferent silence of the night?

The length of their acquaintanceship could still be measured in minutes, so any notion of "sweet love remembered" could certainly not apply to them, even by the broadest of interpretations. That didn't stop her from wanting those words to be true, though.

Her hands trembled a bit as she typed her response:

> Too beautiful to be porn. But if this is foreplay...
> holy crap. We may have to unfurl the hoses.

She looked at the text for a long time, and then deleted the last two sentences before hitting SEND.

———

The front desk clerk on duty the next morning was the same sweet old lady who had checked Sarah in the evening before. Her name was Dottie. She was eager to help Sarah learn all about San Diego. She even dug out an old map from an extremely cluttered antique credenza behind the desk. The map was printed on the back of a tattered take-out menu. Dottie marked the roads for Sarah with an almost completely dried-out yellow highlighter.

The closest beach was just a couple of miles away. Sarah made some quick calculations in her head: Central Park is two miles long; fifty blocks from north to south. She had walked similar distances without breaking stride many times, especially when the weather was nice. "I'll walk it," she said to the woman.

"Oh, no," Dottie said to Sarah. "It's much too far. And there's really no easy way for people to walk there from here. A little closer to Pacific Beach, yes, you can walk, but not from here. You'll want to drive. Trust me." She patted Sarah's hand and smiled with her eyes squinched.

So Sarah drove.

About halfway there, her palms began to sweat. She became aware of her own heartbeat. She wasn't exactly hyperventilating, but her breathing had definitely changed. *This is not a panic attack,* she told herself. But whatever it was, it wasn't right.

She made a right turn at the next intersection. A few blocks up, she saw a shopping center. She parked the car in a space in the middle of the lot, but kept it running with the air conditioner going full blast and the vents aimed directly at her face. Gripping the wheel with both hands, she took a series of deep, slow breaths with her eyes closed, willing herself back into a calm state. After a couple of minutes, the anxiety subsided.

When she felt she was in greater possession of herself, Sarah made her way to the coffee shop near the center of the row of stores. She picked up a newspaper from the stand near the door and ordered the biggest and iciest coffee concoction they could make for her.

There were only a couple of people at the shop, both seated at a table near the back. Sarah picked a place to sit by the window at the front, as far away from them as possible.

She flipped through the newspaper without really reading anything, feeling utterly foolish about everything, but not knowing what else to do with herself. She had no idea at the moment how long she could or would stay in this town, or what she would do when it was time to leave.

It occurred to her that she had been playing hide-and-seek with herself, moving from one moment to the next without thinking too much about what she was doing or why, her only point of focus being to get to the Pacific. Keeping her sights on that goal had helped her to block out nearly everything else for long stretches of time. But now that she was here, it started to feel like nothing in the world would ever make sense to her again after this, that once this adventure was over, the only thing left to do would be to go back to a life that no longer existed, or invent for herself a new life entirely from scratch. But no matter which path she took, she would have to live the rest of her life knowing that, through her own carelessness and inattention to what really mattered, she had been responsible for her child's death.

As noon approached, Sarah still sat in the coffee shop. Between bouts of watching people come and go, she pretended to read the newspaper, moored to her seat at this little table. The longer she stayed, the harder it was to get up and take those last few steps of her trek to the edges of America. That thought served only to anchor her more firmly to this spot because, well, what was she going to do after that?

It was the "after that" that filled her with terror now.

————

Sarah's cell phone buzzed. It was a new message from Jackson.

Lunch?

She debated whether or not to accept the invitation for a moment, then texted back:

Talk?

When the phone rang, she tried to sound as casually happy as possible. "Hey, Jackson." She wasn't sure she succeeded.

"Everything okay?"

"Yes. Of course."

"Are you there yet? Where are you? What're you doing? What's for lunch?"

"Too much. Too much."

"Sorry. Sorry." Jackson inhaled and exhaled loudly. "Hey, Sarah," he said slowly, his voice smiling.

"Hey."

"So… where are we today?"

"San Diego. I made it."

"Good for you! Congratulations. How's the ocean? Big enough?"

"I haven't seen it yet."

"What?!"

"I can almost smell it from here, but I haven't been down to the water yet. I stopped for coffee—" she heard herself say the word New

York-style, and made a face. "Pardon me—*caaahh*-fee."

"You making fun of my accent?" he said in his Jimmy Jakes voice.

"Nope. Just trying to blend in with the locals. Although… turnabout is fair play."

"Foreplay?"

"*Fair* play."

"Ah. Damn…" he said only half under his breath. "Heh-heh-heh…"

"Funny you should mention that, though."

"Yes?" he said brightly. "I'm listening."

Sarah was embarrassed all over again, the way she felt last night when she deleted the last two lines of her text message to him, only now she had spoken the words and there was no way to delete them. "That sonnet you sent me last night…"

"Yes? You liked it?"

"Well, I had to read it seventy-nine times, but when I got it… holy cow. It knocked my socks off. Definitely not porn. So much better than that."

"I knew it. I wish I could convince the jocks. Say—how would you like to be a guest speaker at one of my classes? Give a live testimonial regarding the effects of Shakespearean sonnets on women's socks? We could act it out. Demonstrations are a powerful teaching tool. If more than your socks come off and you get me fired, it won't matter. The school year's almost over. I'll have all summer to look for a new job. What do you say?"

"No. Not in front of an audience."

"Aha! In private it is, then!"

What are you doing? said the voice in her head. *Your life isn't complicated enough? You haven't made a big enough mess of it? Now you're flirting with some stranger you met in a diner in the freaking middle of nowhere—a diner! Really? Really?!*

"I'm sorry," Jackson said to her. "I didn't mean—"

"No, no," Sarah said quickly. "Nothing to apologize for. I just... I don't know, Jackson... This is all a little weird, don't you think? I don't know what I'm doing. But I like it, too. And it feels like I shouldn't. So I have these terrible arguments with myself in my head."

"Ah, Sarah, Sarah... Let's see if we can be a little nicer to you. Tell me what's going on."

She squeezed her eyes shut and winced.

what if this man is part of what you need to find your way back to normal?

(nothing will ever be normal again)

not if you keep running

Sarah took a deep breath and let it out slowly. "Well," she began, "what's going on right now is that I'm about ten blocks from the ocean and I can't make myself go the rest of the way. I drove all the way out here from the other side of the world like my life depended on it, and now I can't seem to finish it. Is that crazy, or what?"

"No... not crazy. It kind of makes sense, actually."

"Yeah?"

"Sure. In your shoes, I'd probably be afraid of being disappointed if the Pacific Ocean turned out to be not as big or as blue as I might have imagined it. Or that, after coming all this way, discovering that the Jersey Shore was actually nicer. ...Is it something like that, maybe?"

"Maybe."

"What if I went with you?"

"What, stay put and wait for you to get here so you can walk me the last ten blocks?"

"That would be nice, but I have a class in forty minutes. Just take me with you now. Talk to me as you walk. Tell me what you see. I'll keep you company."

"Hmm," she said, considering his offer.

"How many miles are in ten blocks?"

"In New York, probably not even half a mile. These blocks are longer, though. Back home, it's maybe a ten-minute walk. Fifteen if you stroll. Three hours if you're sightseeing with out-of-towners."

"You really don't like tourists, do you."

"I know… I should be nicer. They keep the city rich."

"I thought the stock brokers did that."

"No. They keep us bitter."

"Okay. But now you're the tourist. And I'm all yours for a little while. So let's go for a walk. Take me sightseeing."

———————

Having Jackson for company made all the difference in the world. She was not aware of the time passing or the distance. It was the hot, white sun that threatened to overpower her senses now, but even that was a secondary concern.

"Where are we now?" Jackson asked.

"I just turned onto Garnet Avenue from…" Sarah looked around for a street sign. "…Jewell. We should make a note of that. It'll come in handy when it's time to find the car."

"Noted. What's on Garnet?"

"Looks like a commercial area. Tire store, pizza joint, flower shop, gas station… Looks a lot like Central Florida, but with sidewalks."

"Florida didn't have a big enough view of the ocean, either?"

"No, they have nice beaches there. I just don't like that state."

"Why not?"

"Too hot. Too weird. Too many bugs." *Too many bad memories.*

"I see. Good thing you decided to go to Southern California. No one ever accused that place of being hot. Or weird."

"Well, it's hot here, too. That's for sure. But it's not humid or crawling with bugs. And the weirdos here are definitely of a much more interesting variety. Aside from that, I might as well be back in Florida." Sarah shuddered a bit at that thought, and made a little "ugh" sound to go with it.

"You lived there?"

"The longest fourteen months of my life."

"When was that?"

"Long time ago. I was in high school."

"That's an odd time to be uprooted, isn't it?"

"The worst time."

"Why'd you move there?"

This dredged up memories she would have preferred not to relive, but she had opened that door. "My grandmother was sick. There was no one else to take care of her. My Mom felt obligated, and, next thing I knew, we were on a plane. I left right after high school, though. Went back to New York for college. My parents ended up taking care of my grandmother for another six or seven years—the 'Decade of Darkness' my Dad calls it, when my Mom isn't listening."

"And your Grandma? What happened with her?"

"She died." *And not a moment too soon,* Sarah thought. *Crazy old bat.*

"Oh. I'm sorry."

Sarah wanted to say, *Don't be. She was a horror movie.* Instead she said simply, "Mm-hmm."

They walked for a few moments in silence before Jackson spoke again. "Where are we now?"

"Still on Garnet. I think Pacific Park is at the end of this street."

"Pacific *Beach* Park," he corrected.

"You know this place?!"

"I'm following you on Google Maps."

"Oooh... Stalker alert..." That voice in her head wanted to start screaming about serial killers again. She squelched it.

There was a little cluster of colorful old bungalows on the south side of the street that had been turned into shops. "Oh, look. A head shop."

"Let's go there!"

"Follow me."

She crossed the avenue at the next corner and went over for a closer look.

The shop that had caught Sarah's eye turned out to be a pleasantly schizophrenic little place, crammed with broken-down antiques, shelves full of tourist-trap trinkets, an entire wall of herbal remedies, and lots of bongs.

A little bell above the door on a rusty wire tinkled hoarsely when Sarah walked in. The air was suffused with the strong scent of patchouli.

The proprietors were an older couple—a very tan, skinny man, and his rosy-cheeked, cherubic wife—both of whom appeared to be a wee bit stoned. The woman behind the counter gave Sarah a warm, dopey smile. Sarah said, "Hi."

"What do you see? Who did you just say 'hi' to?" Jackson asked impatiently.

"I'll tell you in a minute," Sarah whispered. Then, in her normal voice, "It's a very cool little shop. Reminds me of the Village in the old days. Ooh! Sunglasses." She walked over to a display near the end of the counter with styles from the middle of the last century. "These are great," she said to Jackson, smiling at the lady.

"Describe, please."

"Pink cat's-eye glasses with rhinestones..."

"Too Dame Edna for you."

"I *love* Dame Edna. Let's see... Some hippie-dippy Flower Power shades..."

"Maybe, maybe..."

204 • CYNTHIA CEILÁN

"Oh. These are the ones. These are perfect: Ivory-colored rims, dark-green roundish lenses, wide... whaddayacallems... legs?"

"Temples," Jackson and the lady behind the counter said at the same time.

"Yes. Temples. I should've known that. My Dad's an optometrist."

"Yeah. The cobbler's kids always go barefoot. Right?"

"Well, that's stretching the metaphor a little, but yeah. Something like that." To the lady behind the counter, Sarah asked, "Do you have a mirror?"

"Absolutely," the lady said, and, without getting up from her stool, swiveled around, reached behind her, and brought out a tarnished old silver mirror with a very ornate handle and back, and offered it to Sarah.

Sarah tried on the glasses. "Oh, these are definitely the ones. Very Joan Crawford. Now all I need are some Eli Manning shoulder pads, and one of those hats with the netting over the face."

"Okay, now you're scaring me," Jackson said. "...You know Eli Manning?"

"I most certainly do. Not personally, of course."

"They're beautiful on you," said the lady behind the counter.

"You hear that, Jackson Jackson?"

"I did indeed. Tell her to take a picture and send it to me."

"I don't know how to do that without disconnecting the call. I'll send you a picture later."

As she was paying for her purchase, a display of handmade figurines made mostly of wood and wire caught her eye. They were about seven or eight inches high. The one Sarah reached for was an ancient, naked hippie on a surf board, bearded, long gray hair and all, smiling ecstatically at the sky, arms held straight out for balance. On the base of the figurine, painted in ocean-blue, backward-slanting print, were the words, "Hang Eleven." Sarah laughed out loud.

"What?!" Jackson said impatiently.

Sarah described the little work of art. Jackson laughed, too.

"My husband makes those, mostly out of driftwood," the lady behind the counter said. "I paint the faces to look like him. And the other parts, too."

Jackson and Sarah laughed again.

Sarah looked at the figurine, and then at the man rearranging a supply of souvenir shot glasses on a nearby shelf. He smiled with a wink. Sarah wasn't sure whether it would be an insult or a compliment to either one of them if she said the old naked surfing hippie did, indeed, look like the woman's husband. "I'll take it," she said, walking to the counter.

"For me?" Jackson asked.

"I'll take two," Sarah said to the lady.

Back out on the street, she and Jackson continued to chat about nothing, and she forgot all about her earlier anxiety.

At the corner of Bayard Street, waiting for the light to change, a warm breeze brought her the first whiff of salt air. She looked toward the horizon. She could just glimpse a dark ribbon of blue at the bottom edge of the sky.

"What happened?" Jackson asked.

"I think I just smelled the ocean. I think I can see it."

"Where are you now?"

"Bayard."

Sarah heard Jackson's mouse click. "Looks like you're almost there."

"There's a big bridge or something out there. Is there an island after the beach?"

"I think it's a pier, not a bridge."

When she arrived at the end of the street, she was disappointed to find herself face-to-face with a closed gate. The pier beyond it was actually a long row of cabins, and the gate belonged to a hotel.

"Can you walk down that street to the right?" Jackson asked.

"Yeah. That looks promising."

She came out onto a little plaza with a set of cement benches facing the ocean. "Oh, Jackson," she said. "This is amazing."

The water was a perfect blue. The sound of the surf greeted her like an old friend. "Oh, Jackson."

"You did it, sweetheart."

He listened to her silence for a little while, smiling, loving the way she said, *Oh, Jackson.* He looked at his watch. Just a few minutes left before the next bell. "Sarah?"

"Hmm?"

"Are you going to be okay?"

Sarah smiled, nodding to herself. "Yes. I'm going to be okay." She walked over to the middle bench and sat facing the water. "I'm going to be okay."

"I wish I was there with you."

"Me, too," she said in a whisper, and found that she meant it. "Thank you, Jackson."

"It was my pleasure. I'll call you tonight, okay?"

"Okay."

She was going to be all right.

We came from a star, Professor Singh said in her memory. *We came from the sea*, said Mr. Vicarelli. "They call us back," Sarah whispered to both of her old teachers.

People came and went all around her, on bikes, on foot, carrying surfboards, wielding cameras. Every once in a while, oblivious tourists stood directly in front of her, their backs to her. They took pictures of themselves, always blocking her view. A few of them handed her their cameras so she could take pictures of them. *They're the same everywhere,* she thought, but this time it made her smile. They'd be gone in a minute, off to take more pictures of themselves in front of something else that didn't hold an ounce of meaning to them, and the ocean would be hers again.

It was four in the afternoon when she became aware of the heat emanating from her face and arms. She'd have to invest in a couple of gallons of sunscreen, and a big hat. Right now, though, she didn't want to move. She had the best seat in the house.

An hour or so later, she began to think about the walk back to the car, and about not wanting to miss the sunset, or walk back to that shopping center after dark. She remembered passing a shop on her way to this place, with a sign out front advertising bicycles for rent. She rose, stretching her back, smiling at the water. "I'll be right back," she said to the sound of the crashing waves.

The ride back to her car was quick and easy, and the rental bike fit neatly into the compartment in the back of the minivan. She had to deflate the air mattress, but she wouldn't be needing it anytime soon... unless she decided to take it back to the park by the beach and set up camp there. "There's a thought," she said to herself. She'd decide later.

People began to wander the shore in pairs, small groups, and some by themselves. They had come to watch the sun set. The benches where Sarah had spent the afternoon were fully occupied by the time she got back, but again she didn't mind. She walked on the sand for a while, then explored some of the shops in the area. When darkness came, she treated herself to a glass of wine and a seafood dinner at a nearby pub.

The sunset over the ocean was as spectacular as that sunrise on the plains had been, but beautiful in an entirely different way. Sarah experienced each of those events as uniquely separate encounters, as if the Earth was possessed of two completely independent suns. The golden-red orb that rose so majestically over the flat Texas landscape had been the watershed moment that allowed her to divest herself, at long last, of the searing anguish that had been crushing the life out of her. The distant sphere now descending quietly, and no less gloriously, into the deep blue of the Pacific was healing beyond all medicine and incantations. *The Universe sleeps, and is at peace,* it said to her.

That night on the phone with Jackson, she spoke of her day and evening by the sea as a person who had just undergone a profoundly transformative experience. Jackson listened quietly, living every moment with her, loving the serenity and simple joy he was now hearing in her voice. "Do it again tomorrow," he encouraged her gently. "And the next day, and the next. Whatever made you do this, it was the right thing to do."

Jackson realized he was speaking to Sarah as if he had known her all his life, as if he knew what her journey was about. He hardly knew her at all, of course, but felt close to her all the same.

He considered himself a pretty good observer of people. She had been hunched over in what he assumed was weariness the first moment he laid eyes her, but there was also something painfully familiar in her face. That was probably why he couldn't help speaking to her. He couldn't make himself look away.

"Maybe someday you'll tell me what that was about. And if not, that'll be okay, too. I'm just happy to know that you found what you were looking for, and that it's helping you find some peace."

Sarah could not imagine that she would never again feel sorrow, shame, or guilt over the loss of Tessie and the way she died, or that there would never be a time when even thinking her name would not break her heart all over again. If she lived a hundred years, she would spend every remaining day aching for the presence of that sweet child, imagining rather than experiencing every milestone and quiet moment.

But something had begun to change today. Sitting on that concrete bench by the shore, she heard the lovely peal of Tessie's laughter in the sound of nearby wind chimes. Today, she hadn't turned away from the noise of children being children as they walked by with their parents, friends, and siblings. She found comfort in their squeals and squawks, and even in their whining and their crying. She felt Tessie close to her in the warm breath of the ocean air, in the evocative summer scents of sunscreen and tanning lotion. She imagined Tessie sitting there with her, her ankles barely reaching the edge of the bench, singing made-up songs to herself and talking to her doll or her imaginary friends, or asking Sarah a million and a half questions about everything under the sun. Sarah had sat there all afternoon, occasionally wrapping a protective arm around the empty space beside her, where Tessie would have been. There would always be some sadness about that terrible and unfillable absence. But there would also be tender moments of remembrance.

"'For thy sweet love remembered such wealth brings...'" Sarah had whispered into the warm breeze.

She was beginning to see that, even in her imagined moments with her lost dark-haired little girl, there might also be the occasional respite from sorrow. With time, it might get easier. Maybe. With time. Lots of time.

"Maybe someday I'll tell you," she said to Jackson. "Not now, though. If that's okay."

"Of course it's okay."

"Goodnight, Jackson. And thank you again."

"Goodnight, Sarah. Sleep well."

Eight

SARAH RENTED ANOTHER BIKE before the hottest part of the afternoon got in full swing. Several blocks inland, riding down a residential street lined with Spanish-style, stucco houses with flat roofs, she came across one with a sign in the front yard that said FURNISHED STUDIO FOR RENT. There was a phone number printed at the bottom of the sign. Sarah pulled over and, straddling the bike at the curb in front of the house, dialed the number.

A man with a little bit of an accent that Sarah couldn't place right away answered the phone. She asked about the studio.

The man told her the place was still available, but someone had come by just this morning and was probably going to come back this afternoon to close the deal. Sarah knew immediately that he was full of shit, but when he told her the rent, she almost fell off the bike. You couldn't rent a soggy refrigerator box in a dark New York City alley for what he was asking. "I only need it for about month, though," she said to the man.

"Ah, no, no, no, no, no," he said with his short vowels. "That other lady want it fo-longa."

"Did she want to move in this week?"

"June."

Sarah thought for a moment. "What if I paid you for the whole month and moved out before June? May is already half over."

"You not even see the place yet!" he said.

"Can I see it now?"

Just then, she saw a very short, white-haired, dark-skinned man wearing plaid shorts that fell below his bowed knees and a screamingly loud flowered shirt whose hem stopped just a few inches above his knees. He emerged from the narrow alley between the main house and what she assumed was the studio apartment, which took up what was left of side yard. He sighed heavily into the phone and asked, "Where are you?"

Sarah heard him say it both on the phone and from just a few steps away. "Right here," she said, and waved.

"Achh!" he squawked, startled, and then laughed. She chuckled with him. He looked a lot more jovial in person than he sounded over the phone. "Okay, come. I show you. Bye-bye now," he said into the phone and turned it off.

Sarah rolled the bike into the little alley between the house and the apartment while the man flipped through a set of keys on a metal ring the size of a woman's bracelet. Sarah saw with approval that the studio was completely detached from the main house, even though a person would probably be able to stand in the alley and, stretching out both arms, almost touch both structures. The neighbor's house on the other side was nearly as close.

The studio was about the size of a two-car garage, which was probably what this small building was originally designed to be. The furnishings were minimal: a wicker basket turned upside down with a decorative tray and small lamp on top served as a side table; a not-exactly-new futon was both sofa and bed. "That a *queen* size," the little man said proudly. "New mattress," he added. *Yeah, sure,* Sarah thought. A white, plastic, three-shelf bookcase adorned the opposite corner of the room; on the top shelf, there was an old wine bottle with a couple of plastic flowers sticking out of it, and three old paperbacks on the middle shelf. A tiny L-shaped kitchen was tucked into the back corner of the room; there were two cabinets above a little metal sink and no more than two feet of counter space to the left. Underneath that counter was a mini refrigerator. On the other side of the L, there was another little bit of counter space with a two-burner portable electric stove on top and shoe-box sized microwave oven on an open shelf underneath. The bright white walls were freshly painted, and the place was immaculately clean. She had seen all this without having to take a single step in any direction.

"Bathroom?" she asked.

The man pointed to the area behind the kitchen. "Back there."

The bathroom, too, was sparkling clean. There was a small shower stall instead of a tub. The sink was about the size of a cereal bowl. The toilet was pink, apropos of nothing. This made Sarah smile.

"Closet?"

The man pointed to a metal shelf with a clothes rod underneath. The shelving unit was bolted to the wall opposite the bathroom door. "You can put curtain here," he said, demonstrating with his hands. "Last tenant did that. Looked nice. But you leave in two-three weeks. Maybe not worth it."

She went into the kitchen nook and opened the cabinet doors. There she found four plates from three different dinnerware sets; two souvenir mugs, one from Las Vegas and the other from Knott's Berry Farm; a medium-sized pot; a large plastic Slurpee cup, and a couple of disposable Gladware containers with lids. Inside the Vegas cup were a few pieces of steel cutlery.

"So you're okay with letting me stay here for just a couple of weeks?"

"Sure. If references check out. For one month rent."

Ah, shit. References. Sarah tried to think. "All my references are in New York," she told him.

"That okay. I can call."

They looked at each other squarely in the eye. Sarah smiled first.

"I'll take good care of your place. I own an apartment in New York. You can call the building manager; he'll tell you. I just need a clean place to sleep and a little kitchen for a few weeks. I won't bother anybody. I'm tired of hotels. This place is perfect."

The man looked at Sarah for a long time. She tried to look as harmless as possible. After a while, he said, "Okay. Follow me." She went with him into the main house, where she learned that his name was Harry Tei and that he was from the Philippines but had lived in Japan for a long time. His wife, also tiny and cinnamon-skinned but a little rounder, was Polynesian; she was busy in the kitchen cooking something that smelled delicious. She smiled and nodded as Sarah and Mr. Tei walked by and sat at their dining room table.

Sarah gave him a list of names and phone numbers, and then wrote him a check for a full month's rent. It was a lot of money to spend for a two-and-a-half-week rental, but still lots cheaper than staying at a hotel for the same amount of time and eating out every night. Before handing him the check, she said, "If you change your mind, I get this back, right?"

"Minus one hundred for reference check."

"You said fifty."

"Okay. Fifty."

"Let's write that down somewhere." She wrote a couple of lines in tiny letters on the back of the check, in the endorsement section.

The man frowned at the check when she handed it to him. "I call you layta," he told her as they walked back to her bike.

Sarah shook his hand. "Thank you, Mr. Tei," she said warmly, and rode off in the direction in which she had come.

When she was safely around the corner and out of sight, she took out her phone and used the GPS app to mark the spot where she now stood. Then she made a few phone calls.

The first call was to the building manager back in New York. The second was to her best friend, Shirley, who was first shocked and then thrilled to learn that Sarah was in California. The third call was to her parents, who kept her on the phone for half an hour and would probably miss the call if Mr. Tei decided to phone them, too. That would be just as well. It would only be a good third reference if her father answered the phone.

Harry Tei called her back at about five that afternoon. She was just coming out of a small shop where she had purchased three sarong-like garments she intended to use as sundresses, a pair of sandals, and a straw hat with a big floppy brim. "Mr. Tei?" she said, pinching the phone between her cheek and shoulder as she undid the bicycle lock.

"Everything okay," he said in his sing-song voice. "You can move in anytime."

"Thank you so much," Sarah said happily.

"You know..." he began, and then hesitated.

"Yes?"

"You have lot of people who love you. Even the super in New York. He scared you don't come back. That something."

"Hmm," Sarah said, almost inaudibly. Manny was a good guy, but he had a big mouth. She wondered how much he had disclosed to her new landlord. Then again, there was Ana. "Yeah, that's something. Thank you again, Mr. Tei. I'll stop by tomorrow morning for the key, if that's all right."

"That all right. Bye-bye now."

———————

By Friday of that week, she had settled into a perfectly predictable pattern, in sync with the tides, with the rising and the setting suns, lulled by the song of the waves. Sometimes she sat on the sand, sometimes on the grass under the shade of her own hat. At dusk she roamed the edges of the water, white foam lapping at her feet, leaving slender footprints in her wake that would fade almost as quickly as she made them, erasing all traces of her passage.

She felt like a creature in the midst of a strange but not entirely unwelcome metamorphosis, a long, slow series of changes beyond her control and most colorful imaginings. One after another, layers of gossamer bindings fell away, as slowly and resolutely as the movement of the hour hand on a clock. She felt herself emerging from the ragged cocoon that had been forged from both ancient and newborn sorrows, and becoming someone previously unknown to herself. She was lifetimes away from the Sarah who had lived day to day in a frenzy of noise and grit, in a city she loved with desperate exasperation. This new Sarah was someone she was only beginning to know; she was still just a specter, as yet too insubstantial to cast a shadow or return a reflection.

Even her body looked and felt different to her now. She had lost quite a bit of weight in the past couple of months, so clothes draped on her in ways that were unfamiliar. The sun and the sea had also begun to change her. Her skin became the color of antique gold. Strands of red and bronze began to appear in her hair, especially where it wasn't hidden under the brim of her hat. Her breathing became slower, deeper, and suffused her body from the inside out with the clean crispness of ocean air. She could taste the salty kiss of the morning mist on her own lips. She tasted it all day long. Her eyes took on a calm, faraway look. Her senses tingled with a hunger for more of this magic, even as the rest of her drifted into a dreamlike state. Her limbs felt longer, more sinewy and graceful, as the long-held tension in her shoulders relaxed and the warm sands taught her a new way to walk, changing her center of gravity.

Whenever and wherever she did sit for a while, she always made room beside her for Tessie. Sarah began to feel her presence more strongly every day. Sometimes at night, as she was drifting off to sleep, she stroked her baby's head where she could feel it resting in the hollow of her shoulder, as real as a phantom limb is to its amputee.

Sometimes, sitting outside on the grass or by the shore, she made room for Jackson on the other side of her, and wondered about lives that would never be lived. What kind of father might a man like that have been to Tessie? Would her little girl have been the glimmering twinkle in his adoring eye, a loving and deeply loved daddy's girl, as Sarah had once been? There was no way to know, but there was comfort in imagining it.

And every night before sleep, there was Jackson.

He spoke to her in gentle whispers, reading bits of literature he loved, or lines from sonnets that moved them both. They made each other laugh at things they might not otherwise have found funny if each one of them had been alone or with other people. They told each other random stories about their lives, each one avoiding those dark and secret corners littered with the jagged shards of dashed dreams and shattered illusions. Each night they became closer, and the timid yearning that had begun to blossom from their earliest conversations became an unremitting hunger that was as wretched as it was delicious.

"I wish you were here," she told him one night.

"Oh, Sarah... Sarah... Not more than I want you here with me."

"I think we're in some kind of trouble, Jackson."

"Nothing we won't be able to figure out. I promise."

———————

By the following Friday, Sarah began to feel the first stirrings of restlessness. She felt unsettled and out of sync with everything. Her phone call with Jackson the night before had been brief; he had seemed distracted and in a hurry to get off the phone. And today, he hadn't called her at lunchtime.

Well, that didn't take long, Sarah thought, remembering all the things she had learned to hate about post-divorce dating. *It doesn't matter,* she told herself. *It's not like any of this was real.*

She tried to get herself off that self-defeating mindset, and think instead about all the other things she could do in San Diego while she was still here. She had spent all this time in an area not much larger than a single square mile. After so much time on the road, so many miles behind her, she thought she needed to stay put for a while and let something become familiar.

She also knew she was avoiding thinking about the journey back. Pretending that this was her life now made it easier to procrastinate.

As much as she was loving this beautiful ocean, Sarah knew deep down that she'd never be a California girl. Blizzards and yellow cabs were part of her natural habitat, not boogie boards and earthquakes.

Every day, she had come to the same two or three spots in Pacific Beach Park, and wandered the shore in either direction in the evenings. She wondered what the view would be like from the cliffs she could see in the distance, if she could find them and make her way up to them. Surely there were paths or roads that would take her there.

While she fought the urge to send Jackson a text and pretended not to be waiting for the phone to ring, she tried to do a little research online. The screen was nearly impossible to read in the sun; she had to bend over her own lap, folding herself almost in half, to create enough shade with the brim of her hat to be able to see the screen.

She learned about a place called the Cabrillo Monument, perched on a cliff about ten miles south of here. That sounded interesting. Maybe she'd do that tomorrow. A little closer to where she was sitting, there was a dog beach at the mouth of the bay, which made her think of Lucy and Ethel, and Bitsy, the last little dog she owned. Maybe, wherever she went or whatever she did next, she would adopt a little stray, and together they would figure out what their new lives should be.

She found herself wishing, as she sometimes did, that she still believed in heaven. Dog heaven, in particular. The thought that Bitsy and Tessie might be keeping each other company was sweetly wistful, but too sad to contemplate for too long. She tried to think of other things.

It was nearly four in the afternoon before she heard from Jackson.

"Hey, you," she said to him. "I missed having lunch with you today."

"Sorry. I missed you, too. I couldn't get to the phone. Where are you?"

"Oh, same place in the park. Hiding under my hat, slathered in sunscreen, sitting on the grass, thinking about visiting a dog beach, even though some of the reviews say that it smells kind of poopy. It might be fun anyway. I like watching dogs play."

"Maybe you can get a gas mask to match your hat. What color is it?"

"What? My hat?"

"Yeah."

"It's a straw hat," she said, taking it off and looking at it.

"What else are you wearing?"

"Jackson..."

"Just trying to get a mental picture of you."

She looked down at herself. "A flowery beach thing. Like a giant kerchief. I'm wrapped up in it. I look like a Hawaiian burrito."

"Hmmm," he said, and then he was quiet.

"You sound funny. Is everything all right?"

"I called in sick this morning. That's why I didn't call at lunch-time."

"Really? What's wrong?"

"Can't sleep. Can't eat," he said hoarsely, sounding miserable.

Just then, a shadow appeared before her. A man approached her and now stood looking down at her. She looked up and saw Jackson.

"Couldn't wait any longer." He dropped to his knees in front of her and sat on the backs of his calves.

Sarah kept the phone to her ear. She took her sunglasses off, as if these were the cause of her hallucination. He was still there.

"I think we can hang up now," he said still speaking into his own phone.

She held a hand out timidly to him. He kissed her fingers tenderly without taking his eyes off her. She felt the blood rushing through her like whitewater rapids in the middle of a flash flood. "I was beginning to think I made you up."

"I'm real," he said. "And you're even more beautiful than I remembered."

Sarah rose to her knees. He did the same. She put the fingertips of one hand on the side of his face and stroked his cheek. He put his hands on her bare shoulders and felt an intense heat emanating from her. She leaned in and kissed him, barely touching his lips at first, but then he embraced her, pressing her into him. She wrapped her arms around his neck and kissed him harder. She pressed her pelvis into his, and felt rock-hardness coming to life.

Jackson took her by the shoulders again and leaned back a few inches. "Sorry," he whispered.

Sarah shook her head minutely. "I'm not."

"I think even in California we could get arrested for doing this here."

"You're probably right. Let's go."

"I just need a minute," he said, leaning down until he was resting on his shoulder on the ground, curled up on his side with his hands between his knees.

"All right," she said as she gathered her things, "but make it a fast minute."

————————

They were barely through the door of Sarah's tiny studio when they began ripping each other's clothes off in a frenzy, hands all over each other, lips, mouths, limbs, searching, hungry, tearing at each other as if the end of the world were only seconds away and the fires of hell were lapping at their feet.

Jackson fumbled with a little tinfoil packet he had pulled out of his pocket while Sarah planted little kisses all over his face, her hands everywhere at once. She looked down for a moment, then grabbed the packet out of his hands and tore it open with her teeth. He kicked his pants off the rest of the way, along with his shoes, socks, and underwear, and before he knew what was happening, she swiftly unrolled the condom down the shaft of his hard-on in a single, fluid motion. He almost passed out, barely able to hang on.

Sarah fell backward on the bed, pulling Jackson down with her, her arms wrapped around his neck, her legs entwined around his thighs and calves like pythons. He entered her in a single thrust. She gasped loudly, breathless, lifting her pelvis with remarkable force to take him all in, all at once, tightening the grip her legs and arms had on him. He slipped both of his arms around her, lacing them behind her, wrists crossed in that curve between her shoulder blades, and pulled her to him, her breasts squeezed between them, swelling and pulsing as she struggled to find her breath. He kissed her face, her neck, biting gently at that little space just to the side of her throat. Her back arched. Her arms fell away limply, but her legs remained firmly clamped around his. He pounded himself deeper and deeper into her. She slipped her arms underneath his and curled them over his shoulders, her fingers digging into the muscles she found there. He wanted to push his way all the way through her, amazed at the way she kept pulling him into her. He grabbed handfuls of her hair and pressed her face into his, breathing her, tasting her, drinking her.

She came in a roiling thunderstorm of primal release, panting, moaning, nearly screaming. "Sarah, Sarah..." he kept whispering to her. Whatever she was trying to say was utterly unintelligible.

He buried his face between her neck and shoulder and held on tight. She had loosened her grip just a bit, but was still entwined around him. He pulled his knees up higher behind her thighs, raising her butt off the bed, and pistoned into her in a hard, purposeful rhythm. As she felt him reaching his own climax, she held him tighter, feeling his body quaking on top of her, tensing, releasing, and then finally, slowly, descending.

They lay like that for a long time, hearts pounding, pulses racing, completely spent, bodies melting into one another. He kept his face buried in the curve of her neck, her damp hair mingling with his. After a minute or two, he rolled over slowly and lay beside her, one arm pinned under her head.

When at last he could speak, he mumbled something that sounded like, "Holy fudge-covered cow..."

"You fall asleep, I'll kill you," Sarah said, already drifting off to sleep herself.

"I think you already did."

———————

Sarah awakened slowly, her face still nestled into the space on his chest just beneath his shoulder. He was stroking her hair, pushing stray strands away from her forehead.

"Hey," he whispered to her.

With her ear pressed against him, she liked the way that sound resonated in his chest. She smiled. "Hey," she whispered back.

"I'm starving."

"I thought you couldn't eat?"

"I can now."

"Heh-heh…" She laid a hand on his chest, feeling his heart beat strongly against her palm. "What did you *do* to me…"

"*Me?* All I did was hang on for dear life."

"Well," she said, sitting up on her elbow, "you did that very well." She gave him an impish little smile. "You think you can do it again?"

"Not without a brontosaurus burger. And possibly some intravenous fluids."

"I think we missed the sunset," Sarah said through a deep, sleepy yawn.

"They'll probably have another one tomorrow. C'mon. Let's go find us a side of beef or something, and a couple of gallons of beer."

———————

Sarah wasn't sure if they allowed alcohol or glass containers on or near the beach, so she hid the bottle of wine in her big purse and poured it surreptitiously into plastic cups. They drank and talked while sitting on one of the benches facing the water along Ocean Boulevard after the biggest meal she had eaten in months.

"You're not married or anything, are you?" she asked looking out at the water.

"Well, young lady, isn't *this* is a fine time to be asking!"

"You're not, are you?"

"I am not."

"Ever been married?"

"Yeah. Once."

"What happened?"

"Ahhhh… That's a long, dumb story, and I come out looking like a jackass."

"That's all right. Tell me anyway."

Jackson shifted in his seat a little. Sarah continued to look out on the water, listening without looking at him.

"We were both very young," he began. "High school sweethearts, the whole bit. We'd known each other practically all our lives. I wanted to leave Kansas. She didn't. So we both went to college as close to home as possible, but far enough away not to have to live at home.

"In our junior year, she missed her period. We both panicked. I proposed… sort of… and her mother slapped together a wedding in no time flat. She got her period the night before we got hitched. But we were both dug in by then, and I thought, what the hell. We were probably going to end up getting married anyway. But deep down, I always held a bit of resentment toward her. I wasn't sure I believed her about the missed period. She had been planning her wedding since she was eight, she told me. She wanted a big church wedding with twenty or thirty bridesmaids or some such crazy thing, and she knew she wanted to honeymoon in Hawaii. I was totally on board with the honeymoon part, but not about coming right back to Kansas when it was over. I wanted to keep going."

Sarah nodded, but didn't say anything.

"I'd been talking forever about wanting to travel the world, starting with every state in the Union and then every country in the Americas. Then Europe and Africa. Asia. All the countries in all the continents, including Antarctica. I wanted to see them all, all the people and places and things I had only ever read about.

"Sally dreamt about staying put.

"She once conceded—probably just to shut me up—that we could move anyplace I wanted, as long as it was no more than an afternoon's drive from her mother's house, the house where she had grown up. I think that was when my resentment started sprouting tentacles.

"When she started talking about having babies—lots and lots of babies—I got really scared. Not because I didn't want kids—I love kids—but when she talked about it, it sounded like each one would be another stake she would pound into the ground, nailing the tent of my traveling circus down, making sure we stayed in Kansas. We'd never leave. Ever.

"I couldn't even get her excited about taking a vacation far away. I'd talk to her about Rome, and she'd remind me about how fattening pasta was, and how she hated spicy food. I'd tell her about Stonehenge, and she'd say it seemed a long way to go just to look at a pile of rocks.

"I wanted take my kids to see at least one ballgame at every stadium in America. It would take a lifetime of summers, but no matter how badly I screwed up as a dad, maybe they'd remember me with fondness for that, if for nothing else.

"I wanted to see the Mediterranean standing on the shores of the Greek Isles, and fall in love with my wife all over again, and have her think I was the greatest thing that ever walked on two legs. I wanted to climb the towers of Notre Dame and touch the gargoyles, and the statues on Easter Island, and the Sphinx at Giza. I wanted to *touch* them. I wanted to lay my hands flat on every one of those things, and feel them push back. I wanted to touch the *ages*, the millennia, and feel them vibrate in my bones. I wanted to touch the things that men had built thousands of years ago, things that, incredibly, are still standing."

As he spoke these words, Sarah felt his body become almost rigid with the passion that pulsed in that deep and mostly secret place in his soul. And then, little by little, she felt him begin to let it go. She was keenly aware of his body against hers, and how the muscles in his body began to relax.

Jackson took a deep breath and let it out slowly, quietly. "Sometimes, when I tried to tell Sally these things, she would look at me like she had married the worst kind of fool. I knew she would eventually get tired of waiting for me to grow up. And I hated her for it.

"In her kindest moments, she told me not to worry, that I should be grateful I had married a sensible woman who would keep a silly dreamer like me with his feet planted firmly on the ground, where they belonged.

"When she was most impatient, she told me I needed to concentrate on getting a 'real' job, that we needed to hurry up and start a family before it was too late. She didn't want to be an 'old' mom in her thirties, and risk having infertility problems or children who might be born sick. We could travel after we retired, she said, when we were done paying off the mortgage and the kids were settled in the world and on their own, hopefully not too far away from home so she could enjoy being a grandma to lots and lots of grandbabies while she still had the energy.

"I stopped believing any of my own dreams would ever come true. I could actually hear her in my head, forty or fifty years into the future, saying we were too old or tired to hike the Great Wall of China, that we should just enjoy our old age and be happy for the wonderful life we had in a place where the people were nice and the streets were clean and the food didn't give you diarrhea.

"I knew then we'd never eat hot dogs at Wrigley Field, never order a pint of ale at a Dublin pub, never take a gondola ride in Venice, never climb the steps at Machu Picchu.

"Funny thing is, I still haven't even come close to doing any of those things."

"Mmm," Sarah said.

Jackson continued. "I started to doubt she was taking birth control, like she said. I applied for a teaching position in Fort Worth, and told her I was going with or without her. She gave in when she realized I was done pretending that I was content to live in Kansas for the rest of my life, and that my subscription to National Geographic was going to be enough to sustain my curiosity about the world. She cried as she packed up all our little things, and was miserable every hour of every day we were in Texas.

"Somewhere along the way, my resentment reached out a long, ugly tentacle, and poisoned her, too. We learned to hate each other without ever raising our voices.

"And then one day, she went home. And I didn't try to stop her."

Jackson took the last gulp of wine in his plastic cup and pinched it by the rim between his fingers. He began tapping it against his knee. "So that's what happened. And I'm still in Texas, I think, only because it's not Kansas." He looked around him, and the people walking the beach, at the waves coming in big and disappearing into little fringes of white bubbly foam at the shore. "This is the first time I've ever seen the ocean."

"What about Hawaii?"

"Never made it there, either."

Sarah nodded slowly, still not looking at him. "What became of Sally? Do you know?"

"Oh, sure. It's a tiny town, where we're from. Not even five hundred people. I run into her now and then when I go back to visit my folks. She married a nice accountant, a guy who was a year or two behind us in school. And they went on to have lots and lots of babies. Well... three babies.

"Her Dad passed away a couple of years ago, and they moved in with her mother. She's raising her family there, in the house where she grew up.

"Sometimes I tell myself, 'well, at least *her* dreams came true.' But those words never sound kind inside my own head.

"I don't resent her anymore. I haven't for a long time. She never deserved that, anyway. Not really. I was the jackass with the big dumb dreams that never amounted to anything."

"Don't do that," Sarah said, patting the hand he had laid over her shoulder. "I like your dreams."

Jackson gave her shoulder a little squeeze.

"Any more wine left?" he asked her.

She poured the last little bit into his cup. It tasted bitter in his mouth.

"What about you?" Jackson asked after a little while. "Is there some husband or jealous boyfriend coming to kick my ass from here all the way back to Brooklyn?"

"Nah. Not anymore."

"Okay, then. Your turn. Let's just get it all out of the way now so we never have to talk about it again."

Sarah didn't want to talk about Vince. She could still smell his girlfriend's sex in her nostrils. "Mm-mm. No." She gave her head a few tiny shakes. "Not tonight."

"Oh, c'mon. No fair. I bared my dumb, ugly soul to you. Now it's your turn."

Sarah looked toward her left, away from Jackson, at the sparkles of light on the water. She leaned forward, gripping the edges of the bench. "I'm divorced," she said, and then was quiet.

"How long?"

"About six years now."

"Any kids?"

Sarah looked at him sharply. Jackson flinched.

"Well… I ask," he said, "'cause of the minivan. I mean, that's usually a dead giveaway. But I didn't see any soccer gear in the back."

"I told you. It's my parents' car."

"Yeah. You did." He wanted very much for her to come back, to lean against him again. But he was also no fan of secrets. "C'mon. Tell me."

Sarah thought about it for a moment, and then said, "One."

Jackson cocked his head, confused. "One what?"

"One child," she said. "A little girl." She took a deep breath and leaned back again, but looked straight out over the ocean. "Her name was Tess."

————

She told him everything, all about having Tessie, and about losing her. She told him about Vince and the end of her marriage, and how she kept their child a secret from him. She told Jackson everything. She told him without looking at him. He never interrupted or asked a question. And then they were both quiet.

"You missing Fort Worth yet?" Sarah asked at last.

"What…? Why?"

"Look," Sarah said with something of a cynical chuckle. "Let's not kid ourselves here. My life's a fucking train wreck."

Jackson took her by the shoulders and made her look at him. "Are you kidding me?"

"I did some terrible things, Jackson. I don't know if I'd ever be able to forgive someone who kept the knowledge of my own child from me, and then, through pure and utter carelessness, let her die."

"Are you *kidding* me?" Jackson asked again, incredulous. "You think *that's* the story I just heard? I don't know how you're even standing up and walking around in the world! I'd be in an insane asylum if only half of that happened to me!" Jackson pulled her to him then, and hugged her tightly. "Jesus Christ, Sarah!" he said, his voice thick with emotion. "Your *baby* just died. For pity's sake, sweetheart. Why didn't you tell me? Why didn't you *tell* me."

For her part, Sarah had been waging an internal battle with just that question, especially in the sobering hours after she had given in to her most primal instincts and jumped his bones with a nearly mindless animal ferocity.

While there had been several hundred miles between them, he was just a concept. Some guy she met at a spot by the side of the road. Each of them had been heading in completely different directions. They had no connection or obligation to each other. He was just someone who showed up and kept her company for a little while, much like countless other people she had met briefly throughout her life, people she had spoken to politely at the occasional social gathering or while waiting in line somewhere. Some people are natural-born gabbers; some are listeners. She and Jackson happened to be two such people, one of each.

For the last few days, he was just a voice on the phone, a temporary but welcome distraction. As attractive as he had become in the tiny space she made for him in her fantasy world, and as captivating as his presence had become to her at a safe distance, she never really believed they would see each other again, much less that they would ever begin to behave as if this were the blossoming of a new relationship. So she invented an imaginary version of herself, too, in that fantasy world. There had been no reason to reveal to him the details of the shattered reality of her life. No sane person would begin a relationship at this time, or become involved with someone so broken and lost, someone who was quite literally wandering the earth without a plan, or any notion of what she would do next, or how, or why.

Now Sarah felt a little ashamed for having pretended to be what she imagined "normal people" were like. There was sadness and anger there, too, and the terrible regret of not having met Jackson at another time in her life. She wanted very much to give him the best part of herself, but she no longer knew where—or if—that part of her existed.

She lay against him limply now, with no idea of how to move beyond this point.

Jackson rocked her gently for a long time, his heart breaking over the loss of a child he would never know. He wanted to find the bastard who had hurt her, and break every bone in his face. "Oh, Sarah..." was all he could say.

But he, too, was worried about the myriad complications this new information had revealed. He had begun to imagine her as the companion who might happily and at long last join him on the fulfillment of his long-postponed voyages to every corner of the world. She was unafraid of going places she had never been, even by herself, and he wanted to latch on to that fearlessness. For Sarah, it had been as simple as getting in a car and driving away.

But she was also in the midst of climbing out of some deep, dark, and scary place, and he was a little afraid of what that could mean. There was nothing in his travel books about that kind of journey.

A strong gust of wind carrying a salty chill enveloped them both. Sarah shuddered.

"Let's go home," he said to her, and kissed her hair. And then, he heard what he had just said. "That sounds nice, doesn't it? 'Let's go home'?"

"Mm-hmm," she said.

They went home.

———————

They spent the rest of the weekend exploring the coast, making love, and pretending they had all the time in the world.

That first night, when they got back to her tiny apartment, he made love to her again, this time as if she were made of gauze. In the morning, it was Sarah who climbed on top of him, and rode him with her eyes closed while he watched her, smiling. On Saturday night, the sex was nearly acrobatic, and they laughed all the way through it. "Trick fucking," he had called it, which made them collapse in hysterical laughter as they pretended they were the stars of their own sex rodeo.

The following morning, the mood was more subdued. Jackson's plane was leaving in a few hours.

"Can't you call in sick again?" she asked, lying beside him after a slow and sweet little session of unembellished lovemaking.

"You broke my streak. You know that? Three years of perfect attendance, all down the drain."

"And worth every orgasm."

"Boy howdy."

"What happened three years ago?"

"What do you mean?"

"The last time your perfect attendance record was shattered."

"Oh. I broke my toe. Playing touch football."

"Hmmm…" she said playfully. "I have an idea…"

"No. Please. I'm a lot more fragile than I look. I cried like a girl for a week. I hate pain."

"It's just one more day. What harm can it do?"

Jackson stroked her hair and kissed it. "It's the last week of school. I should be there. I still have final papers to grade, school dances to chaperone, horny teenagers to hose down…"

"What if you were really sick? I mean, not *sick* sick, but, you know… *loooove*-sick." She poked a finger softly into his ribs.

Jackson jumped up and squealed as if she had stabbed him. "*Yeeeoooahhh!!!* No. No tickling. Never." But he said this laughing. "It makes me… flatulent. I was saving that for later."

"Oh. Nice. *There's* something to look forward to."

"Holy crap! I almost forgot!" He got up quickly and started digging through the small duffel bag that was serving as his luggage. He found what he was looking for in one of the outside pockets. "Awwww, no… it's ruined!" He held out a small Styrofoam container for her to see. "I'm sorry. I'd been planning this since the night I met you."

"What?"

He opened the lid of the crushed container. Inside were the demolished remains of what was once a perfect slice of apple pie.

"Ohhhh, noooo!" she laughed. "Let me see."

"Nah. It's inedible. I can't believe I forgot about it!" He closed the lid and put it in the paper bag in the kitchen they had been using for garbage. "Get dressed. We're going to have apple pie for breakfast." He held a hand out for her as she got out of bed. Jackson spanked her on the bottom as she bounced up.

"Ow!"

"Oooh, that's nice," he said, grabbing a satisfying handful of tawny butt. "Nice and ripe. …You been sunning yourself naked?"

"Nope. That there's a natural-born tan. Handed down through generations of wandering Mediterraneans and a few industrious Caribbean merchants."

"Oh! You habla español? Français? Italiano?"

"Just a *poquito* of each. Mostly the bad words."

"Hmm. That might come in handy someday." He smiled at her, his head full of dreams. She smiled back, but tried to dismiss it.

Jackson followed Sarah into the microscopic shower stall, where they splashed more water onto the floor than they managed to get on each other.

————————

Jackson sat on the steps in front of Sarah's door, his duffel bag slouching sullenly at his feet, and tried to think about anything other than the fact that, in about four and a half hours, he'd be on a plane headed back to Dallas-Fort Worth. He thought about what he might order for breakfast. He marveled at the San Diego climate: sunny, warm, and beautiful. He wondered what bad weather looked like here.

Inside, Sarah was busy mopping up the water in the bathroom with wads of paper towels, also trying not to think about saying goodbye. Instead, she let her mind worry about what Mr. Tei would say if he saw this wet mess, and what he'd think of her promises to take good care of his little apartment.

A small sound, almost like the squeak of a baby's toy, caught Jackson's attention. It seemed to be coming from the space between the side of the studio and the house next door. He went over to investigate.

Crouched and trembling among the sea urchin-shaped leaves of a row of yucca plants, Jackson spotted a tiny kitten. It had the faint markings of what might someday become tiger stripes. Right now, though, the kitten was mostly covered in wispy apricot-and-cream-colored tufts of hair, scant and fine.

When Jackson got closer, it mewed a little louder, but didn't flee. "Hey, little fella," Jackson cooed to it. "Are you lost?"

The kitten mewed plaintively in response.

"Awww... I'll be right back," Jackson told it.

He went inside and poured some milk into one of the Gladware containers. He hurried back outside, almost running on tiptoe, trying not to spill any of the milk. The kitten was still there.

He placed the container on the grass, just a few inches away from the plants. "Here, kitty-kitty. It's all right." He took a few steps back and hunkered down, giving the kitten enough room to feel safe.

The kitten looked at him through enormous green eyes. More hungry than afraid, it ventured out slowly, but without taking its eyes off Jackson. It was following its nose to the scent of fresh milk.

A little more trusting now, it drank thirstily from the container, and continued licking the bowl long after the milk was gone.

Jackson tiptoed away and went back inside.

Sarah had just grabbed her bag and was about to join Jackson outside. He went to the fridge and got the container of milk. He shook it a little to see how much was left. "I owe you a quart of milk."

"Where're you going with that?" Sarah asked.

"Follow me."

Sarah followed close behind, crouching and tiptoeing like Jackson, and not knowing why. Then she saw the kitten. "Oh, Jackson…"

The kitten took half a step back when it saw them approach, but didn't go all the way back into the plants. Jackson poured a little more milk out for it. The kitten lapped it up in no time.

"Do you think it belongs to somebody?" Sarah asked.

"I don't know. He looks kind of scruffy. Poor little guy…"

By small and careful increments, Jackson gained the trust of the tiny animal until he was able to pick it up. It was barely bigger than the palm of his hand. "Oh, pardon me. You're a *she!*"

The kitten gave him a dainty little squeak in response.

"And you're half starved to death," Jackson said, mostly to himself. He looked at Sarah apologetically. "I can't just leave her here."

"I don't think I'm allowed pets." Sarah said, though the look on her face was very close to mirroring Jackson's. "What should we call her?"

Jackson thought about the countless puppies and kittens—and even much older animals—that he had taken in over the years, growing up on that farm in Kansas. People would drive by and throw them from their cars. They still did. He didn't know what could diminish a person's humanity to such an extent that it allowed them think that was a perfectly reasonable thing to do with a defenseless animal. Jackson could never sit by and do nothing, not even as a kid. He and his grandfather had taken many of them to a shelter three towns away, but there were plenty of them that he kept, quietly ignoring his mother's protestations. He would save food for them from his own plate, preferring to go hungry himself so they'd have something to eat. Eventually, his mother relented and pretended not to notice when she saw him building yet another little dog house with his grandfather in a patch of ground just beyond the back garden. She offered to raise his allowance on the condition that he do an extra chore or two a week. This made them both feel better about feeding his pets with money he had earned himself. Grandpa also always seemed to have a couple of extra bucks in his pocket to help make up the difference.

"If you name her, you'll have to keep her," Jackson told Sarah.

"What-choo got there?" said a sing-songy voice behind them. They both turned around guiltily, like burglars caught red-handed, Sarah clutching the container of milk, and Jackson cupping the kitten protectively in both hands. All three of them looked at Mr. Tei with wide-eyed uncertainty.

"Hi, Mr. Tei," Sarah said. "Is this little guy yours?"

"Girl," Jackson corrected out of the side of his mouth.

"No, no, no, no, no, no, no. No cats," but he approached the bit of fur in Jackson's hands with curiosity all the same.

Mrs. Tei came waddling behind her husband with a large watering can in one hand. She put the can down immediately and went over to Jackson. "Oooooh… May I?" she asked him, holding out her own cupped hands.

"Sure." Jackson, who was roughly twice as tall as Mrs. Tei, bent at the waist and gently put the kitten in her hands.

Mrs. Tei began cooing to the kitten and speaking to it in a language neither Sarah nor Jackson had ever heard.

"Ahhh... Now look what you did," Mr. Tei said to Sarah. He reached a hand out and began stroking the kitten's head with just his index finger. "How much rent you think you can pay, cat? You not look so rich to me."

"She was hiding in the plants over there," Sarah explained.

"No need to hide anymore, Tipis," Mrs. Tei said and turned to take the kitten inside.

"What does that mean, 'Tipis'?" Sarah asked.

"Little fluffy creamy thing, soft and light."

"Tipis," Jackson repeated. "See? I told you. Now it's hers."

———————

The drive to the airport was piercingly quiet. The question on both of their minds was, "What happens next?" Neither one of them wanted to ask it. It was Jackson who dipped a toe into those waters first.

"How long do you plan to stay?"

Sarah sighed deeply, and adjusted her grip on the steering wheel. "Well, I have the apartment until next week, at least. There was an alleged tenant who's supposed to move in sometime in June, but Mr. Tei hasn't mentioned her since he tried to get me to sign a long-term lease. I might stay at least that long. I'm not sure, though."

It won't be the same without you here, she thought. *And I think I'm done doing what I needed to do.* "Maybe it's time to head back home."

"Will you be driving back through Texas?"

"Probably." She wanted to stop by Ed and Linda's again, check in on Reverend Owl. And maybe see one more sunrise on the Texas Panhandle.

"Do you think you can take a minor detour through Fort Worth?"

Sarah smiled at him, then put her eyes back on the road. "I don't know, Jackson…" she said in a regretful tone. "How's the apple pie in Fort Worth?"

"Only the best in all of Texas! But not as flat as the one I brought you." He reached over and took her hand, and kissed her fingers. "Say you'll come to see me."

But she couldn't say it.

He let go of her hand slowly and sank a little deeper into his seat.

"Jackson—"

"No, no. It's okay. I get it. Really."

"I don't think you do."

"It's the timing. It's the distance. It's… complicated. I get it."

"It's all that and a lot more."

"What then?"

"If I go to Fort Worth…" She never felt more exposed in her life, but she forced herself to say it anyway. "If I go to Fort Worth, there's a pretty good chance I'll have to stay. Or you'll have to come home with me."

Her words hung in the air for a moment or two. "Yes," Jackson said at last.

"And if I stay, Jackson, I'll never know for sure if it's because I'm running away from my life or I'm just pretending I've found a new one. I'm tired of running. And I don't want to live a pretend life."

"Mmm," he said.

"And if you come with me… I don't even know what it is I'd be inviting you into." Sarah started to feel that big purple thing in her chest begin to fill itself up again. Would she never be rid of it?

"Do you know it would break my heart in a million pieces if I never saw you again?" Jackson said finally.

Sarah smiled ruefully, without looking at him. "Me too. A million pieces."

Nine

THE GPS APP BROUGHT Sarah right to Ed and Linda's house. It was just past nine in the evening, later than Sarah would have ordinarily knocked on anyone's door without an invitation or forewarning, unless that door was attached to an apartment in New York City.

The lights were still on all over their house. Under the circumstances, she thought it might be okay to ring the bell.

Linda peeked through a sheer curtain in the living room with a slight scowl on her face. When she saw who it was, her face lit up immediately. A moment later, the door flew open and Linda threw her arms around Sarah.

"Look at you, look at you!" Linda said joyously. "You're... *glowing!*"

"The California sun and sea did me a world of good." *Not to mention three straight days of some serious boinking.*

"Come in! Come in!"

"I know it's late—"

"Hush. I said come in." She pulled Sarah into the house and

pointed her toward the kitchen. She leaned into the living room doorway and said, "Ed, put your pants on. We got company."

"Oh, my goodness, Linda, really I don't want to disturb—"

"Hush, I said. He's in his pajama bottoms. We were just watching the TV." Linda put on a pot of coffee for them. "I hope decaf's okay. I'll never get to sleep if I make the regular stuff."

"Sure, sure. No problem. Oh, hey, I brought you something." Sarah handed a paper bag to Linda.

"Ohhh… you didn't have to do that." But when she saw what it was, she burst out laughing. It was the old naked hippie on the surf board, hanging eleven.

"They didn't have one that looked like a cannibal, but I thought this was pretty close. A little something to remember me by."

Linda hugged her again. "Like I'm ever going to forget you. In fact, you're coming to our family reunion next month. Clear your schedule for the Fourth of July. Bring your air mattress."

They chatted over coffee for an hour and a half, way past Linda's bedtime. Sarah told her how her days on the Pacific had renewed her, cleansed her, helped her clear her mind and ease her soul. There was still a long road ahead, she knew, but she felt better prepared to face it now.

Linda patted her hand when Sarah told her this, and said, "Listen, sweetheart. There'll be good days and bad. But then one day you wake up, and discover that you can say your child's name and smile instead of weep."

Sarah looked into Linda's eyes. It was like peering over the edge of a dark canyon. There was profound sorrow in those eyes. But there was also love, and acceptance, and courage, and strength. Sarah didn't have to ask the question. Linda nodded, and she knew.

"Whether you believe it or not, I think the Lord did send you here. I don't think it was an accident or a coincidence at all. He put that plane on the highway, and made that trooper point the way to our road. And that sunrise you fell in love with? That was a gift just for you. You can laugh at me if you want. I know this must sound simple and silly to you—"

"No, no," Sarah said, and squeezed Linda's hand.

"—but I truly do believe that. I believe it enough for the both of us. And I'm grateful enough for the both of us. Now I want you to go out there and live, Sarah. You're a precious, precious child, and I want you to live. I want you to be happy."

―――――――

Sarah made it back to her parents' house in two days' time. Halfway there, somewhere in Indiana, she stopped for the evening after dropping the minivan off at a full-service station where they promised to replace the tires, change the oil, and replenish all of the fluids before noon the next day. The last stop she made was at a gas station in Ridgewood, where she filled up the tank and ran the minivan through an automatic carwash. It would probably take two or three more passes to get the vehicle as clean and shiny as it had been when her father first handed her the keys nearly a month ago, but this was good enough for now.

It was just past midnight when she drove up to the house.

Sarah could see grayish-blue lights flickering behind the curtains in her parents' bedroom windows, indicating that they had either fallen asleep watching TV, or Ana was up watching a late-night show. Sarah phoned from the car, and watched as lights flicked on all over the house as Ana made her way downstairs, talking excitedly into the phone.

They sat in the kitchen and talked for hours. Dan and Ana both marveled over the change that had come over Sarah in the course of the past few weeks, and thanked God for taking care of her and putting so many good people in her path. For her part, Sarah believed that for every wicked person, there were at least a thousand decent ones, maybe more. The odds would always be in favor of meeting more of the good guys than the bad, with or without divine intervention. But she didn't want to quibble; she kept that to herself.

Sarah told her parents everything. She didn't get into too many details about the darkest night, the one in that motel in Oklahoma, but she didn't keep it a secret from them either. "It was bad," was all she said about that.

When she got to the part about Jackson, both Ana and Dan's expressions changed, mirroring each other perfectly without having to look at each other.

To Sarah's surprise, they were both quiet. She had expected a more emotional reaction, especially from Ana. They were just quiet.

"I don't know what'll happen, if anything," she told them. "But I'm glad our paths crossed when they did. He seems to be a good-hearted person, a man of decency. He was a friend to me at a time when it hurt too much to connect with people who know me better. I couldn't take any more condolences and pitying glances. I didn't know it at the time, but a new friend who didn't know anything about me was exactly what I needed. He knows the whole story now, but it's different. Telling him about it after the fact was different from living it with people who know me, and who knew Tessie." The mention of her little girl's name made all three of them draw a deep breath. Sarah continued. "Maybe he'll come to New York someday. Maybe someday I'll go visit him in Texas. Maybe we'll just be phone pals for a while, until we run out of things to say, or until life takes us in other directions. But I'm glad I met him when I did."

Dan nodded after a while. Whatever he thought about this situation, he kept it to himself. Ana struggled to keep from blurting out her fears and anxieties about her daughter hooking up with some strange man she met in a diner in the middle of nowhere, but managed to save it for later, when she could unload it all on her husband in private. To Sarah, she said, "Well, time will tell. If it's meant to be, it will be. I'm just glad you're home safe." She got up and hugged her daughter tightly. She whispered into Sarah's ear, "How did you get so brave?"

Sarah chuckled and hugged her mother back. "I don't know, Ma. Is brave the same as crazy?"

The following afternoon, Dan offered to drive Sarah back into the city. Sarah thanked him, but declined. There was still one more thing she needed to do on her own: she needed to find her way back home.

———

Sarah took a commuter bus from Ridgewood to the Port Authority depot on 42nd Street, and immediately upon putting her feet down on the sidewalks of New York, fell in love all over again with the city that makes each of its inhabitants earn its welcome through sheer, mulish obstinacy.

Rather than hail a cab or ride the train uptown, she walked the forty-five blocks or so back to her old neighborhood, thankful once again for her mother's ugly gardening clogs and thinking she could walk a million miles in these magical shoes.

She actually found herself smiling at the herds of clueless tourists who blocked her way or ambled in slow-moving, gape-mouthed clumps on the wrong side of the sidewalk. She wanted them to love her city, too, so, for the first time, she politely stepped aside for them.

When she finally stood before the door to her apartment, she simply stared at it for a long time, keys in hand, unsure of what she would find behind that door, or how she would feel about it. Several minutes passed before she was able to summon the courage to open the door. She stepped inside, closed the door softly behind her, and listened to the silence.

A few windows had been left open, and a hint of warm breeze blew through the apartment. Slowly, she walked in and out of rooms, the only sound that of her own muted footsteps against the hardwood floors. She breathed in familiar scents that lingered ghostly despite the fact that the apartment had been empty for almost a month. She smelled the fragrances of her own soap and shampoo in the bathroom, the smell of crayons in the corner of the living room where Tessie's tea party and drawing table stood empty, the scant scents of early summer wafting in timidly through the windows.

She walked around like this for a long time, coming close but not looking into Tessie's little room. She touched the edges of her furniture as she walked from one room to the other and circled back again. She knew there were things she needed to do, things that needed laundering or cleaning or dusting, things that needed to be put away or discarded, but now was not the time. When the time was right, she would know it and she would do it. For now, there was no need to hurry. For now, everything felt all right just as it was.

She walked over to the window at the end of the living room where, in the winter, when the leaves were gone, she could see a little bit of Central Park through the bare branches of the trees that grew on the side street outside her building. She couldn't see the park now, of course, with summer in full swing, and maybe that was a good thing.

Then she noticed something on the window sill: a perfect white feather, about five or six inches long. The window was open, but the screen was down.

Sarah tried to imagine how that feather might have gotten inside and landed there so neatly. Perhaps a dove or a pigeon had perched on the ledge, right next to the screen, which may or may not have been closed all the way down. Or maybe the wind had lifted the feather from some other place and made it slip through the same slim gaps where the occasional fly or mosquito found its way inside the apartment in spite of the screens. She picked up the feather and examined it. It was pristine in its whiteness.

She walked over to the bookcase and laid the feather gently next to a picture of Tessie.

Behind every miracle, there is a perfectly logical explanation.

"Mm-hmm," Sarah said to the voice.

Sarah turned around slowly, taking it all in, her home, her surroundings, her furnishings, her things, Tessie's things. She took a tentative step forward. And then she took another.

Ten

THEY HELD OUT FOR a whole two months.

Around the second week in August, Jackson made his first trip to New York.

Sarah did her best to give him a little taste of the world. She taught him how to disappear into the gray blur of humanity, to stand quietly on street corners and listen to the sound of a thousand passing voices, snippets of conversation spoken in a kaleidoscope of languages from every corner of the Earth. She took him to tiny eateries where they could sample foods with names they couldn't pronounce, infused with the same aromas and fragrant herbs that had been pleasing the palates of peasants and of kings since antiquity. She walked him through the neighborhoods where Dutch settlers had built their brownstones centuries ago, and where people still strived to keep that architecture alive. She showed him the Gothic cathedrals, buildings, and monuments where vigilant gargoyles kept watch as they had in medieval times and places. She took him to Coney Island and introduced him to knishes and salt water taffy. They got up early one morning and scored a pair of free tickets to see Shakespeare in the

Park. They rode the train up to the Bronx and saw a game at Yankee Stadium. "Here's one you can check off your list," Sarah told him. "Next time, we'll go with my Dad to Shea to see the Mets."

"It's called CitiField now," he corrected.

"It'll always be Shea to me."

They went to New Jersey one afternoon, where Jackson charmed the pants off Sarah's parents and Ana fed him until he begged for mercy. "I like your cowboy," Dan whispered to Sarah when they were hugging goodbye.

"Me too," Sarah whispered back.

Jackson never commented on the little table and chair in the corner of Sarah's living room, the one with the spill of crayons over a dusty pile of construction paper and drawings whose edges had begun to curl. He also noticed but didn't mention that there were a couple of little containers of chocolate milk in the refrigerator that had expired.

Late one night, when he had gotten up to get a drink of water, Jackson found himself wandering around Sarah's apartment, reading the titles of the books she kept on her shelf, peering at unknown faces in small framed photographs.

Sarah got up a few minutes later when she realized he wasn't in bed beside her. She found him peeking into the little nook that had been Tessie's room. The space was originally intended to be a small breakfast area just off the kitchen. Sarah had used that space as a home office in her first few years in this apartment. Just before Tessie first birthday, Dan had helped her create a partition, separating it completely from the kitchen. On the open side, she put up a beaded curtain instead of a door. They took the crib out of Sarah's bedroom, reconfigured it into a child's bed, and moved it into the new little room where it fit quite snugly, though there wasn't room for much of anything else in that space. Sarah figured she would eventually need to move to a bigger place, but that could wait until Tessie was older.

Of course, that was all moot now.

"Hey," Sarah said quietly from the edge of the living room. Jackson jumped, even though she had spoken barely above a whisper. "Sorry. Didn't mean to startle you."

"It's okay."

"That was Tessie's room."

Jackson nodded.

"Someday I'll get around to... changing it. Or moving. Or something. I'm just not ready yet."

Jackson nodded again.

"I can still feel her here, you know. With me. I'm afraid that if I change anything, that feeling will stop."

Jackson nodded again. "Yeah. I can feel her, too."

"You can?"

"Umm-hmm. Maybe I'm just sensing you feel her. Sometimes I see you looking around behind you, before you take a step, like you're trying not to bump into something. Trying not to step on... something."

"Huh," Sarah said. She hadn't been aware of doing that.

"You can talk to me about her, you know. About Tessie. I won't mind."

Sarah smiled wanly, and looked away. She started to walk back to the bedroom.

"Marry me, Sarah."

She spun around on her heel. "What?"

"Marry me. I don't want to go back to Fort Worth without you. I don't want to leave you here. I want to stay here. With you. I don't care where, geographically. I just want us to be in the same place. Together."

"Yeah, but... marriage? That's... a bit rash... don't you think?"

"I think I knew it the moment you swapped those two glasses of water at the diner. I knew it the first time I heard you say '*caww*-fee.' I knew it when you made friends with that barn owl, when you wanted to name that kitten, when you nearly killed me the first time we made love. I knew it all those times. And I know it now. I know it now more than ever."

Sarah looked at him for a long time. "So you're just going to walk away from your life in Texas and start all over again."

"Why not? You did it. Sort of. I want to do that, too."

Sarah smiled. "What'll you do for a living? New York is expensive. And I only barely have a job."

"I'll apply for a teaching certificate here. And while I'm waiting, I'll tend bar. Or go play dueling banjos with the Naked Cowboy in Times Square. Or mow lawns in your parents' neighborhood. Or walk dogs fourteen at a time. Or wash windows. I'm not afraid of hard work, Sarah, or of getting my hands dirty. I'm afraid of my own empty house, of my dreams only ever being dreams. I'm afraid of a life far away from you."

Sarah wanted very much to say yes, to run up to him and scream yes, *yes, YES!* But she could only think of her own brokenness, all of the shattered pieces of herself, the few she had managed to gather up, and the many more that still lay strewn all about her. Jackson's visit had been a wonderful diversion, a homecoming all its own. But she feared this was a momentary happiness, as fleeting as a wisp of smoke, an illusion for them both, that real life was going to come barreling out of a dark tunnel like a runaway train any minute now and crush the life out of them both.

"What are *you* afraid of, Sarah?"

And then it hit her: What if she had already lived through the worst thing that was ever going to happen to her? She had survived more than a horror or two in her lifetime so far, and she was still standing. She had not lain down and given up. She had come close, but she had not given up. She had gotten up and found a way to keep putting one foot in front of the other. Even the things that had scared her or beaten her down had not succeeded in killing her.

"Nothing," she said simply, somewhat surprised to hear herself say it. "I don't think I'm afraid of anything anymore."

Jackson walked over to her and wrapped his arms around her. "So marry me, Sarah."

She pressed a cheek against his chest. She felt his heart beat, strong and true, their breathing in sync. "Okay," she said. "But let's take it slow, okay?"

"Okay."

———

The next morning, they went down to City Hall and applied for a marriage license.

———

It took several months, but Jackson's modest little house in Fort Worth finally did sell.

Sarah accompanied him on this trip for the closing. Once all the paperwork was done, Jackson's life as a Texan was officially behind him.

Before heading back to New York, Sarah called Linda and asked if she and Jackson could stop by for a quick visit. Linda was delighted to welcome her back, and couldn't wait to meet the fine young man who had swept her off her feet.

Linda and Ed prepared a wonderful meal for them on the backyard grill. Sarah didn't ask if the cow had a name before it became steaks, and tried not to think about that aspect of life on a horse and cattle ranch. They talked and swapped stories like old friends for hours afterward, and even big silent Ed brought out his guitar and sang in a beautiful tenor voice for them for a long while before they called it a night.

————

Sarah lay in bed for hours in the guest bedroom in Ed and Linda's house, unable to sleep. She felt simultaneously at peace and restless. Her body was calm, but her mind churned in a slow whirl of disconnected thoughts.

Jackson was snoring lightly beside her on the other side of the bed, a sound she found oddly comforting. But even that couldn't lull her back to sleep as it often did.

Eventually, she crept out of bed. She dressed in the dark, and quietly stepped outside for a bit of cool air.

A sliver of moon shone brightly, almost directly above her. The sky was a vast spray of twinkling diamonds against a backdrop of black velvet.

Sarah spun around suddenly and went back into the house. She retrieved a set of keys from the dresser, where Jackson had dropped them when he undressed. On her way back to the rental car, she grabbed one of the little solar-powered lamps from Linda's flower bed. She then drove down the road, toward the barn.

She parked several yards away from it, and holding the lamp out in front of her, she peeked into the dark barn. "Hello?" she called timidly, and listened. "Click, click?"

Nobody was home.

Sarah trudged back outside, disappointed that she wouldn't get to see old Reverend Owl. She imagined he was out hunting for dinner, and was secretly glad she didn't have to watch him kill something.

Almost on impulse, she pushed the lamp into the ground and climbed up to the roof of the car. She lay flat on her back, looking straight up at the sky. From this vantage point, with the barn far enough behind her, she had a completely unobstructed view of that infinite Texas sky, so full of stars. It gave her the sensation that she was floating through space. Small wisps of clouds occasionally floated by, backlit by the light of the moon.

All those suns, all those planets with their own moons, she thought. *What goes on in all those places? Or is it really nothing more than silence?*

Sarah thought again of that old Chemistry professor from her college days, Dr. Singh, the one who told the class one day that every element in our bodies—all of us, every person, every living creature, everything in our world and the galaxies around us—everything was once contained in a single star. That star had exploded in one magical burst of immeasurable energy, sending little bits of itself hurtling into every corner of space. "We all come from a *star*," Dr. Singh had said dreamily, in nearly a whisper. It was a notion that struck Sarah as utterly poetic, the one lesson from her entire student career that she could still remember verbatim, and would remember forever. She remembered, too, the look on Dr. Singh's face as he spoke those words, a man of science, so full of reverence for that wondrous moment that marked the beginning of life, the creation of the universe as we know it.

The idea that we are all connected to each other, in the present and the past, through uncountable millennia and into the future, was more beautiful and moving to Sarah than any description of heaven, faith, or eternity that had ever been pounded into her head in the guise of religion.

Looking out on this dark, velvety sky, speckled with its dense spray of brilliant lights, she was moved once again by its beauty. "We are all connected," she whispered to herself, repeating the lesson learned so long ago, "through time and space, we are connected."

But we've also all been blown to bits, just like that long-ago star. Lives shattered. Fragments scattered. Like shards of glass and jagged bits of stone, we hurtle along unknown trajectories, not knowing where these pieces of us will land, whom they will cut along the way, or what will slash our own souls to shreds.

"And still we survive," she marveled.

For no reason that she could discern, she found herself thinking of the little mobile that had hung over Tessie's crib when she was a baby, the one that looked like a tiny carousel of little birds and butterflies, the one Shirley had given to her when Tessie was born. The image came to her in such crisp detail that it almost hurt to remember it. Its music box melody played clearly in Sarah's mind. She heard it now exactly as she had when she stood over Tessie's crib, watching her baby sleep, filled with wordless awe at the perfect miracle of that tiny life, her heart feeling like it would burst with all the love she felt for that extraordinary little creature.

"Where are you, Tessie?" she asked, searching the stars for an answer. "Where are you, my sweet baby girl?"

Just then, Sarah caught site of old Reverend Owl.

He made a slow, silent descent toward the barn, gliding in a wide arc. He narrowed the angle of his flight, and flew a bit closer to Sarah. Twice he encircled her overhead, with barely a flap of his wings.

A single white feather, small and fluffy, floated down toward her. Sarah reached out and caught it.

On his final swoop, the beautiful, silent bird disappeared into the barn.

"Thank you," she said to no one in particular. "Thank you," and then closed her eyes.

Acknowledgments

I am fortunate beyond all imagining to have the love and support of dear friends and family, people who happily cheer me on, who give generously of their time, energy, and talents, and, best of all, who aren't afraid to tell me when I've gone off the rails.

I want to thank especially the following people: C.J. Sullivan for letting me borrow (steal?) the story of his grandmother Sadie's Irish wake, and William Gorta for answering my questions about police procedures under special circumstances.

My love and gratitude also goes out to Elizabeth Benedetto for her eagle-eyed editorial assistance, her unwavering friendship, and her joyful exuberance. And to Kathryn Carissimi, whose artistic sensibilities and perseverance finally led me to my Helen Keller Moment, thank you for being my Anne Sullivan!

About the Author

Cynthia Ceilán is the author of three internationally published books of nonfiction humor: *Thinning the Herd: Tales of the Weirdly Departed* (Lyons Press, 2007); *Weirdly Beloved: Tales of Strange Bedfellows, Odd Couplings, and Love Gone Wrong* (Lyons Press, 2008); and *Unlucky Stiffs: More Tales of the Weirdly Departed* (Lyons Press, 2010). Her works of short fiction have been published in a number of literary magazines, including *Potpourri* and *The Sun*. She was also a named contributor in Smith Magazine's *Six-Word Memoirs on Love & Heartbreak*, published in 2009.

Ms. Ceilán lives in New York City. *Myths of a Merciful God* is her first novel.

www.ingramcontent.com/pod-product-compliance
Lightning Source LLC
Chambersburg PA
CBHW020553180626
46810CB00007B/2481